Praise for

"[The Great Chameleon War] is hypnotic . . . creatively ambitious, un-willing to sacrifice its undulating, organic sensibility for a more typical scifi aesthetic . . . for people who prefer *Annihilation* to *Gravity*, *Sunshine* to *The Martian*."

— *Polygon*

 "Writing of a New Storytelling Production"

— 2020 Audio Verse Awards

THE
TIDE WILL
ERASE ALL

JUSTIN HELLSTROM

**DEAD
POND
SWAN**

DEAD POND SWAN PRESS

05 :: *Fhe* - Garden Exoquadrant :: 17-19:95

This is a work approximating true transdimensional occurrences that will one day burn this book from your hands. Names, characters, places, and incidents are both a product of the author's imagination and encoded in the temperature fluctuations of the CMBR. Any resemblance to actual persons, living or dead, should warm their hearts forevermore.

First paperback edition July 2021

Frontispiece by Jordan Long

Book layout by Dead Pond Swan Press

Fonts Used:

Body Text: Fanwood

Chapter Headings: Raleway

Prologue & Numbers: Roboto Mono

Library of Congress Control Number: 2021907111

Dead Pond Swan Paperback ISBN: 978-0-578-85803-6

ISBN 978-0-578-89305-1 (ebook)

www.DeadPondSwan.com

Cover Illustration: Ori Toor

For Marielle and all girls
who brave beyond their sleep.

THE TIDE WILL ERASE ALL

SINGULARITY PLAYTIME SAGA

Book One

```
OSGO::// XX::111::XXX
Altitude::// 592.32 km - 610.10 km
Time::// 23::13::09 X-X 07::07::35
Milky Way Apoptosis::// 79.xx Days
Log Date::// 183 Days Post-Mouth of God Permeation
```

The sky above the observatory was heartbroken. Bleeding gold, violet, and seashore blue in all directions. If the universe were an organ, it was failing one cell at a time—each star infected by an unseen emotion. One which sheared the bonds of particles with exotic violence, and from the most fundamental units of matter, released a molten terror from beyond the boundary of perceptible existence. Alu stared through a porthole in the observatory at every possible reality condensed, heated, and spewed into the night from broken constellations. An extinction event of unknown mythlogies colonizing our own. Somehow it reminded Alu of a starfish pulling its arms off. She tossed a rubber duck at the window, and it bounced away in the weightlessness of low Earth orbit with a solitary squeak.

"Hey, Captain. They're back on the mirrors." Alu held her middle finger up to the floating duck. Captain Juneau drifted out from her quarters and pulled a torn, stained sweater over her head. She shook free a bundle of frayed cables wrapped around her foot and set aside the automated resuscitation module.

"Whose turn is it?" Juneau typed into the control panel, but some of the keys were stuck. The week before, Earnest had sent a bolt from the rivet gun through his neck while watching the monitors, and Alu and Juneau had been too exhausted to clean the panels. The rest of the station's bridge was in similar disrepair. Cracked touch screens. Screwdrivers lodged in light fixtures. Pipes and conduits spilled in a tangle of irreparable system failure. The hydroponic network had been compromised months earlier, so vegetables and berries were now grown from punctured station paneling arranged around the circumference of the command center. Eighty percent of life support systems were now concentrated in this central hub—a broken circle choked with vine and vegetation, star chart debris, and blood, as if the chamber were the site of a sacrificial ruin. A site of ritual gone wrong.

"You know I love bird-watching duty," Alu said. She pointed to a paper calendar. Birds were drawn in pen on every Saturday of June. Doodled with their heads cut off and tumbling into other dates.

"I would lose consciousness out there." Captain Juneau hugged herself.

"And I'd go out and drag your sweet, tiny, broken body back into the airlock. Stop feeling bad about nearly getting crushed to death by that beluga billboard on the last raid."

"I hate satellites."

"You hate birds more." Alu took Juneau's hand and pulled her through a wreath of budding blackberries to the other side of the command ring. "Maybe Rostov is doing better. Let's take a peek and see if we can get him to stop drawing and help."

Rostov hadn't left the viewing cupola in two weeks. Sketches and notes drifted around the dome-shaped module and its broad windows, the glass blue with Earth's ocean locked in its gaze. Monitors showed footage from an array of

Earth-pointed cameras with resolution high enough to identify one species of ant decapitating a different species of ant on a small leaf. Alu and Juneau knew better than to use the cameras now. Once you looked at what was happening down on the surface, it became impossible to look away. The subject of their observations was astronomical—not planetary—and exploding through space in the opposite direction.

"He's watching that giant animatronic yeti wading out in the middle of the Pacific Ocean," Juneau said.

"Still? The ape thing with an oblique pyramid for a head?"

"Yeah."

"It's getting worse. MoG phenomena are maintaining form for longer. Fuck."

Rostov let out a frantic moan and pulled a knitted cap tight over his head. Then he scribbled on a few scraps of paper. Alu grabbed one of the free-floating drawings and inspected it. A colossal robotic primate held a splintered cruise ship in the air, its passengers plummeting into the triangular jaws of its nonsensical, geometric head. Rostov sketched it well. Some of the fuel tank detonations dented the water with pressure.

"Looks like that thing nailed one of the Haven Vessels fleeing California." Alu released the sketch back into an orbit around its creator. "I don't think Rostov can feel emotions anymore."

"No. I saw him cry when that gigantopithecus ate a pod of whales a few days ago."

Alu laughed. Then gave her captain an embarrassed shrug.

"Let's get you out there."

The gear room by the airlock hummed shrine-quiet with primary life support subsystems flushing coolant and recycling oxygen. An exploded canister of sealant clung to the ceiling. Several of Elroy's teeth were embedded in the foam stalactite material. Burn marks scored the enclosures for the Extra-vehicular Mobility Units, but the spacesuits were undamaged. Juneau's stomach growled with a small echo.

"If I catch you not eating again, I'll have to spoon feed you. And I will *coo* like a baby the whole time." Alu tweaked the captain's ear and took out a crinkled and baggy EMU suit from its plastic locker.

Izumi's EMU dangled inside the same locker. She'd gone on a spacewalk to calibrate the observatory's positioning thrusters. After a few hours she'd stopped moving. Alu retracted Izumi's tether to pull her back into the station, but crystal blue ocean water was all she found inside the suit. A herd of tiny manatees grazed among corals, snails, and sea slugs on a yellow meadow of kelp in the suit's hard-upper torso. Colonies of wolf eels peered from the cavernous junctures of armpit and crotch. Captain Juneau shone her headlight on an egg sack where a developing shark of some sort pulsed inside.

"Have you been feeding the fish in Izumi's EMU?" Alu asked. Behind the helmet visor the small sea bubbled. A chunk of protein bar drifted by a starfish chewing on a wide-eyed manatee.

"Well, if a part of Izumi is still in there, I need to take care of her."

"You're precious." Alu trembled.

"You don't really care about discovering the source of all this *connerie* anymore, do you?"

Captain Juneau pointed out a porthole at the reef of blistered color propagating through intergalactic space.

"I mean, do you?" Alu replied.

They floated there. Alu pet Izumi's helmet visor with the miniature manatee being digested on the other side. Juneau tugged at a hole in her sweater. Some creature sloshed deep within the spacesuit, and Alu pulled Juneau close and kissed her. They fell asleep for a short time as the sky outside the airlock continued to trickle and burn, outlining their quiet, huddled bodies with a thin sheen of treasure. The partially-eaten manatee watched them—mouth open to sing.

When they woke, Alu suited up, fastened her helmet into place, and entered the airlock. Her voice inside the EMU transmitted to Captain Juneau's headset.

"No, I don't care anymore," Juneau told her. She handed Alu a telescoping-arm tool and sealed the airlock for her, releasing the other door that opened into vacuum. "I'm just doing this for *her*. Our little robot."

"Yeah, same."

Alu exited the station and drifted toward the rear of the mirror-array shielding sphere—falling snowflake slow to the backside of an immense white and paneled eyeball. She toggled her thrusters to avoid the husks of satellites they'd cannibalized to keep the observatory operational.

"What do you think she'd say? About bird watching duty?"

"She would say this mission was *totally burnt pancakes.*" Juneau patted her microphone with a pretend spatula.

"That's spot on." Alu flailed stiff-limbed while passing a gutted billboard satellite. Some corporate beluga whale watched her with furrowed scorn from the curved sea of neon diodes. "She'd say I looked like a *no-legged platypus rolling in a dumpster*, floundering around out here. That I could use a *happy hamster* in my pocket. Something weird like that."

"Hey, we have that one tape saved in the backlog. Want me to play it?"

"You bet your toasted marshmallows I do."

Alu skimmed along the shielding sphere, peeked around its lip, then positioned herself on the front side of the mirror array, each hexagonal surface the length of an Olympic swimming pool and set in the gigantic protective cavity. But the mirrors weren't collecting starlight. Instead, they were covered in a feathery white substance. A mass of soft, downy pulp shifting in unconscious clots. Alu extended the tele-scoping tool and passed over the first mirror, swatting at the white masses. She spanked one of the birds, which raised its long neck and orange beak to hiss at her. Soundless. Alu kept smacking until it took flight, impossibly so, beating broad wings on the nothingness of space. Thousands of swan necks rippled outward from the first as a disturbed arctic lagoon —and in that single wave the whole gathering of birds took flight. The sunlit bevy rose from the telescope in a migratory spire of plumage to rupture the great eye. The birds blocked out distant galactic eruptions and star-cluster froth with their aerobatics and murmuration. They glided in lines and dove and climbed again, beaks parted in unheard calls, flocking as a ribbon of synchronized swans around the entire station with their diamond tears trumpeting in blue glissades.

Rostov smeared charcoal on his face as the birds crossed the cupola's ocean view. Alu held a gloved middle finger to the sun-gold jet stream of swans. Juneau touched her lips, clutched her sweater, and hit play:

○
.00

"*Good evening my bold math knights of untold zoom and fury.*" The static-crackled voice of a young girl whispered in Alu's helmet and echoed through the observatory.

"*Here's your nightly radio wave skin thunder: Today I cut open a bouncy ball and wondered if there's a rainbow hiding inside of everything. I felt sad that there's a shadow in a crack of Europa I'll never get to touch. My emotion level is a little Dead-Lemur Midnight. I'm trying to be okay with that. Like how I have to be okay with knowing dinosaurs never discovered metallurgy or got to eat ice cream. Or how I want to give swordfish legs but deep down I know that's a terrible, terrible idea. Still, I want to see that. I want to know. Like how I want to know if up there, with all your hyper-detectors and wonderful height and majestic soaring through the thrashing cosmic surf of the universe's imploding memories, if you can calculate the speed of light inside a dream.*"

PART ONE

—✕—

WITCH-CURSE PANCAKES

CHAPTER ONE

The Order of My Memories
Inside the Belly of a Lion that Never Ate Me

We called it the Mouth of God, what happened to the sky. It just sort of appeared one day—a Friday. I was at a younger kid's birthday party and it was *bo*-ring. The piñata's llama face was ripped, the pool was full of kiddie pee, and the lawn itched fresh and sticky. Birthday boy Tyler was the most annoying seven-year-old to ever climb out of Time's primordial pudding pit, and he went into full toddler meltdown mode over his tube floaty species being a dolphin instead of a shark. I wanted to kick his bottlenose-hating butt into the pool. Instead, I lit a napkin on fire with a tiki-torch. That's when I noticed the night sky. Totally normal. The stars shining like they always did. Twinkling in their usual const-ellation neighborhoods. Then there was a flash—a great one that painted everyone and everything on the planet with speckles of what looked like blue firefly butt-goo. When I could see again, all the stars had changed position. Teleported. Moved instantly from one point to another.

Some a little bit, and some a lot.

Orion's constellation gained a hundred pounds and his belt bloated out. The Hunter's club-arm shredded, hung limp, broken in half by an unseen spell. The Big Dipper kinked its handle and spilled. Every point of light above us twinkled wrong—rearranged as the night sky of a far off and uncaring alien planet. A total nightmare. Terrifying. Some people fainted. Others screamed. New stars were being born, too. Changing color and blooming like small neon yellow thunderclouds.

Seven called my dad as soon as it happened. He told me all the stars and galaxies had moved to what he called "true-position" and that those closest to the edge of the universe had just started exploding. And I mean *exploding* exploding. Seven was an astronomer completely in love with the stars, so I know it hurt him to see them suffering such horror and violence. His favorite nursery rhyme would never be the same.

Twinkle, twinkle little star, how I wonder what you are.
Up above the world so high, in the place where you'll all die.
You won't shine anymore, now that heaven shut its door.

I walked right up to Tyler. His stupid mouth open and gasping with that dolphin inner tube snug around his waist. I shoved him hard with my foot clean into the pool, *so hard* his swim trunks slipped down to his ankles when he went underwater. He flailed naked in the deep end, the dolphin floaty smiled a secret smile to me, and I took the polka dot bow out of my hair and tossed it in the water—a tiny funeral ceremony for the old world.

Yep. There weren't any rules anymore. Even I could tell that much.

People panicked right away and my dad drove me straight home, which was fine with me. That party *sucked*. Just a bunch of little kids running around being brats with Tyler wanting to open his presents before having cake. He got what he deserved. The roads were a bumper-car deathmatch warzone though, and my pops drove us behind looted supermarkets and through a golf course undergoing a full sprinkler splashdown. After leaving an abandoned park, we saw some hooligans set fire to a giant inflatable gorilla on top of a car dealership. I'm telling you, it was every platypus for themselves out there. Then a deer leapt out of the woods with a square of metal fence jammed in its antlers like it was trying to send a signal to deep space. A school bus swerved around a flaming tire rolling across the highway, just having a random adventure all by itself, and the bus hit the satellite-dish deer head on—

—transmission terminated.

The yellow machine skidded sideways, tipped over, and the whole thing rolled down a hill. Lunchboxes and camping stuffs flew out the windows along with a whole kid or two, maybe a detached leg even. We drove by and the bus litter scattered across the sky spelled out a message I couldn't read. It was like the stars had always been guiding our fates, and with them gone all our souls were exposed. Just empty juice boxes, as if no one alive or dead had ever really made a choice for themselves.

In the days to come, scientists and astronomers found out that it wasn't only stars and star neighborhoods on the edge of

15

the universe dying, but closer ones too. Seven said there was a membrane moving through space. Wherever there was a planet or a star or a moon or an asteroid—or any little particle, like a molecule or atom—the same amount of energy was released regardless of its size. More energy, he said, than there'd ever been. It was coming for us fast. Trying to swallow us whole. And that was that. He told us it was the Mouth of God, so that's what we called it.

Seven said we shouldn't even be able to see what was happening because light travels so slow. The only way this was possible, he thought, was if something bigger than our whole universe had overlapped with ours, something invisible and huge. Like if everything in the sky, the whole cosmos, was your friend underneath a blanket. Then you said, "Hey. I want to be safe and snuggled under a blanket too." So. You put an even bigger blanket over you and your friend, then took theirs off so you could see them. Seven said that the big blanket had other rules in it. Science rules. And when our blanket was taken off, some of our laws of nature merged with the big blanket's—just by being seen, by being observed and blinked at.

Discovering the source of this infernal galactic tidal wave was what we were after. A mission to find out who or what was sneaking a gaze through all the star saliva to watch our tiny, shivering world. Seven and my pops both set out on adventures to reestablish contact with the Great Seeker—the largest space telescope ever, so we could peek into that collapsing fire blanket. Use it to stare right back into whatever extracosmic glare had microscoped us and our fragile lives. And after Sevs and my dad located the heart of that monster, we were gonna find a way to eat it. Double-Donut-Sunday style, baby.

I lost my dad early on in our adventure and I was all alone for a while. *Alone* alone. Eating pop-tarts out of dumpsters every day because there wasn't much food left and the big city was sorta still on fire and stuff. The tall buildings and markets had always been my home, but now it was more like a jail or the dentist's when you have to sit in a funny-smelling chair and not get up and move even though you want to. And since I was stuck, go figure, all the things that'd been trapped before the Calamity were now set free. Just fate and physics hard at work.

The city had a big zoo. I loved it. Every time I visited, my dad let me pick out an ice cream popsicle from a vendor stand beside the lion cages. One of those carts with an umbrella and someone wearing a white visor to take your money. I always picked the lion-shaped one and ate it in front of the big cats in their cages. Not to make them feel bad, but to show the mega-kitties how much I liked 'em. And there was this one lioness with a big brown spot on her neck. She always took note of me when I was there, and I always waved to say hello. I named her Duke Ellington, which is weird. Because I know Duke Ellington made jazz and was a guy—not a lioness. My mom played his songs for me when I was in her belly. But also, Duke was some sort of title for old fancy-pants rich people back in the day, but I didn't really know what a Duke was, so I thought that girls could maybe be Dukes, too? And Ellington

17

was a pretty name for a lioness, no matter how you looked at it. So bite me.

When the city collapsed everyone went full golden ape-shit. Flipping cars, lighting fire hydrants on fire, stealing electric scooters, and peeing wherever they wanted. Some level-nine derptron went into the zoo and let all the animals out, including my lady Duke Ellington. I knew because there were zebras and elephants and weird birds in the streets. I even saw a giraffe pick a fight with a traffic light.

I was in this mini grocery store, munchin' on my pop-tart, when Duke Ellie popped out from behind the counter. She had a paper coffee cup stuck to her head like a hat, and I thought it was the cutest thing I ever saw. I wasn't scared though. I was too out of it to be scared—just trying to pick up a few of the cupcakes I'd lost and put the sprinkles back on the ones I'd found. Yep. Just your typical traumatized eleven-year-old making friends with a safari predator. I waved to the lady lion like I always did and felt kind of happy. But then she climbed on the counter and knocked over a rack of Skittles and scratch-off lottery tickets, which are my two favorite things at stores like that. Scratching off those numbers is a lot of fun, but don't sniff your fingers afterward. The number dust makes 'em smell funny. Having spilled everything, Duke got down real low and wouldn't stop panting. I heard her claws scrape against the counter, which is kitty sign language for *I'm gonna nibble your earlobes off.* I got up and ran into the lobby of the building next door as she launched herself into the refrigerator with all the soda drinks and things.

She was certainly upset with me. That I always ate those lion popsicles right in front of her at the zoo—teeth gleaming in summer sun. It was time for her to return the favor. Show me what her favorite kind of popsicle was.

She hunted me for two days.

I slept on the floor of a dirty bathroom, but it wasn't too uncomfortable after I found a roll of toilet paper to use as a pillow. Broken air-conditioning tubes became my escape tunnels. Piles of filing cabinets worked well as hideouts. I kept going up and up through the offices to try and get away, but she never called off the hunt. I couldn't trick her well enough to get back down the stairs either. Duke Ellington could go down them faster, just a little zoo fact I learned the hard way. I only managed to escape because there was a fire extinguisher in the stairwell. I'd first used one of those foam blasters on my eighth birthday—without permission, of course, and all over my neighbor's pet goose, Croissant—better known as my childhood mortal enemy. I taught that honk-nosed feather muncher that no one pooped in my wagon and got away with it. So. Duke Ellie took a triple-whipped-cream faceful of the cold foam and got scared, but only a little bit.

I ran into a room full of desks and chairs and papers with all kinds of numbers on them. One whole side of the building was collapsed, and you could see right through to the other skyscrapers. Even the street if you dared to get that close to the open edge. I found a closet full of mops and brooms, so I dove in and closed the door. But Duke Ellington didn't like me leaving her out of that closet party. She slammed against the door so hard the wood split and bent. Her yellow eye peered through one of the cracks, waiting, patient and hungry. I caught my breath while purrs hummed into the closet to try and lure me out into the hallway.

Come play with me, her purrs said. *Crawl inside my mouth so I can show you a secret. It'll make us both stronger. You'll have claws like me to tear apart the whole world. You can see through my eyes. Pump the blood through my heart. Come now. Let me whisper in your ear—ancient and warm, a song that'll merge our lives into one.*

I was no fool though. To Duke Ellington, I was nothing but a robot-flavored pop-tart. But I was a tad more intelligent than most breakfast pastries, and I sincerely mean it. Just a *tad* smarter at that point. So I knew I couldn't stay put for long. Janitor closets don't have food supplies. Plus, all the cleaning chemicals smelled like a heap of dead penguins. And yes—I know what a pile of murdered, flightless flipper-flappers smells like. What the closet did have were a bunch of hand-held vacuums on a rolling cart for spray bottles and trash bags. They were the little battery-powered things you use to suck up bugs or dirt from underneath your couch, maybe a whole quarter if you're lucky. I stomped on a broom and snapped the handle into a sharp point. I turned all the baby vacuum cleaners on, one by one, then powered up the mother of all carpet destroyers and loaded her on the cart.

Poor Ellie. She hunched her back in a cower when I busted out the door with all the vacuums roaring, my broom-lance cradled tight and a bucket on my head. Yep. She didn't want in on my closet party anymore. No kiddo-flavored pop-tarts for her. I thrust my cleaning spear hard into her jaw, and she bolted with the mother of all vacuum cleaners eating her butt with turbo-whirred bristles. Her claws gripped carpet fibers with the same genetic fear all kitties have around vacuum cleaners. I chased on, but it didn't matter.

My lady, Duke Ellington, galloped valiantly over the ledge of the open wall. She tumbled straight down twenty stories to the wet street.

I braved it to the edge and saw her sprawled out on the ground. She looked like a stuffed animal. A little soggy, sleeping peacefully beside the giraffe having his battle with the traffic light. Mr. Giraffe was mad that the signal wouldn't stop flashing red—another modern concept well outside a simple zoo animal's understanding. I watched him for three rounds. One of his eyes popped out of its seeing hole after a particularly heroic headbutt lunge, and then Mr. Giraffe conceded victory to the stoplight. He closed his one good peeper and lay down beside Duke Ellington to tuck himself in for a forever nap, too.

I could've handled how sad me and Duke Ellington's final encounter was. Kept on moving and chomping on Skittles while never looking back, but I did my best to make up for killing the Lion Queen. I went down to the street and petted Duke Ellie for a little bit. Put my head right to hers and tickled those floppy, furry ears. Even pulled a few broom splinters out of her gums.

"Now, you're one with me," I told her. Duke Ellington's head was heavy and wet with blood, but I put it on my lap and let it soak my leggings anyway.

"You can roam free through the plains inside my head. There are memories for you to hunt down and sink your saber teeth into. I won't blame you. Because I knew your secret before you even told me to crawl inside your mouth. *You were scared.* Scared of the mysterious universe guts that are catching fire and spilling all over our world. I'm right there with ya, 21 sister. So was Mr. Giraffe. Our little wind-up toy brains are getting blown away together. But it's okay, now. I'll teach you how to deal with whatever grand wizard is spilling lava from their summoning pit overhead, all the monsters and sick light raining down on us. Your claws are my claws now, and we're gonna tear open heaven's belly and find somewhere warm to make our nest. So. Listen. I promise, one day I'm going to find the prime origin of all popsicles—hold its flavor ice to the sun—and lick that frozen, tasty embryo core so hard that its soul will shoot through all known times, mutate every popsicle that'll ever exit, and morph all that cold sugar into lion shapes with a brown neck spot of bubblegum. Not so you can be eaten forever, but so you can have your revenge through an endless winter of brain freezes."

After I sent Duke Ellington to the Chasm of Eternal Solitude, I met the girl who saved my life. Allie. She fast became my best friend, a proper ten-year-old library witch. Allie knew exactly what was going on. I mean, we lost almost everyone. So many things went wrong right in front of us. Buildings crashed and broke apart all over people, whole herds of 'em. Have you ever seen a chunk of exploded building? They're huge! I know I'm still small, but even the tallest person on earth would look very tiny next to skyscraper parts. Even a dinosaur couldn't live after the top floor of a hotel fell on them. They'd be totally extinct, just like we were going to be. Many people weren't strong enough and decided to end themselves before bad things got to them. It happened all over the place. On swing sets in backyards. At the mall. Men and women jumped out of windows with babies under their arms or crawled in front of speeding cars. One guy even fed himself to the cranky alligator at Kangaroo Bob's Putt-Putt —right beside the pirate cave skeletons on hole sixteen. People couldn't handle it anymore. Lost their shit, yes they did. All of their marbles and their cupcakes, too.

Sprinkles and everything.

Killing Duke Ellington messed me up. Left me shuffling aimless and zoned out toward a crashing sound that echoed through an island chain of suburban parks. A sound like prehistoric turtles falling out of clouds onto a marble bell tower.

Shuffle, shuffle, shuffle. Shatter, crack, splat.

When I got to the source, all I saw were mountains of factory-perfect refrigerators. Whole hillsides, heaps, and polished porcelain dunes. A tall white tower of rectangle stood as a proud sculpture at the center of the landscape, watching over the food tombs with its blind, flat face. Oranges spilled out of all the refrigerators—each and every one filled from crisper drawer to freezer with the fruit. The massive monument created a refrigerator at its peak every few minutes. Most of the time they just slid off onto a ground platform. Sometimes they popped off into the air, doors flung wide open with tropical fruit spiraling in sheets of colored rain.

Allie sat atop one of the refrigerator mounds and waved me over.

"What a spectacle," Allie said, handing me half of a peeled orange. The climb was tough and left me out of breath, but I scooted onto the fridge beside her and pulled a string out of the hem of my dress—casual and confident.

"I heard this from miles away. Thought it was giant turtles maybe being eaten."

"The world is too weird for something like that to happen now," she said with a fingertap to her glasses.

She was cute. A genuine book worm for sure. I saw novels and magazines spilling out of her backpack, and she had a pink worm on the center of her sweater.

"Watch this," Allie said. She patted the electronic panel for dispensing ice and water. Pushed down on a button that glowed in the shape of a fruit. Baskets, armfuls, and whole wheelbarrows of oranges poured out, tumbling and spilling in citrus cascades down the appliance mound. "I think there is an infinite number of oranges inside."

I offered a wet slice to her sweater worm. "Welcome to Produce Paradise. Now your wiggler will never go hungry."

"I guess you're right," she said, then gave a careful nibble to the top of her sweater. Real serious and thoughtful. Probably contemplating if a worm could handle a tube-tummy full of tangerine acid without dissolving.

"Oh, hey. Do you know that person down there?" I asked.

Below the white tower was a woman. She took off her clothes all the way naked and held her arms open wide.

"No," she said, and Allie and I started shouting at the lady. Throwing oranges and banging the fridge door open and closed to make a commotion. She heard us alright. Turned around as the sound of statues hugging rang hollow and crisp from the tower peak. The lady curtseyed to us, elegant as a ballerina. Then she stared into the sky, hands clasped tight as a refrigerator toppled off the monument pinnacle and crushed her naked body flat. Left her arms twitching in a pile of oranges that weren't really orange anymore.

This moment would define the both of us, Allie and me. What kind of people we were. Our friendship. What horrors our trauma-cores were capable of comprehending. Whether or not we were gonna be strong enough to make it as things got worse, because they absolutely were.

"This looks like the end of a really bad play," I said to her. "One that doesn't make sense on purpose."

Allie cleaned her glasses off on her sweater and *hmmm*'d.

"No, I don't think so. I think this is the start of a fantastic play. It's not supposed to make sense. It's just supposed to make us *feel* something. That's all that matters anymore." She bit into a raw orange and slurped.

That's my girl right there. I kissed her wet and hard on the cheek and pressed down on the orange button—overflowed groves of infinite fruit to make the world as strange and wild as it could be.

A few weeks later our new adventure group was formed. After Allie and me watched a brave pilot burn to death in a hot air balloon, Seven found us on a playground at the top of a hill. A miracle beyond any other I'd seen since the Mouth of God yawned open to swallow that kind of hope. He had two other kids with him that he rescued from what they all called Space Camp. They were traveling to a control center for the Great Seeker telescope, but Seven was also looking for me. My dad used to work with Seven, and before I lost my pops we were headed Seven's way to help him find the Great Seeker.

"So, were you gonna be an astronaut?" I asked Mackenzie.

She was six years old, a big mess of blond hair stuffed in overalls with an old sweater spilling out. Mackenzie scrunched up one of her eyes and patted both of her knees twice.

"I was gonna be's a *hippaplotamus*." She smelled my finger and nodded. That was it. I loved her right there and then, all her nonsense-filled brain and snotty sweater'd body. The new world had broken her in just the right ways.

Toby was a different story. He was twelve years old, which pissed me off. He flaunted that one year like it made him crown emperor of the solar system. Really, he was only the king of being a moron. He wasn't always the strongest out of us kids, but he sure pretended to be. He didn't even make faces when we passed a candy store, one with bodies—or at least body parts—sticking out of the chocolate and bubble gum bins. Look. Sometimes you just have to throw up, and that's okay.

We left the rim of the smoldering city and headed for a neighboring forest. In that forest, we got pinned down inside a rotten treehouse on the edge of a classic hotel-painting hillside. A herd of people ran across the nice open meadow. Screaming. Clinging to bags of treasure and photo albums. Typical frightened newbie behavior. We peeped through the crooked treehouse windows as the herd was torn apart and flung into blue sky and clouds. Stomped and smeared on the late-summer lawn by a glimmering slug-silver entity. Torpedo sleek. Tangles of feelers grazing through dirt, pasture grasses, and body fluids. Its sea-monster jaws munched on clumps of bodies and then snorted, much like a bored horse would while gnawing on an untasty treat. Then it winked out of existence in a clap of bubbles, as most random Mouth of God phenomena did. The only sound to be heard was the obnoxious slurping of juice through a straw. Toby squeezed the empty carton as he observed the bright playdough carnage mashed into the slope. He spit the plastic tube out the window and smacked his lips.

"Ah, that's some *damn* fine juice."

There's Toby for you. He'd hold Mack and Allie's hands until they fell asleep, sometimes. No way I was gonna let that goober touch me though. I tried to tolerate his presence in the group, since he was the other refugee from Space Camp. They made a point to never explain or talk about it—Tobes, Seven, and Mackenzie. It must've been a bad party. Mega traumatic. Maybe the reason why Mack-a-Doodle was so derped out all the time. Anyone left alive had some secret terrors they needed to keep to themselves. I myself had the ghost of a lion prowling the plains of my soul, and that was okay. I think.

Seven was the only adult supervision we'd had in months. Our shining stellar compass and bold astronomer-leader. Our substitute teacher and bravest friend. I was the only one who knew him before the Mouth of God appeared—my real dad got him to come to my school and teach some classes about space. Seven was the first friend my dad made after moving from Japan to America so he could work on telescope mirrors, and the two made for a goofy pair. I befriended Seven right away. Part of that was because I asked *a lot* of questions while most of the other kids in my class were picking each other's noses. Seven was easy to make fun of, too, which he seemed to find amusing. This kid who thought she was clever enough to make him look like a navel-gazing baboon looking into a telescope from the wrong end. He took me home from school

27

somedays and on the weekends my dad and I hung out with Seven at the city's observatory. Those two would party some and let me run around the massive telescope. I'd ride on my dad's shoulders and battle Sevs with laser pointers. They let me string up constellations from the balcony and drink sparkling juice while they talked about life on other planets, what kind of bizarre solar systems might exist, and what secrets the never-seeable-heart-core of a black hole held dear.

"If we could see inside the event horizon," Seven asked me, "what do you think we'd see?"

I sat between Sevs and my dad on the observatory's lawn, staring up at constellations and wondering who were the first people to name each one.

"I think we'd see a garden."

"What kind of garden?" my dad asked, sprinkling some grass on my knees.

"The kind made from everything that'll ever be. With an impossible fountain at its center where everyone is swimming but no one can remember each other's names. But still—*but still*, when two friends see each other, they know. They hold hands and all their memories come back to them, for the tiniest moment, before being lost to the fountain forever."

Seven was more than just another adult to me. He was more than just a way older friend, too. With my mom leaving my dad and me, Seven was like a second dad. Father number two. He knew that. Knew all about the weird lines families make when one of the pillars goes missing. How it makes a lopsided temple that some people can't seem to understand, even though it stands up totally fine. Even though it feels like the rightest, most sacred thing ever—where magic from all dream worlds is pooled and protected by a circle of golden tigers that'll let you gaze upon the sparkle of its waters—but never let you get close enough to touch its source.

I named our new family unit the Lost Star Children, and we followed Seven from that rundown treehouse to some railroad tracks nearby. We followed the tracks for a week. Drank from a stream that ran beside the iron rails. Slept in the living rooms of long-abandoned houses. Practiced firing weapons so we could protect ourselves if something happened to Seven. Then one day the Conductor found us when his train rolled by Allie, a bunch of books on her lap, squatting by the tracks, trying her hardest to go number two.

"No right-minded rail chaser could let a bookworm use proper literature as toilet paper," the Conductor said, after he stopped his train and the three rail coaches behind it. He'd kept the train hidden for months in the station where he worked so he could make it to the west coast. "Gotta see that Big Blue Lady of mine one last time."

I thought the Big Blue Lady was his girlfriend, but Seven said he was actually talking about the ocean. I wasn't so convinced. Two other groups were in railcars behind the train engine and they scooted back to the middle car and the caboose to make room for us, letting us have the first-class cabin. But they didn't come out to greet us. Just one wild old man who jumped out, pissed off the Conductor, and told us his name was Captain Frumpy Butt before letting out a long *brap* of fart.

29

"Hey, you. Mr. Kindergarten Teacher," Captain Frumpy Butt said to Seven. "You ready to accept the promotion to be this parade's Grand Monorail Marshall?"

"No?" Seven replied, pulling some pine needles out of his back pocket.

"Say *no*, and I'll smack that ear right off your head and string it 'round that toddler's neck." Captain Frumps pointed to Mackenzie.

"Okay—" Seven said, but before he finished his sentence, Captain Frumpy Butt pulled a party popper from the front of his pants, the *crotch part*, and blasted Sevs in the face with confetti and streamers, before giggling like an idiot, pulling a whole giant pack of poppers out the seat of his pants, and running back onto the train after leaving them for us.

Yeah. I wasn't the only one whacked out of their mind, but that's why we were the only ones left alive. No totally sane person was strong enough to make it. Maybe when the Mouth of God first appeared they could, but not now. You had to be ready for a blood-stained stardust banana to appear out of nowhere. You had to smack those naughty peels with a baseball bat before they screamed at you, and then keep moving forward like it was no big deal. Just another Tuesday.

We boarded first class and invited the others over for milkshakes and heartfelt thank yous. Mackenzie had held onto a few bags of milkshake powder for months and hadn't told anyone about 'em. She hid them in her overalls, but we were all okay with it. The group from the caboose was quiet and unimpressed by our snack offering, dressed all in black and looking cool with bandanas and scarves. Hands in pockets. Guns slung to backs. One woman and two guys. I decided to call them the Black Bandits because it looked like they were about to rob the *choo choo.*

Captain Frumpy Butt stole the show for the middle car group. A true gem of the end times. He wore a sweater with a moose head on it and argued with it, the moose head, whose name was apparently Randy and whom Captain Frumps seemed to blame for the Mouth of God appearing. His pockets were full of plastic dinosaurs, glitter, and old candy wrappers. Kind of a grandpa version of Mack-a-Doodle if I sit and think about it. Captain Frumpy Butt helped Tobes make a milkshake. When Toby hit the blend button, Captain Frumps lifted the lid and sprayed chocolate gush all over himself to stain the moose on his sweater. I thought it was hilarious. His group was a little less amused.

"Boy howdy *hey.* I sure hope that makes Randy shut the ole up fuck," Captain Frumpy Butt said. He proceeded to suck the concoction out of his sweater. "One day I hope me and him become a stain—just like this. Smooth chocolate drizzle in the brain. Do me a favor though. Don't you let anything lick us up when that happens."

After trying to clean up the milkshake mess, everyone returned to their train cars. Some of the chocolate still dripped down the window though. It looked like a flock of birds. Broken necked. Wings crumpled. Gliding slow and sad over the horizon to find somewhere to cry—probably nesting inside the Great Seeker's armored eye of orbital telescope—letting their tears flood magnificent and brave to extinguish the violence eating away the stars. Tears can do that, I think. Cleanse the sadness from any heart. Any universe. Any dream where God lurks on all fours, naked and insane, waiting to eat.

CHAPTER TWO

*I've Got Enough Curse Words
in My Pockets to Vaporize Your Eyeballs*

I chewed my stuffed monkey's ear and watched Seven kill a spider on the train window with a chess piece. He pressed his knight down on the glass, and the bug's black legs squirmed and scrabbled as trees passed by. When the spider's smooth skull popped, I didn't flinch. I was scrunched up in the chair across from Seven holding my dress over my knees. My feet didn't touch the floor and I hated the way it felt when they dangled. Why don't train conductors have shorter seats for kids? I guess we'd complain about not being able to see out of the windows. Especially if there were an animal like a bear or a fox peeking out from the forest. We'd be mad if we didn't get to see a rare animal and someone taller did. Can you imagine that? Having to hear your parents just *talk* about how *amazing* the wolf looked in the woods and how *sorry* they were you couldn't see it. But they shouldn't be sorry. It'd be the kid's fault. It'd be my fault for wanting my feet to touch the ground and whining to the conductor for a shorter seat.

If I ever behave like that, the universe has full permission to squash my tiny piñata brain until it gushes all over its sunglasses.

Seven held my beat-up dinosaur walkie talkie and sent a message out into the stars. "The Itsy-Bitsy Spider [blip] has been banished to the Chasm [blip] of Eternal Solitude."

Seven could've seen out the window even if he was in a short kid's feet-on-the-floor chair. You'd think he was a grown-up, since he was thirty-three—just past the big three-oh. He was way older than me, but he didn't act like it. Not like the other grown-ups. Not like the professor and teacher he was supposed to be, either. If I missed the majesty of a deer walking outside, he'd tell the conductor to stop the train. If the conductor didn't pump the brakes, Seven would drag the rail captain's coal-stained body behind the train until it derailed. Sevs would go outside and pretend to be a deer. Just so I could see something neat. He'd go on all fours and walk around real careful. Sniffing the air or a tree. Even put his hands up to his head to make antlers. It wouldn't matter if it was snowing, raining, lightning storming, or volcanoing. He'd do it for me.

"You didn't have to do that," I said as he scraped off the spider husk underneath the table between us. He placed his horse-head knight back on the chessboard. I couldn't remember if it was in the right spot though.

"Really?" He pretended to be scared and pointed at the smudge on the glass with the walkie's antennae. "That thing was looking right at you guys. He sized you two up and was ready to leap straight for Mr. Banana's throat." Seven scratched his armpit and made some monkey sounds. *Ooo Ooo.*

"He doesn't scratch himself like that, he doesn't make that kind of noise, and that's not his name. You will address him as

Sir Galileo." Galileo's button eyes looked at me and I patted his monkey head.

"Ah, Galileo was an okay astronomer. But he got soft about his work when the church threatened to torture him. Tycho Brahe had some good astronomical observations, even though he couldn't accept that the Earth orbited the Sun. But Tycho looked way cooler than Galileo. He had a metal nose."

"Well, Sir Gali doesn't."

"Well, he should."

"Whatever you say, Eight." Oh, he didn't like that much. His parents named him Seven, which was awkward enough, but it seemed that the universe nicknamed him Eight. Anyone who met him would eventually come up with it on their own. They probably thought they were clever and all, calling him the number that comes just after his real name. No one ever called him six, the number right below seven. They always added one instead of subtracting one—like it was some deep mathematical truth hidden on the dark side of atoms and mapped on the exoskeleton of the universe. I'm sure he didn't mind at first, but I guess it got old fast. Why was six afraid of seven? Because Seven would punch you in the face if you tried to make stupid number jokes around him.

"Alright," Seven said. "Next time a blood-thirsty arachnid comes clambering for Galileo, I'm not going to stop him. Or his little fangs. Got that, Robot?"

"I am not a robot!" You could see him cheer up right away. One day he simply decided to call me Robot. The story behind it involves me filling up his water bottle so perfectly that it blew his mind. He claimed I had to tilt the bottle at an impossible angle at the water fountain to get it to-the-brim full, and some other boring stuff like that, but it convinced him that I had to be made of computers and gears in order to pull off such an exact refill. On that day, with his overflowing drink in my hands, I became Robot. Sometimes he'd use clever names like Microchip, or any other word that meant I was made of wires and batteries. Pocket Calculator. R2-D2. Game Boy. Optimus Prime. He said I looked like a cute little machine, and if he wanted my attention, he'd make stereotyped robot sounds. *Boop boop beep.* I acted like I hated the name, but I really thought it was awesome. I'd make an excellent robot. I'm good at math and can make lots of weird noises. I even know that people use little bits of electricity in their brains, so I guess we're all kind of robots. But I knew how much Seven hated being called Eight, so I wanted him to think I got annoyed when he called me Robot. You know. So he didn't have to be alone with the whole not liking his nickname thing.

Sometimes people need stuff like that.

"Hey, Short Circuit, it's your move." Seven fired off an imaginary laser from his finger and cracked his neck.

A chess board wobbled on the table with our pieces all mixed up. He played as the black pieces and I commanded the white. He'd been letting me win. I'd taken one of his murder horses, one rooky-rook, and a handful of pawns. He'd only taken my piece with the funny nipple hat. As I pondered my next move, a hand pushed through the gap between my seat and the next. The hand opened and closed like the mouth of an ostrich as it surveyed my habitat. Mackenzie peered around the edge of the aisle seat behind me, and she made a tired sound. A little bird squeak.

"Yeah, Sevens, we're tough. I ain't afraid of no spiders."

When she talked her bird-hand did too. Typical six-year-old tough guy act. Mackenzie was the youngest of us and usually dragged a little behind in all our conversations. One of her eyes would stay scrunched closed until you responded to her. She kept pirate-eying Seven, and I squished her hand-bird to stop her from talking.

"That's right," I said. "We're tough as a band of blind teddy bears battling a *motherfucking* sea monster to the death."

"Die, foul beasties." Mack-a-Doodle pretended to stab him. Seven covered his eyes.

"Your curse words have blinded me. Vaporized my eye-balls. And corrupted Mackenzie too. Great."

Toby popped up from behind the bar counter where the snacks were. Powdered chocolate dusted over all the empty passenger seats around us. He licked a chocolate-milk mustache off his lip and took another sip. Then he gargled while saying, *son of a bitch.* Just your typical twelve-year-old acting half his age.

A toilet flushed. Allie stepped out of the bathroom and found her seat across the aisle from us. She sat on one of her books and grunted. After pulling it out from under her butt, she played with her glasses while eyeing Seven. Real smart-like and all. A little librarian a little annoyed with the book she just sat on.

"Really?" she asked. "Curse words don't *vaporize your eye-balls.* They give you strength and let you know that other people are okay. That you made it through everything. Don't be an ignorant."

Seven got this big smile on his face. He got that way when he told us grown-up secrets—stuff kids aren't supposed to hear, which is stupid, of course, as if not telling us would make those things disappear. Adults can be so very childish. Seven put his hand to his chest.

"*An ignorant?* Well, sticks and stones will break my words but bones—no, unicorns . . . shit, how's all of that go again?"

Mackenzie tried to gargle like Toby but only managed to contract a severe case of the hiccups. She gave up on her ostrich hand puppet, but instead of burying its head in the cushions, she pawed at my back. She was bored and wanted attention. Mack purred and then said, "Rawr—*hiccup*—I'm the Lion King."

Mack's cub roar reminded me of Duke Ellington. I imagined Duke at the bottom of the Chasm of Eternal Solitude. Sulking through big leaves. Lapping up dirty pools of water. She was on edge, alert. Something stalked her in the black jungle floor-mist of the Chasm—booming with low sound that shook beetles from the trees. A cry of hunger and bad things and a continent ripping down the middle forever putting two friends just out of arms reach at the edges.

Then Captain Frumpy Butt entered our car and slammed the platform door shut behind him. Hurricane hair wind-frizzed. Fingers wiggling over imaginary piano keys. The air suddenly filled with crazy, like Captain Frumps had shepherded in a pack of carnivorous and invisible gnomes that were hopping around and gnawing the seats.

Mackenzie clapped twice. Hooted. Then Captain Frumpy Butt picked her up and placed her on his shoulders.

"You. Grand Monorail Marshall," he said to Seven, handing Mack a handful of glitter. "There always has to be a dinosaur leading the parade. Else those peasants and dirty

37

pigeons won't get outta the way, you hear me?" Mackenzie threw the glitter at Seven and pointed with courtroom accusation.

Seven turned slow, mouth open to me. Looking for help. I shook my head—he was on his own.

"Um, of course," Seven said.

Captain Frumpy Butt pulled three plastic dinosaurs out of his pocket and placed them on the table between me and Sevs. He explained what each one was. The first dinosaur had a dome-plated head meant for ramming, a Pachycephalosaurus. The second had a swooping head crest meant for making loud calls, a Parasaurolophus. And the third was a swift and nimble predator, a Velociraptor.

"Choose the wrong one and I'll pop your weasel dead." Captain Frumpy Butt pulled out an orange-capped toy gun and held it to Seven's forehead.

"Oh, this is awesome," Toby said and hopped up on the counter to watch. Allie surveyed the situation, then put her headphones back on and kept reading. Seven thought hard for a moment. Cycled through rounds of Jurassic Olympics to test each dino's attributes against one another. Then, without hesitation, he picked up all three dinosaurs and *put them in his mouth.*

"Hey!" Mackenzie yelled.

Seven got up into the aisle and roared with the plastic dinos clenched in his teeth. His hands turned into claws. His butt swooshed a make-believe tail. Captain Frumpy Butt gave Mackenzie the pop-gun and transformed into a dinosaur himself—bellowing like a beached whale. He and Seven grappled while Mackenzie fired off crackle rounds from the gun.

Two grown men pretending to be ancient lizards is a weird thing to see. I mean, Seven was drooling all over the place, and I was afraid Captain Frumpy Butt would never return to normal again. Well, whatever normal was for him anyway. Bad behavior and bad example at its finest.

The fight calmed down and Seven spat the dinosaurs into Captain Frump's hand. You'd think some sort of explanation was in order, but no. Those two nodded in approval of each other and it was over with. The extinct souls of noble reptiles left their bodies and returned to whatever tar pit tomb they'd escaped from.

"See. I told you," Captain Frumpy Butt said to sweater-moose Randy. "He's done us proud. I think we'll sleep just fine tonight." He left us and went back to his car, spanking himself on the way out the door. All of us tried to remember what we were doing before the ultimate distraction appeared, and we took our seats again.

"Avery. It's still your move." Seven used my real name when I zoned out or got lost in the horror circus of my own memories. That's me. Avery Lucille White. Lover of animal-shaped chocolates and ass-kicker aficionado. Known to enjoy cartoons with spaceships in them and scaring people from behind doors. Honestly, at that point I didn't care about the chess game anymore. He was letting me win so it didn't matter. How was I ever supposed to get better if Seven took it easy on me? I'd rather think I wasn't good and work hard to get better. To beat him at his best. Murder all his wooden minions and decorate my chess throne with their corpses.

"Sevs?" I asked. "What's the most powerful piece in chess?"

"That's easy," Toby said. His hand was fist deep in the milk glass and he pulled it out to lick chocolate off his fingers. "It's the king, doofus. If you lose the king, you're done."

Allie threw a hand towel at him. "Wipe your fingers off, Tobes. That's gross. And the king can only move one spot at a time. Not tactically superior to a piece like the knight. It can jump over any other piece to attack and evade."

"Knight, my ass," Toby said and shoved the towel into the glass. "I'm sticking with the king." He pulled the soaked towel out of the cup and sucked on it.

"Well, the queen can move far and in any direction," I added. "And I like that a girl is one of the strongest pieces."

"You're all kind of right," Seven said. "It depends on the situation, you know, what kind of hole you dig yourself into. One might be more powerful than another at different times. But I think the king sucks—sorry Toby. Kings aren't real. They don't exist and shouldn't exist. Not much different from a pawn, moving one space at a time. They're more like a pawn with a big ego. Knights are good but can miss crucial pieces from hopping around so much. The queen is beautiful and mighty, but if you rely on her too much, you'll be devastated when you lose her." He looked at me and sagged his face into a big frown. "But if I could be any piece, I'd be a pawn. It's definitely the coolest, in my opinion."

"Open what?" Mackenzie asked.

"Nothing," Allie said. "He said opin-ion." Al Pal tossed Mack a tootsie-roll and she put it in her mouth. Wrapper 'n' all. Mackenzie kid-slobbering all over that candy was a spectacle to behold, but I wasn't going to let that distract me.

"Why do you think so, Seven? Pawns get killed all the time in chess." I wanted to know the secret so I could use it to beat him one day. He perked up and leaned in close over the table. His fingers rolled a pawn back and forth and he had this look he got sometimes. It made him happy, sharing stuff with people. Thoughts. Sharing his thoughts with me.

"Who taught you to play chess? An ignorant, clearly. Anyway—if a pawn survives long enough, sometimes the other player will be too busy dealing with other threats on the board. And if you're careful and sneaky, you can make a run for it and get your pawn all the way across the board."

"What happens when you make it to the other side of the board? Can you jump off?" He laughed at me and placed the pawn in my hand.

"Well, kind of. It does disappear. When your pawn makes it to the last square of the board it can be promoted and transform into any other piece in the game. So, it could bring back a knight or a bishop—"

"A king!" Toby yelled. Allie threw a whole blanket over him this time.

"No, Toby, it can't. The king should burn in hell for eternity and I don't think they are real, anyway. A pawn can bring back the queen though, in all her rapacious splendor. Any piece it desires. Just like magic."

"More like cheating," Mackenzie said, one hundred percent serious and with some brown saliva leaking out her mouth.

"But what happens to the pawn?" I asked. He lost a bit of his smile and patted me on the head like I couldn't understand what he was going to say.

"The pawn goes away. Sacrifices itself for the greater good. Dies. Lives forever. Maybe goes on to catalog every aquatic mammal in some distant ocean moon. I don't know." 41

I was tired of holding my knees. My right leg had fallen

asleep and my butt was a little sweaty. The war against small uncomforts never stops, even when the sky starts exploding. I stood up on the chair, and then thought I'd go ahead and stand on the table. I stepped up and planted a foot in the middle of the board and looked down at Seven.

"So. The pawn gets to be kind of like God?" I toed over his king on the board. He stood up in the aisle and looked at me. My head was almost as tall as his with me standing on the table. It felt good.

"No. Not at all. I'd say that God—most fundamentally —means omniscience. It should know everything, right? So, even if God gave up its life, God shouldn't be scared, since it would know what was going to happen. And that's it. That's the real force that makes you scared. The unknown. God would *know*, and it would be no different than if God held the door open for you or fed your cat while you were on vacation. The pawn isn't the same—the pawn is the most scared out of everyone on the gameboard. Ready to poop a dead parrot in its chainmail at a moment's notice. But that doesn't matter. Despite not knowing what will happen, pawns charge forward through massacre and graveyard. Never turning back. For all the pawn knows, its death could be meaningless, or only lead to more violence, even on planes of existence it doesn't understand—like in the world of the chess player sliding the pieces across the chessboard. Fear and unknowns are the substance which lets pawns pierce a hole through time and space to thwart entropy, to manifest dreams, to perform the grandest miracle imaginable."

"Goddamn," I said. It's my favorite curse word. See, I think about God all the time, and I like knowing what other people think God is too. So. When you say *goddamn* to someone—you get to see what they think of the big, mighty bearded fellow. It's like I'm giving someone a present to unwrap, only I'm more excited to see what's inside because I don't know what they're gonna say. Goddamn is the final cosmic mystery, and every time I use it, someone hands me another one of God's puzzle pieces to fit together. So. I said the big GD. It was pretty much the end of the whole world with the Mouth of God singing its holy bastard hymns and we had the all clear to curse away, so I took full advantage. Dropped the holiest of word bombs.

"Goddamn," Seven repeated. "My dear Robot, one day the grand sum of all that is sacred will slump down before you. Eviscerated. With entrails strung through your fingers and its soul dead, damned, and dangled from your jaws." He gave me a big hug and spun me around. I looked at chocolate-finger'd Toby, at sleepy and constipated Allie, and even at herp-derped Mackenzie chewing on Sir Galileo's head. It felt like Seven flipped over the lid of the puzzle box and showed me the whole picture. Over his shoulder and out the window I saw the sun go goodnight. The sky filled with the trickling gold fire leaking through space where the stars used to be. Where all of the pieces to the puzzle were jumbled up now.

CHAPTER THREE

Show Me a Picture Where
Even an Ant Can Lift the Sun

H ello all you brave and fearless telescope knights floating up there, it's me again," I said into my dino walkie-talkie. It was a stupid kid toy with dull yellow spikes on one side and triangle teeth on the other. A sleepy reptile eye painted on the speaker hissed with crackles and static. The radio signal it sent out was super weak, but it was my nightly ritual. To call out to the astronaut scientists aboard the Great Seeker in orbit around the planet. Even if they could never hear me, maybe my record would be stored somewhere amongst the vast vibrating strings of the universe.

"Everything was pretty okay today [blip] This train is nice. I'm standing on the toilet looking out the window at dark trees. I'll pet one for all of you once we disembark. I imagined a gigantic walking donut this afternoon—chocolate glazed with pink sprinkles—terrorizing a community of old people with its very bad donut dance moves [blip] I imagined a herd of horses sprinting off a sea cliff and the sound they made on the rocks and waves below. My emotion level for the day is Sneaky

Tapir Wizard. I guess I feel a little anxious. About what happ-ens next. But who am I to say that to you?"

I tapped the window with the antennae.

"Seven killed a spider today. I feel weird about it [blip] Do you have spiders up there in the station? What do you do with them? I hope you don't airlock-eject 'em out into the Chasm of Eternal Solitude. I've been thinking more about that, the Chasm of Eternal Solitude. I don't think it's some sort of mid-night graveyard or volcano pit where all the lifeguards have pitchforks and flamethrowers. I think it might be just like this world. Only you're aware of it [blip] That no matter how close you try and get to someone or something, you always feel the space there. The space between two things. Anyway. Keep your pancakes fresh. Your hamsters happy. And your eyes on the core of forever eternal. Robot out."

After Seven and I cleaned up the chess pieces from our match, he saved Mackenzie from choking on some candy, and then decided it was bedtime for everyone. Allie and I got under a sleeping bag and watched the sky fall out the window. You didn't need the Great Seeker's mountain-top control lab to see it—the blowing up was a firework show now. The grand finale. You couldn't even see the stars anymore. The celestial erup-tions were too bright. Long clouds of light reached out and bubbled in big swirls over the tops of forest trees. Every now and then you could see a cooled energy blister pop, like gum in slow motion, into sharp shells of silver and blue. But I knew those bubbles were larger than our solar system, or even

45

billions of them. Whole galaxies vanished in an instant. A few patches of black splotched the sky, but they were getting smaller all the time.

Allie put her finger to the window and traced edges around the boomed light. I wondered if she missed someone, or was mad, or if she was pretending to be a wizard. But I didn't want to intrude on her thoughts and ask. They seemed private. So. I traced the intergalactic boom on the window with her. My finger smudged grease on the bright bulges and blurred them into the little bits of remaining black. I used my thumbnail to highlight the thin color around the edges of all the gold and purple heat. Sometimes Allie's finger and mine would touch. When that happened, we shared something we never could by talking. Whispering secrets. When our finger-tips collided, it felt as though we were the ones guiding all that holy fire out there. It was nice. Thinking we were in control. Because if we were, then I could make it all mean something. I could tell Seven about what the Mouth of God was and he'd figure it all out. Save everyone, just like he always did.

Sev's arm hugged Toby and Mackenzie—who I allowed to sleep with Galileo that night. My monkey pal looked over at me with his head squeezed through Mack's elbow. Just for the night, little buddy. Hang in there for me.

Allie was conked the hell out. Fast asleep clutching her sweater worm. Drooling enough to make damp ponds that could terraform her pillow into a habitat most suitable for a salamander slumber party. I made sure her glasses were secure in their case, gave her a goodnight head pat, and then slipped out into the aisle.

I snuck a juice carton from the fridge and drank it. The train rocked our car back and forth like a big crib. Quiet forest rushed by the windows as soft yellow light from the sky splashed on the shut-eyed faces of my friends. It's a little weird. Watching people sleep, I know it is. But who else is going to protect you while you dream? Seven and Toby. Allie and Mack. They all did so much for me during the day. Saved my butt more times than any seat ever had. Night was the only time I felt like I watched out for anybody. Made them feel safe. So. I stayed up all night, as long as I could to keep a secret patrol. I loved it. The way a shadow felt when I stepped into its cool puddle, or the way the moon was still in orbit, trying its best to block the universe from smashing into us.

I spent those nights wishing I could watch everyone in the world sleep. Pull a billion blankets right up to a billion chins to keep 'em warm, or however many chins were left alive. Make sure no monsters came to pull the covers off and make anyone cold, or something way worse. If you woke up nice and safe with your body parts still attached—all snug and warm under your comforter—you'd know I'd been there.

I won't lie. It got boring every now and then. Staying up so late. But that's why I played games. The table was collapsed to the floor so Seven could rest his feet on the seat in front of him. I sat down beside his footsies and tugged on his sock a little to make it straight. Seven was leaned back with his mouth open. I could've thrown a peanut in it and choked him right there. I checked the clock and saw it was 2:30 a.m., or what I liked to call: *Imaginary Conversation Time.*

"*Seven,*" I imaginary-said, "*all the numbers on the number line have decided you are no longer needed. They, after much*

47

deliberation, declare war on your most comfy and cozy spot among them in the top ten. Their army is infinite. Their hunger is deep. How will you defend against them? Against what you're a part of? Against all of the endless other Seven Point Ones and Twos and the numbers they've joined?"

I held out my dino walkie-talkie to his open mouth and sleeping head.

"*I don't plan on fighting,*" he imaginary-replied. "*I'm just going to make some pancakes. Maybe some bacon. Then I'm going to make a pancake hat and wear it around with a bacon mustache. The numbers won't know what hit 'em. Captain Breakfast doesn't take shit from anybody. Not from French toast and powdered sugar, and especially not from numbers. Numbers are for calculators and birthday pony rides.*"

I brought the microphone back to me.

"*Professor Oulglaive, your defense strategy could use some work. We're talking about a sky-filled armada set out to destroy you. Physics and probability. Time and space. You can't possibly think a plate of breakfast will save you! And what do pony rides have to do with anything?*"

I dropped the walkie and threw my hands in the air.

"*Your mom is a birthday pony ride, but you're also right. I've got it all wrong.*" Seven snored a bit and then continued. "*There's no way I can get bacon to stick to my lip. What I'll do is put the bacon in the pancakes. That will really throw them off.*"

"*Again, your plan seems a bit—*"

"*Delicious. Do you know how many numbers there are in maple syrup? I don't, but it's at least, hmm . . . twelve. I could probably take out a dozen of them in one bite!*"

I giggled and Seven started to wake up. I drooped my head and pretended I was out cold. Started breathing nice and slow. Even changed the look on my face to cute and peaceful. He didn't say anything, but I sensed him look around a little, so I woke up with a fake yawn and caught him gazing out the window at the Mouth of God. He was thinking about stuff I could never understand. Real smart people stuff. About all those numbers out there trying to kill us. He could think up a better plan than making bacon pancakes for sure. If he had his telescopes with him he probably would've figured it out by then. His scopes were neat. One was so big I could fit right inside its polished magnification throat—but he didn't have a telescope with him then. Just food and water for us, camping stuff, and the weapons.

Anyway, the Great Seeker would cast any telescope we could've carried on our backs straight into the primordial-flux plasma of the Big Bang—spanked it all the way back through time to our universe's star-blind and egg-laying grandma. The Great Seeker's orbital station was crewed around the clock by the best astronaut-astronomers the world had ever known, and whole arrays of radio-dish 'scopes and gravity-wave detectors and special particle catchers on the ground were linked together with the magnificence of its behemoth galaxy-gulping eye—one made of hexagonal mirrors the size of swimming pools all protected by a sphere of white armor—its sensors locked in horror upon the spontaneous combustion of our reality. Our home.

I teared up at the thought of the Great Seeker. All lonely up in space, surrounded by its dead telescope friends whose simple-circuit-minds couldn't handle the Mouth of God's introductory particle barrage. Seven saw me awake and gave a concerned eye scrunch.

"You should be recharging now," he whispered. "We don't want you to run outta batteries."

"Real cute," I whispered back, sounding a little annoyed and still sleepy.

"You're okay?"

"Yeah, I'm good."

"Beep boop?"

"Beep . . . boop," I conceded.

He did a happy wiggle. Gently pulled his arm out from behind Mack and Toby to rest one behind the seat and the other in his lap. So relaxed. Sitting in a chair with a finger in his bellybutton looked like the coolest thing if you watched him long enough.

"Seven, are you okay?" He didn't answer right away, which if you don't know, meant he was not okay. Even sleepy-headed Toby and Mack could tell that. They snoozed away in agreement.

"Of course I am," he said, and pouted his lower lip.

"Can we go outside for a minute?"

"It's cold out there. We got on the train so we wouldn't have to shiver anymore."

"What's wrong with shivering every now and then?" I hugged myself and shook.

"I don't know. It makes me feel like I have to pee."

"Well, you can whiz off the railing onto the train tracks."

"You can go outside in the morning. After we sleep."

"I'll give in if you tell me what's really bothering you."

He thought he was clever, but I could see broken thoughts

through that paper skull of his. Little figures dancing on the inside of an old flimsy lantern. I'd never seen him upset. Not even once. After all the people he lost, his friends, his family, you'd think he'd get sad from time to time. He only got serious if one of us started a Great Fall. You know, when you start missing the people who aren't around anymore. Seven would see us plunging down that big hole into bad feelings and thoughts and he'd snatch us right back up. Stop us from falling all the way to the bottom of a well where there were things that smelled like wet toad goats regurgitating movie-theater popcorn. He could do that better than almost anything else. Better than he could name stars, find hidden planets around them, or imitate our favorite animals. I think he could only do this by keeping his deepest feelings hidden, drowned beyond the edge of a black hole somewhere inside him.

See, everyone has a black hole. Something hidden below their smooth surface you can never glimpse. Because if you ever did see it—you'd be lost inside whatever garden grew there. You could never return to yourself once you peeped something as precious and secret as that. You'd just wink out of the world and all your friends would forget that you ever existed at all. The way you wake up from a dream and a golden flood sweeps in to destroy that entire world trembling inside your head.

"Am I doing a good job of being your bodyguard?" he asked me.

"Sure. But I still think of you as a professor. Just a weird-ass astronomer my dad dragged to class one day and was easy to make fun of. But, yeah. You're Star Captain numero uno for all of us. Pilot of the crashin' spaceship. Don't mess it up."

51

"I'm trying not to."

"Good. But I want you to tell me what you were *really* thinking before I caught you staring out the window all . . . all lonely like and everything."

"My mom," he said.

"Your mom?"

"If you look out the window you might be able to see it. Blinking way off over the treetops." Far away over the frilly pine-needle canopies were a few red lights blinking on a tall tower. One of those that's real thin and held up by cables.

"*That is not your mom,*" I said.

"No, it isn't. But she told me about those towers once. When I was little like you. She told me that if you stood underneath one, and closed your eyes tight, that it would launch you. Not through the sky, but through other people's dreams. Like flying on a spaceship into someone else's mind, all the worlds sleeping there. She said those towers would let you dip into a never-ending imagination if you believed they would."

"Did you ever try it?" I asked.

"Once, when I was a lot older."

"What happened?"

"Well, I was waiting in my car out in the woods one night by a tower like that, listening to some music."

"Waiting for what?"

"A girl."

"A girl?"

"Yes, we were supposed to meet out there."

"Was she your girlfriend?"

"No. I wanted her to be, but I guess I wasn't her type."

"Hmm, can't blame her."

"You don't even know what I'm talking about," he said. Silent and calm, he raised a long finger and wagged it at me. I *hate* wagging fingers.

"Yes, I do."

"What do I mean by *type* then?" It was obvious this conversation was going off track.

"It's like you're an octopus and she's a whale. They can be friends, but secretly all you want to do is eat each other alive." He nodded and the conversation hopped back on the rails.

"Alright, alright. One breathes air and one doesn't, I got it. Well the girl never showed up and I got pretty bored."

"Never showed? What a stupid idiot."

"What?"

"Nothing. It's just that if someone is waiting on you at night in the woods you should show up."

"Even if they're a whale and you're an octopus?"

Damn. He really knew how to corner me with my own words.

"Yes, Eight. Even if you're a dumb, gimpy, sandal-snarfing octopus and they're a stupid barnacle-pooping whale."

"Exactly. Now let's continue." He inflated his chest with victory like he was about to barf it all over the place.

"Nah. I'm bored now. You're a good storyteller, but this one blows."

"You keep interrupting me!"

I put a finger to my mouth. "Shhh."

Mackenzie tightened her grip on Galileo and Toby wheezed. Seven shrugged and pawed at his eye. I tickled his foot a little and he toed me under my armpit. He looked at me and I looked at him. We could stare at each other all night and all day like that. It was a game he made students play when he came and visited my school.

The Unseen World game he called it.

Here's how you play: First you sit down in a chair, feet on the floor, of course, across from someone else. Then you stare into each other's eyes. And I mean really, really stare into them. Seven told us to look hard at the eye color, and then to peer even deeper past that, past striations and rifts and patterns and microdots of hue. Then we'd draw worlds based on our observations of the other person—recreate the plants, animals, lakes, and landscapes we'd seen inside. How they interacted. How the world formed its atmosphere and how that planet or moon orbited in its solar system, where the solar system was in the galaxy, and finally, where Seven thought our worlds were located on a big image of the universe—a picture taken from the Great Seeker called the Liemlar Ultra-Deep Field. It was a clever game and I thought about Unseen Worlds all the time. I wondered if his mom had taught him how to play when he was young like me.

I stared at Seven. Into the big grey seas in his eye holes where stripes of blue surf peeped through the foam. There was a whole ocean world inside there. Full of islands with monkeys playing coconut drums and happy dolphins saving drowning sailors. Exploring that ocean was one of my favorite things to do. I had a rowboat and would paddle around in the waves, use a little spyglass to look at stuff from far away, searching for a special kind of treasure I knew was buried in there somewhere. His ultimate core. But I didn't want to open that treasure chest and see what was inside. *Remember*, seeing something like that will annihilate your soul. I just thought I could maybe tell him where it was. Mark an "X" on his map. Help chart a path to his own blackhole and let him see for himself what mystery burbled inside.

I wondered if he remembered the Unseen World game, but was too embarrassed to ask. Maybe he didn't imagine a world in my wide-open peepers and thought something was wrong with my brain when I stared at him for so long. But thinking my eyes were empty made me sad.

So. I thought the opposite. I decided that when he looked at me, Seven saw not just one world—but all of them. Everything that could ever be. That's why we could stare so long at each other, because there were forever amounts of things to find in me. A little presumptuous, I know. But I wanted it to be true not just for my sake but for his, and also for Allie, Toby, Mack-a-Doodle, and even the Great Seeker and planet Earth and all the trembling galaxies. We needed all the worlds we could get if we were to survive.

The train passed a line of sharp cone trees with human bodies impaled on their tips. Long streamers stretched from their chests out to the faraway space-lava of the Mouth of God, but we ignored them. Same sprinkles, different donut. We were busy making our own reality, and I focused so hard that Seven's skin split with jets of water that flooded the whole cabin until he dissolved into a full blue-blooded sea. My seat hardened into a boat and I paddled around in his world as he made his way through my universe. I bobbed by an island where the girl that didn't meet him in the woods brushed her hair on a fallen palm tree. With a slap of my paddle on the water, a black and white killer whale beached itself on the sand in a shiny arc. The killer whale bit the girl's leg and shook her back and forth like a dog with a sock until her plastic Barbie arms flew off into the water. Splish and splash.

In my universe, I imagined Seven climbing an icy mountain with two ice picks, sticking one and then the other into the snowy cold before taking another step up. At the summit was a pond full of swans swimming upside down underneath the surface. The water was made of all the tears from their crying. It scared me. Not the swans, but whatever made them weep.

Seven's ocean flashed away under me in a puff of steam and slid back into his body, smooth as rain. My interior swan world faded—the mountain slinking back into the Earth to form a flat desert, but still the pond remained. Sad and rippled by paddling bird feet.

"Hey, Sevs, will you tell me a story?"

Storytelling was one of his favorite things to do. I loved listening to his tales. Everyone did. They were good right from the start, even better after they ended. They grabbed you by the hand and led you into a perfect dream. Huge ones that felt small and small ones that felt huge. He turned your heart into a heavy gate and slid it open, nice 'n' slow. Took you to places inside yourself you never knew were there, but always were. Made you feel things you'd never felt before. Happy and sad. Connected and alone. All at the same time. At the end you felt like a different person. Like the stars shifted just from his words to make you the center of the universe, casting their light so you could see all your shadows—but never be able to pick out the one that was the core of you.

"What kind of story?" He tried freeing Galileo from Mackenzie's elbow, but she only squeezed tighter.

"I don't know yet. Lemme think."

"Anything you want, Robot." I brought my knees up to my chest and wrapped my arms around them. Seven took the blanket off his lap and tossed it to me. The fabric was warm and smelled like cedar trees from the woods. I put it over his feet.

"Machines don't get cold," I said, moving my arm up and down.

"Please, Miss White." I pulled the blanket over my legs but made sure to keep his feet nice and cozy. Being under that blanket made me feel safe.

"I don't like this," I said.

"Don't like what?"

"Not knowing if we'll get to the Great Seeker or find it in time. Not knowing what's gonna happen, or how many body parts we'll be munched into."

"You're worried about all of us getting snacked on?" I nodded and got a shiver out of nowhere, but unlike Seven, it didn't make me feel like I had to pee. "I'm going to keep you as safe as Mr. Banana is in Mack-a-Doodle's arm right now."

"But Mackenzie eats bananas."

"So?"

"So? We're not safe. The Mouth is going to eat us like Mack is going to eat Galileo. I saw her try to do it earlier." I put my hands together and made them bite down.

"The Mouth of God is not going to eat us."

"Are you going to stop it?" My hand chomper opened up again.

"No," he said. My hands chomped hard. Seven leaned forward and pulled them apart. "I don't think I can do it. But you—"

"Me?"

57

"Yeah, you. I think you're gonna bust its teeth out, implode the sky's whole stupid face into an oblivion of curved sorrow." He opened his mouth and bit down. "The Mouth of God is going to totally shit its pajamas after you're done with it. When we get to the Great Seeker, I'll show you exactly where to fire your robo-lasers." He booped me on the nose and rested back into his seat.

"Hey, Professor Oulglaive, I know what story I want to hear now." I tugged on my necklace with a pendant of the Little Dipper constellation, or as me and astronomers call it, Ursa Minor, or Little Bear. Sevs blinked, overly quizzical, stroked his chin, and sat up. Tugged on his own necklace with a pendant of Ursa Major, also known as the Big Dipper and the Great Bear. I tucked my stars away and let him know what was on my mind. "I want you to tell me the greatest story ever told." He stopped being dumb and his head went a little sideways, real sneaky like and thinky. I caught him off guard. Ten points for Robot.

"What if it's sad?"

"I don't care."

"Or people get hurt?"

"Everyone does." He got all serious then. His seas went flat with not even a wave or a ripple. It let me know he did indeed know the story I asked him to tell. "Let me hear it."

"I can't," he said, and then covered his mouth with a finger. Like that was going to keep the story in there.

"Don't mess with me, Eight. Tell me the story." He pulled his feet off the chair beside me and shook his head back and forth. He was scared of it, the story.

I slid forward in my seat. "Tell me already, you lopsided

monkey puncher," I whispered as nice as I could. Nudged his knee a bit. But he didn't budge. He knew I meant business and was going to pry it outta him. Every last nail out of the story's coffin. "Tell me."

He whispered, "I can't."

"Seven." He looked up again. Branches from a tree brushed by the window. I held my walkie-talkie up and transmitted my request to the Great Seeker astronauts—to the whole gaping cosmoverse. "I want to hear the story all fiction stems from."

That really shocked him. Jolted wrinkles right into his forehead.

"I want to hear the bedtime story that tucks God in for sleep, swaddled and warm. Then sets its bedroom on fire. I want to hear the last breath of a sea-monster prince. A song that pulls the arms off starfish. Tigers paddling through sunken temples. All clocks on fire. Starship fleets colliding. Give me the lone knight atop a tower—the eyeless giant biting cannon balls and castle walls. Blood-prayer summon a dinosaur extinction. Show me a picture where even an ant can lift the sun. Tell me why every soul has its own garden in heaven, but no matter what we do, all are forbidden from entering."

Seven looked out the window to watch the sky's solar-war march toward our home. Then he scooted forward to take my hand. His cheek had a wet streak on it. He was crying. A tear followed the trail until it landed on the back of my hand. His seas were gone. Poured right out onto the carpet with the last drop on me. His oceans were all dried up with the sharks and fish and whales flopping around on its muddy floor. Gasping for water. It looked like they were singing a song I couldn't hear.

59

"Okay, are you ready to hear it?" Sevs asked. "Listen."

He took the dino walkie and nodded at the window. At the trees and the ground and the sky. The train clicked and clacked like pages being turned and the wind howled the chapter titles. Then Seven looked all over the train car. At Allie. Drool spilled out of her mouth in a puddle of ink. He watched Toby and Mack. Their little snores and booger whistles punctuated sentences and spaced paragraphs. He remembered to look at Captain Frumps' chocolate milkshake stain on the wall and at super-squeezed Galileo. Seven took in the tiniest details, and at last he looked at me. Brushed away some of my hair and cupped my cheek. Tweaked my ear a little.

"You're inside of it, this story you want to hear. The main character is sitting across from me right now. I'm not the one who's going to tell it to you. You're going to be the one who tells it to me."

Seven closed my hands around the walkie and sat back. Put his feet by me again and shut his eyes. I stared out the window. At the shadows of trees and the Mouth of God peering through them. I watched the breathing of Seven and my friends, how their chests inflated like balloons that could never be filled. I read our story a while longer, and then pulled my bookmark out of a magazine. Put it in my lap to save my place for when I woke.

CHAPTER FOUR

Piku Bo-Bebop Tucan Maru

I woke up because Toby, with his head inside a paper bag, was drumming on my shoulder with an eggbeater. I didn't appreciate him moving my bookmark to this page in our story. Mackenzie helped Seven make food in the kitchen. Well, in her mind anyway. She wore a dirty apron over her overalls and shoved anything she could get her hands on into the apron pocket. An eggshell. A handful of flour. Some plastic wrappers. Seven had food steaming up on the stove where he spatula-spanked an array of breakfast wonders. Allie drowned out the noise with her headphones and bobbed her head to the music. A perfect morning. Outside the sky slunk blue and cloudless, but I could still see the Mouth of God's yellow ghost bubbling and popping in a faraway mist—a thermal reef boiling far below water.

Oh yeah, and Toby was still whacking me with a kitchen utensil. I guess with the bag over his face he couldn't tell I was awake. So. I rolled over real quick, assumed an attack pose, and with a tiny *hiyaaa* gave him a flawless ninja kick that sent him headfirst into the seat. Assassination complete.

61

I left him and took my small ladybug bag into the bathroom. Peed and brushed my teeth, but not in that order. I tickled my armpits with a mini deodorant stick. I know that stuff is meant for grownups, but when you go weeks without bathing it can make you smell like fresh laundry. I paid little attention to my hair. Pulled out a few knots with my fingers and then called it quits. Looking fashionable in those days didn't get you anywhere. I like to think it never really did. My dress stopped in a sharp cut at my knees and fluttered in its usual state of dirtiness. The fabric was tan, which helped make mud and stains blend in, but you could tell the flower-bud pattern was starting to fade. Makenzie had colored some of the struggling petals with a marker in hopes of bringing the buds back to life, but her Crayola gardening hadn't been fruitful. My leggings rounded out the outfit, a little torn and holey and blood encrusted. I could've changed into new ones, but I liked looking tough.

When I came out, Toby was busy adding fangs and eyebrows to his bag mask while bothering Allie about her music, so I checked on breakfast. Whaddya know? Pancakes, rice, and bacon. Yeah, it was kind of a weird combo, but it beat sucking on tree bark and hacking down grubworms. A pancake and bacon burrito was going to be the tastiest thing I'd eaten in a month. I propped my elbows up on the bar top and knelt on a stool. Mackenzie let out a sneaky *hee hee* before taking something out of her apron. She pulled the string of a small party popper and shot confetti streamers all over the stove. Little paper caterpillars curled and died black-charred deaths on the burners, having only known life as an explosion and split-second freedom of air.

"Hey!" Toby shouted from inside his bag mask. "Those are only for special occasions."

Seven pulled a massive pink tube out of his back pocket —the big mama party popper that gave birth to all the other ones in the pack Captain Frumpy Butt gave us.

"All hail the *Prometheus Popper*," Tobes said with a salute.

What a dumb name.

"Well Toberkins, um," Mackenzie said. Picking her nose with the spent confetti popper. "Maybe you should like all the pancakes more."

I ignored the rest of their arguing and pet my stomach. "It's feeding time at the aquarium. Who eats first? The whales or the octopi?"

Seven flipped a pillow-fluffed pancake and caught it on the plate. "The whales are going to have to wait a minute for all the meat to cook."

"Whales don't eat meat."

"All whales eat meat, and killer whales sure do."

"You told me killer whales are a kind of dolphin. Besides, they only eat girls who don't meet people in the woods under cable towers."

Seven tossed a pancake in the air but missed it with the plate. The serving of breakfast food bounced off Mackenzie's head and landed flat on the floor. "Wait, what?" he asked.

"Nothing, Captain Breakfast. Don't take shit from anyone." He twisted the spatula back and forth like he was gonna unscrew my brain to see what was wrong with it. It took me a second to realize I was using lingo from *Imaginary Conversation Time*, and Seven didn't have a clue as to what I was talking about. I rolled with it though.

63

"Hey, let's give that flapjack to Mack." I pointed to the pancake on the floor. He nabbed it off the ground and put the contaminated pancake somewhere in the finished stack.

"We'll never know who eats it now!" Seven began his signature mad-scientist *muahahahahahaa-bwahahaha* laugh as he shuffled all the pancakes like cards in a deck.

Allie took her headphones off and gazed on in confusion. Mackenzie skipped over to her and snatched a napkin from under the seat and shoved it in her apron pocket, which now also contained Galileo—plunged headfirst into its depths. That's borderline animal cruelty if you ask me. Seven took notice of Galileo's primate plight and stopped Mack with a spatula to the chest. Then he grabbed a metal spoon and held it to his nose.

"I don't think, I don't think Tycho Brahe can breathe down there." Seven snorted and wheezed on purpose. "*Mu-ahahaHahaha-BwuahahaHahahahahahaha!*"

Sevs choked a little and then pointed to the spoon.

"Metal nose, I tell ya. Tycho-friggin'-Brahe." Mackenzie laughed along, too, but only because she discovered the un-attended bowl of batter felt good with her hands inside it. Allie nibbled on her headphone cable.

"Honestly," she said, "Hubble is a better name for the monkey. The name of an astronomer *and* the space telescope dedicated to him. Those two are classic."

"The librarian speaks the truth." Toby got on his knees and held his hands high in the air. "Bow to Lord Bookworm." He bent over, and it almost didn't seem fake. Real reverent and respectful. Then he passed gas.

I ignored Toby's salute to Allie.

"Seven, do you need any help?"

"Not right now, Jane Goodall." He whipped up the last of the batter.

"Can you do me a favor?"

"No, maybe. Yes."

"Will you put some of that bacon inside a pancake, please?" I asked.

"Roger that."

Imagination turned to reality I tell ya. Easy-peasy. All those numbers self-combusting in outer space didn't stand a chance against my breakfast weapon. I joined my only sane company on the trip and let out a huff.

"Allie, how were we going to ditch all these weirdoes again?" At that, Toby stopped being a moron and got off the floor. He opened his mouth to talk, and then closed it. I'm sure he was about to say something not very nice—maybe something about my "*squinty*" eyes again, although the two-hour-long lecture on race and body types Seven gave him after his last comment probably made him hesitate—a ninth wonder of the world in its own way for sure.

"What?" I asked. Toby shrugged and kept quiet, which was for the best.

Al Pal said what he'd been smart enough not to. "Ditch *these* weirdoes? You're one of the weirdoes, you know that, right?" She winked, but I still wanted to get her back some-how. I thought about making fun of how she was having problems going number two, but then I'd have been the only one who'd really said anything mean.

"Hey," I whispered. "I've got a secret to tell you."

"About what?" she asked.

65

I made sure to look back and forth to ensure no one else could hear.

"About my room in our Super Ultimate Treehouse."

Allie dropped her pen to the floor. Yep, this was serious business. We started talk of this future treehouse when it was just me and her, before Seven found us. We only discussed it when we were alone and never let anyone else know what we were up to. Of course, we planned on inviting everyone over to the Super Ultimate Treehouse after it was built. We were legally obligated according to an agreement scrawled on a napkin that I forced Allie to sign after Toby put a squashed-flat and sundried frog inside of her notebook.

Allie made a roof over her head with a book and wrinkled her nose.

"Let's take this outside," she said with a finger to my lips.

Seven huddled over a skillet on the stove, working delicately with a flippy-scraper and fork as if he were calibrating some special clock to run time backward. Mack and Toby sat on the countertop beside him. They both let out a long *aaaaaaaaaah* in awe of whatever sizzled in the pan and, I must admit, smelled especially tasty.

"Seven," I said. "The ladies are stepping outside for a moment."

"Good god," he replied, still staring at the food. "Hal," this was another nickname I didn't understand, "please don't jettison me into outer space. Not before you see *this*."

Seven turned around with the skillet in his hand. In its center was what I'd asked for. A pancake with bacon inside it. Three slices ran parallel to each other through the fluffy circle. He scraped it off onto an empty plate—a big gesture, him not mixing it in with the pancake contaminated with Mack's hair and floor germs. "Robot, you should've told me a genius programmed your breakfast food routines."

"I will be the one to take that honor," Toby said, real regal and important sounding. He took up the eggbeater as his magic wand. "I reprogrammed her this morning."

I tried to give him my worst look, but he was too busy basking in his self-coronation with a scepter used to stir up liquid chicken babies.

Seven held the bacon pancake high in the air. "May absolute despair and annihilation befall all who gaze upon this miracle."

Syrup drizzled from his offering.

"Hear the drowned leviathan gasp. If starfish sing, they perish. Tigers sink, hide, and laugh. All clocks on fire. All starships cratered. A tower marked with giant's teeth. The reptile tomb unseals. Blood insect sunrise. Swaddled-myth-extinction. Circuits searching, lance aflame, robots breach the garden gate—unmake heaven, and prune the lost grove of golden fruit."

His incantation complete, Seven set the now ultra-sacred breakfast food back on a plate. Mackenzie raised a finger to her face, as cautious and confused as the rest of us, then plunged it straight into the core of the witch-curse pancake.

"Have fun with that," Allie said, and hooked me under the arm.

We went through the door that joined our car to Captain Frumpy Butt's car. Their train cabin had multicolored lights hanging in the windows. I called it the Fiesta Car. We stepped out to the transfer deck and found Captain Frumpy Butt on the connector, snacking on some sunflower seeds while the stained moose head on his sweater eyed the wilderness. Outside on the platform the air was cool and crisp and the forest saluted us with still branches. Clackity clack went our little train over the railroad. The mountain air was good, not like the fumes from the city. This was fresh. Alive and free of destruction—Grade A nature. Lord Bookworm and I leaned up against a guard rail and observed a cluster of white rocks jutting from a hill.

Captain Frumps finished his last seed and then sputtered the shells out of his mouth in machine-gun fashion. "I fought a Quetzalcoatlus last night in my dream. A full-blooded pterodactyl complete with a fifty-foot reptilian wingspan. Stood taller than a giraffe. Had this knife-edge beak the size of a surfboard. You girls know what I'm talking about?"

We let loose some anxious chuckles and shook our heads.

"Listen. This thing was Mesoamerican deity incarnate. Huge." He pulled an orange pterodactyl toy out of his pocket and made it hop on the handrail. "She ran at me through a baseball field swarming with badgers, her knuckled fingers flinging the furry fuckers high up over the stadium lights. Gnawin' on a few of 'em, too. I stood at home plate with my arm cocked back, baseball bat stirrin' little circles in the air. That behemoth craned her head all catawampus to peep me real good 'n' proper, but I'd had it with that prehistoric condescension gazing down on me."

He pulled a smaller two-legged dino out and made it fight the pterodactyl with swooping headbutts.

"So, I stormed the mound. Brought the fight straight to her gaping wide gullet. Beat her in the beak and smashed her claws after she tried to pop my head like a porcupine. I managed to gouge one of her big black eyes right outta its socket, but she scraped me up real good. Chomped off summa my fingeys."

Allie yawned. Captain Frumps and myself assumed expressions that snapped her jaw closed.

"Well," he said, "you gals know why I'm telling y'all this horror show stuff?"

"Because it's *freaking* awesome," I said with an enthusiastic arm pump.

"I'm pleased you approve of my subconscious, sanguine savagery, but I'm trying to teach ya something too." He took in a deep breath to help carry the weight of his words.

"*Piku Bo-Bebop Tucan Maru.*"

Trees bent heavy in the wind. Grass bowed in long zagged waves. Some falcon circled high before an archway of cloud-kingdom summer. The pterodactyl toy and two-legged head butter scooted close together on the railing and embraced softly with all the love the end of the world could hold, tiny and tight, in plastic dinosaur arms.

Allie was not impressed with this wisdom.

"Captain Frumpy Butt, that doesn't make any sense."

"It doesn't, does it?" he asked with some secret wildness twinkling in his eye—the falcon divebombing that sky-door of cloud. "If the world won't make sense anymore, why should *we* have to?"

Captain Frumps stared right into the sun for a second. Blew it a kiss. Then he tossed the dinosaurs off the train into a creek.

"When that one-eyed pterodactyloid bit my arm off, I knew I was done for. She gripped me good and flew up high, through cloud and lightning and space and stars, right into the seething heart of eternity. She burned me alive all the way down to that hollow pit where your soul should be. Where your dreams end up when you've solved your own secrets. But it was okay. I had fun the whole time—kept a smile on even after it dissolved from my face." The good Captain Frumpy Butt hooked an arm up in his sleeve to make his elbow a stumpy appendage. "Try 'n' smile back from time to time for me, will ya?" His fake arm stump struggled to wipe away the damp creases around his eyes. He took a shaky breath. Waved to the nature rushing by, then ducked back into the Fiesta Car.

"That old man needs adult supervision," Allie said. "Remember when he blasted the milkshake all over himself and said he wanted to *become a stain?*"

"Oh, I remember. I think that's why I love 'em, right down to that dirty moose hanging out on his sweater. What's its name—Randy? You can't let your moose get hungry, ya know? Or else it'll eat your babies."

Al Pal nibbled on the sleeve of her sweater and mumbled. "Do you still want to have a secret passage from my room to yours? In the treehouse?"

"Of course. We'll put one behind some bookshelves, or a big mirror."

"Okay, good. I was worried maybe you didn't want one anymore." Nibble nibble.

I nudged her. "Don't be a ridiculous rhinoceros."

"You know, we could have a zoo down on the ground level." She stopped munching on her sweater.

"Yeah, or even in the lobby."

"No cages though," she said.

"Definitely no cages."

"A zebra receptionist and an alligator doorman." Dimples popped up on her cheeks as she smiled into the woods.

"Lemurs can deliver room service with tiny top hats and pockets full of mints." I made my fingers leap along the railing.

"Dolphin swim coaches in the pool." Allie waved her hand and arm up and down in slow dips.

"We'll be the zookeepers, Al Pal."

The train pulled around a bend and crossed a bridge where the river below crashed and frothed on big oval stones. Several large trees plunged down the flow. They'd been torn in half and were splintered real bad. One sported a dark red stain on its bark, a color we were starting to see more and more of. Upstream, I could feel the upside-down swans from the pond in my imagination with their necks craned, weeping beneath the current. Beyond the river a meadow full of green grass and yellow flowers stretched out to the base of rocky mountains.

"So," Allie asked, "what's the secret you wanted to tell me?" I had a few to choose from but hadn't really picked one out.

Flowers in the field bent and bobbed, and I smelled them with a deep sniff. Life. It didn't make much sense to me—why you decorate the dead with them, flowers, that is. Why kill them just because something else died?

"I know that once we're safe we'll build the Super Ultimate Treehouse." I spit over the railing into the river. "But that doesn't mean bad things will stop happening. We're all going to bleed to death from our ears sooner or later."

"That's not a secret," she said with a tap to her glasses.

"Right. Well, when I'm gone, whether I fall off the deck on the third floor and crack my back on a branch, drown in the hot tub, or accidentally get stomped on by a life-size dinosaur toy, I don't want a grave."

"No grave?"

"Yep. They're sad. They make me sad. They make it seem like you're in one place and that's a lie. After you're gone, you're in all kinds of places." Al Pal reared back and spit into the rushing grass now that we were over the bridge. "Exactly. See? Part of you is out there now. I hate seeing the tacky graves made out of debris and ripped-up clothing all over the place. I don't want rubble to remind you of me."

"Bookmarks," she said.

"Huh?"

"Even when you're not around, bookmarks remind me of you. All the ones you've made for me. How it feels when I play with the tassels and strings on them while I read. All that reminds me of you."

I put my arm around her and pulled her in close. Pinched her sweater worm. "That's right, Lord Bookworm. I want everything to remind you of me, not some silly hunk of stone or even a bookmark. I want you to see me in falling leaves and icing on birthday cake decorations. In funny movies and shooting stars. When I'm gone, I don't want you to think that I'm really gone at all. I want you to think I'm part of everything, trying my best to make the world a good place for you. Nothing sad about that."

Allie nibbled on my sleeve for a second. "Nothing sad at all. From a distance, the garden and the graveyard appear the same."

A door flew open behind us. The Conductor ran out onto the platform and bent over. He was a geezer with a thick white beard, usually calm and cool while stroking his face hairs with a little patch of velcro. Right then it looked like he was about to mess his pants. He was panting, sweating, and making awkward gestures to the Fiesta Car. His baseball hat flew off his head and he didn't even try to catch it.

"One of them is heading for the train." He covered his eyes with a hand, then wiped his mouth. "A Messenger."

The Conductor pointed to the empty pasture and then raced over to the Fiesta Car. Allie went back inside, but I stayed at the door and watched weapons and ammo spill off the tables. Playtime was over. Mack took the regular bullets out of the rifle and tried, unsuccessfully, to put the red tipped projectiles in. Those were the ones that blew up when they hit. Reserved only for Mouth of God emergencies. Toby busted out a window with a skillet and propped the grenade launcher's snout outside. He wasn't supposed to use it, since when Seven showed him how, Tobes had 'naded our car and blown its tires into a swimming pool—but he'd use it if he had to. Seven strapped his sword to his back and unhinged the Dance Party. That's what we called his double-barreled shotgun. One night, we went into a house and this boom box wouldn't stop playing dance music. So. He turned it off with a round from the gun. Hilarious, I know. Seven filled the weapon tubes with ammo. Two red shells blessed with drawings by Mackenzie—a rabbit head she liked to doodle every-where. If you pulled up her overalls you'd see her legs covered

73

in the furry buttheads, all floppy-eared, scrunch-eyed, and with their tongues stuck out.

Allie sucked hard on her sweater neck, trembly and nervous, but she rushed to Mack and helped push the heavy bullets in the rifle magazine. Mackenzie thought Allie was cold because she was shaking so much, so Mack threw a blanket on her. There they were—all my friends preparing for battle. Saving me again.

My hand rested on the rung of a ladder that led to the train roof. I decided the least I could do was yell when it was coming. Plus, I'd never seen one of the Mouth of God's *Messengers* up close and operational. Just blips of weird geometry lodged in skyscrapers or electro-burning in muddy pastures. I climbed to the roof and fought against the wind to earn my footing. I looked out at the yellow-spotted plain for the pair but didn't see anything at first. Nothing but boulders, grass, and flowers. Then I noticed something that didn't fade away with distance. It kept in step with the train. A black sphere the size of a car hovered a few feet over the ground about a soccer field or two away from the railroad. It zoomed in a straight line, occasionally dipping down to make tracks in the grass and kick up a dirt wake. Flower petals tore apart and fluttered away in the breeze behind it. On fire. Black fire.

Our group called them Halos. The Conductor called them Messengers, but everyone had different names for 'em. That's what Seven told us. He said they could be in lots of different shapes and colors—but they were all unique and bad. Very bad. The Halo shot down into the ground and disappeared. I could see the humped trail of its burrow as the Halo headed for the train. But its owner was nowhere in sight and that worried me. Out of everyone we'd met, Seven was the only one who'd taken on what we called an Angel, and its Halo, alone. He'd killed a single pair of them. An Angel and its Halo. Beings sent from the Mouth of God.

"Get down," the Conductor shouted from the platform. I shooed him away and yelled back.

"Tell Seven it's burrowing and will be here in thirty seconds!" The Conductor ran back into our car and I kept my eye on the Halo in its Bugs Bunny tunnel. I was a little scared, even though I knew Seven would take care of everything. He'd sworn promised oaths to protect my motherboard and memory cards, and that was long before the Mouth appeared. We were in for a fight, alright, but Sevs had some special equipment that would tear 'em a new one. Good old Seven's head popped up over the ladder rung. He clambered to his feet and covered my heart with a hand to hold me back. The Halo burst up beside the train car. Pebbles rained down on us with tiny rocks splashing into the seethed wetness of the Halo's black-globe surface, singing unbelievable and high-pitched from puny gravel mouths. Singing because upon contact with the Halo—the rocks had become suddenly *alive*, aware, and microscopically horrified.

Seven's hand stayed over my heart. Covered it. Protected it, and I wondered if he could feel it beating. If that made him feel stronger, like it made me feel stronger.

Foaming waves calmed and died, settling dead-pond perfect into the Halo's surface. It became a smooth sphere of void that glinted in the sun. The most perfect ball ever made. The black mirror drifted down to the next group's train car and holes opened on its sides. Thick rubber power cables shot out from the Halo, long and dark, and punched through our windows and latched onto the caboose car behind our neighbors—the Fiesta Car—grabbing hard onto our train cabins. The Halo's new cabled legs bent and flexed as its body reared back.

It looked like a spider. The Demon Soul Emperor of all spiders. A graveyard-born granddaddy longlegs that crawled out of the Chasm of Eternal Solitude to exact vengeance upon us for the spider Seven killed—the one he squished on the window with that chess piece. I told Sevs he didn't have to do it! We were all going to pay now. The Halo tightened its spider-cable grip on our cars and metal groaned. It reminded me of how his little spider buddy's legs scratched at the glass.

Yep. The Halo definitely knew what we'd done, but it had the wrong train car in its sights. An orange ring extended from the front of the sphere and glowed some sacred shade of sunset I'd never seen before. Steaming neon. Drooling hot orange juice. I think it was the Halo's mouth. The thin circle floated there and then the Fiesta Car began to float, too. Like magic. The whole train car turned a little sideways with all its party lights flickering, and because it was still attached, our car began to tip, but the connection under the platform broke and we slammed down with wheels sparking and screeching on the rails.

Seven steadied me and I saw through the windows of the levitating Fiesta Car. The other group huddled together in a single pile of wobbly arms and legs. Just a big awkward yarn ball of shivering scaredy-cats, which you couldn't blame them for. Captain Frumpy Butt rubbed the fanny of someone trying to burrow deeper into the huddle. Took out one of his little plastic dinos and tucked 'em in for a pants-pocket nap. Captain Frumps left his group and pressed chocolate-stained Randy against the glass. Nothingness deep within the Halo reflected him and his sweater-moose in its terror-zone emptiness—but Frumps gazed back—right into that hollow pit where his dreams would end up after he solved his own secrets. Captain Frumpy Butt stuck his tongue out at the blackness. Raised his cap gun with the most flamboyant and dramatic French cowboy stance—then slammed its hammer down in a puff of smoke.

A sound appeared. You could feel it lick your skin. This tremendous hum that roared from a billion harps inside the orchestra-mouth of a faraway golden monster. Blind maidens plucking the strings and harmonizing with haunted opera *OoOoOo*s. The Halo's floating ring splashed back into the sphere and the sound dripped—made the earsplitting echo of a frog bouncing down a deep black well. Old Frumps exploded from the cone of sound. So did the other passengers. All the windows in the Fiesta train car were painted red from the inside, so thick I couldn't see anything but a torn bit of sweater-moose plastered to the glass right where Captain Frumps turned into a stain on the wall, just like he wanted.

I know it's sad to think about Captain Frumps' death that way. But it makes me happier to think he got what he wished for in the end. He earned that much. Never gave up, even when *Piku Bo-Bebop Tucan Maru* infiltrated all his amoebas and shredded him apart.

The metal of the Fiesta Car caved inward, red-hot and molten, until the whole thing blasted off into a patch of trees beside us with an insane scream that sparkled the air. Hot wind blew my hair back as the passenger car rolled through tree trunks like they were twigs, straight into the steel hammerhead of an oil well. Now the caboose car of the train was only connected to our car by the Halo's cable-wrapped legs. The Black Bandits inside the train's butt opened fire. One guy with a red scarf covering his face ran out the door with a rifle. He took a knee on the blood-soaked caboose platform to aim. This immediately earned him the title of *Lone Ranger* in my mind. His bullets splashed into the Halo with the sound of rain on a roof, but not the kind of rain that helps you get to sleep. Muzzle fire flared out from underneath me. Mack and Allie had the assault rifle out the window, with Allie aiming and Mack helping to hold the gun still as their shots flashed inside the Halo in black-and-red explosion claps. I'm glad Seven made them practice on a bunch of cacti the week before, otherwise Mackenzie probably would've blown her hand off.

Then the Halo *smiled.*

A U-crease opened up and spread like a wave lip peeling back. From inside, the Angel uncurled with two arms folded over its chest. A cape flared out in a dazzling sheet of white like fine-feathered bird skin. Like something with a mind. A face materialized from the cloak—emerging smooth, brilliant, drool-soaked and rejoiceful as a swan parting the ripples of a pond spotted with dead fairies. Electrostatic opera-singer soundwaves boomed with volume. The Angel had two eyes. Blond, short hair. One nose, one mouth. Completely naked other than the feather cloak, and yes. It had a penis. The Angel was so beautiful I almost passed out. Seven hadn't lied. They looked just like people. Like you and me. And they didn't have wings like I first thought they would or golden rings floating over their heads.

Shaded grass filled the Halo's mouth as a black garden bloomed around the Angel. The Halo was a self-contained ecosystem, for sure. Those plants, they were certainly succulents from the Chasm of Eternal Solitude's jungle floor where this machine prowled, wrapping up whole prides of lions in cocoons to drain the life from their pregnant bellies. The rainforest stuff grew and sizzled out of the Halo's fleshy insides. White. Pulsing like a soft tarantula wrapped in liquid armor, its orange ring-mouth salivating and glowing with God's final promise.

The Halo's cables flexed to close the gap between the caboose and our car with wheels skidding and whining. We were close to the Angel, and I looked into its eyes to see what sort of world lived inside them.

I was crushed well before I could see all the way into its peepers. Drowned. That's how it felt to be in the presence of a being that'd come from universes away, from places I couldn't even imagine. An instantly appeared ocean pushed against the thin blanket fort of my lungs. I felt the pressure of its reality bursting my eardrums. The Angel's gaze showed me how small a creature I really was, how unimportant a thing my existence was before it. Holy. That's the only way to describe the Angel. Even with it naked, I could tell that thing was on another level from us—from living beings. The Angel was a supermassive black hole and we were flaming action figures falling into it, stretching down into forevers we could never understand. This one Angel had to know more than all of mankind ever did. Times infinity. It was so deadly smart there

79

was no reason for me to even think about how to beat it. No logic my little cupcake brain could produce would be of any help. Seven said we were only able to fight the Angels because they were still restricted to some of our laws of nature, the ones they invaded. He thought they were responsible for the Mouth of God closing. That there was no reason why they should even be on the planet with us. No reason for them to come down and poke us until we popped.

Unless they were looking for something. A something they couldn't find anywhere else. Not in all the anywheres-elses.

Seven left me behind. He charged to the roof edge and leapt onto the Halo. With a few lunges, he climbed up the cables and stood eye to eye with the white-caped birther of swans. I don't know how Sevs managed not to be crushed by the Angel's presence—he hadn't even drawn his sword yet. He just grabbed a fist full of tar plants from inside the Halo's curved jungle and yelled something. The Angel didn't respond. So. Seven, in his never-ending wisdom, pulled a long pink tube out of his back pocket. The *Prometheus Popper*, as Toby called it. He aimed point blank. Twisted the cardboard and pulled. Streamers, confetti, and glitter plastered the Angel's face with a puff of speckled magic that stuck to shadow ferns, grass stalks, and midnight moss, staining the whole extradimensional garden with piñata guts.

History books would forever tell of this moment.

The moment of a fearless, moron astronomer who wangle-blasted party trash all over a being from another dimension standing on its front lawn—marking humankind's territory beyond the brim of space-times unknown.

The Angel was not amused.

A thick, rubber cable arm latched onto Sevs and cocked back to throw him over a snowcapped mountain. But a dead thump whooshed from underneath me as the grenade tube launched a projectile that meteor-splashed on the side of the Halo. Seven was flung onto our car's transfer platform where the Black Bandits caught him. They'd boarded our car and, I could only imagine, helped Toby aim the grenade launcher to stop him from blasting us all to hell with the big-time boom-stick. I climbed down the ladder only to be covered in shadow as the Halo primed itself for another train-destroying scream. Its orange ring extended in an uneven wobble of drool while black astroturf leaked from the sphere in a bushy trail. The Angel abandoned its polluted garden with an almost-levitating dismount and glided onto the roof of the caboose.

"Mike, hurry up!" The scarf-wearing Lone Ranger waved his friend over to us. His bald buddy handed him a duffel bag with wires sticking out of the canvas. A gym-bag bomb.

"Hey, Superman," the Lone Ranger said as Sevs wiped blood from his nose, "it's time to drop some hammers."

I held onto Seven while the Halo cried out another beaut-iful symphony to burst our organ sacks. But before the skin melted off our faces, another grenade blew a titanic bubble of lawn from the Halo's mouth. We felt the impact. The comp-ression. A blast so powerful that it dropped all the lion coc-oons from those jungle trees in the Chasm of Eternal Solitude. The Halo's invisible sound attack missed us and burrowed a lava tunnel into the ground. Stuff flew out the train car door. Bullet casings. Spoons. A pillow. And my primate in crime, Sir Galileo. The debris clattered against the caboose and my dirty monkey flew high over its roof, probably making his escape from poor living conditions—thanks to Mackenzie. I saw a hand reach into the air and catch him. The Angel gripped tight, held on, and pulled Sir Galileo close to its face.

Seven saw it, too, and he patted me on the head. Then he snatched the gym-bag bomb from the Lone Ranger and jumped to the caboose car.

"Wait," I yelled, but he didn't. Seven ditched the bag through a broken caboose window and headed to the roof. He drew his sword and walked out of sight. The Lone Ranger had an old walkie-talkie in hand, primed to initiate the dropping of *hammers*. He wouldn't look at me, so I knew he didn't want to light the bomb fuse but would anyway. Everything was out of control. Totally beyond my powers.

I sniffled. Slapped my hand to the platform. And there I found something warm and sticky. The bacon pancake had flopped out of its stack and was covered in dirt. My imagination gave birth to it, a real thing that only existed because of a *very* unscientific plan. Stop the hyperintelligent, naked murder entities with breakfast. It didn't make any sense, but I thought that's why it could work.

If the world won't make sense anymore, why should we have to?

There's always a path to the splintered and pointy peak of the tallest playground, if you don't follow the rules. But it takes great risk to get there. You've gotta jump high off the swings and aim for the sun, even if you'll probably just face plant jaw-first into fire ants and mulch. I grasped the pancake and crossed to the caboose car before it spread apart from ours. The gap opened up again, and the Lone Ranger made like he was going to come get me, even though he couldn't make the jump. I gave him a taste of my middle finger to let him know I meant business.

Pancake clenched in teeth, I climbed the ladder and bent over on the roof. The sound of metal on bird skin was quiet as Sevs fought the nude Angel with its cape flapping in the wind. Seven's sword was a little wider than the credit cards I used to steal from my dad's wallet. It was about as long as me, segmented like one of those super-sharp exacto blades parents and teachers try to keep hidden from you. The Angel fought without moving. Feathered tendrils lashed out from its cape, just long bird necks without any heads that blocked every strike Seven made.

With two hands, the Angel inspected Galileo—which punched me *right* in the *fucking* heart. The way the Angel did it—the way it pet Galileo—running slender fingers through his monkey fur like Galileo wasn't actually mine at all, but instead belonged to the Angel. A sole treasure worth setting the universe on fire for.

Fluff. Swoosh. Whiff.

The full-on slumber-party-pillow-fight sound of sword on feather whips. Without effort, the Angel dodged Seven's sword and lunged. Sevs spun down the length of the Angel's arm until his elbow entered its eye socket. The Angel didn't flinch, Seven jumped back, the wind gusted, and Sevs spotted me. Frozen with his weapon at the ready.

"*Oi oi oi*," I said.

The Angel turned and locked on to the tiny target known as Robot. Right away, a crystal church the size of Jupiter crashed steeple-first through my brain. Confidence in my plan drained into the world behind Angel's eyes, a primeval ocean where emerald whirlpools bathed a glorious paleo-white sea monster—one with a pink and maze-toothed mouth. It was a calculated look. A face commanding me to bow before its royal form. Offer myself as a curled shrimp to those jubilant whale-chomping jaws in worship of a crowned and naked majesty. And I came real close to kneeling before it and giving up. To closing my little eyes in wait for the seaweed-covered teeth of a prehistoric monster prince to press through my skin. But I'd come to terms with the fact that there weren't any real thrones or crowns. Even sea monsters could drown.

As Seven put it, *Kings aren't real.*

"Do you know how many numbers are in this maple syrup?" I asked its holy nakedness. Seven swung and the Angel caught his blade without looking. I was onto something. So. I pointed to the Angel, and then the pancake, and took a big gritty bite out of its flesh. Put my birthday-pony-decapitation-festival face on. "At least *twelve.*"

I held my pancake up to the sun and imagined a ceremony. Rows of spotted ponies wearing cone-shaped party hats reared their hooves into the sky as blood spurted from so many severed and neighing heads. The Angel braced against some invisible force, some truth in the nonsense I spoke that only it could understand. My words made it take a step back, horrified.

"*May absolute despair and annihilation befall all who gaze upon this miracle. Hear the drowned leviathan gasp. If starfish sing, they perish. Tigers sink, hide, and laugh.*"

A fuse blew in the Angel's head and it covered its face. Pretend pony blood flashed to steam.

"*All clocks on fire. All starships cratered. A tower marked with giant's teeth. The reptile tomb unseals.*"

Horse jaws split. Branches spiraled out with budding oranges the size of basketballs.

"*Blood insect sunrise. Swaddled-myth-extinction. Circuits searching, lance aflame, robots breach the garden gate—unmake heaven, and prune the lost grove of golden fruit.*"

Invisible machines rumbled beyond the clouds. Palace columns toppled and crushed blind maidens hooting operas. All those tangerines squirted with imaginary nectar to spill their treasure inside my mouth.

I threw the double-witch-cursed pancake and it smacked into bare Angel chest. The pancake stuck there, then *foamed* and fused to the Angel's ribs. An alarm sound clanged from the Halo, loud and deep, like the sound of a glacier becoming alive in slow motion. Bright orange light poured from the Halo's cockpit and pulsed with the noise. It was a siren. Deep within the Chasm of Eternal Solitude, Duke Ellington was free from her cocoon. Prowling. Something hot and wet shrieking in her mouth.

The Angel reached out to me, and Seven put the *Dance Party* to the Angel's ear and turned on the music. Splish and splash.

The Angel shivered. Long colored streamers shot out its back. Sapphire blue water gushed from its exposed rainbow spine and fanned hundreds of feet in the air. The force of the newborn geyser pressed the Angel flat against the roof of the train car, which moaned and buckled under the pressure. Some of the spray misted into my mouth and I could taste salt. Moon-sea blood algae.

Aquamarine dolphin-death blueberry lemonade.

Seven grabbed me and backed up as the geyser spouted water higher and higher. The Angel turned into a fountain.

85

A malfunctioning super soaker. While its naked body raged with water, smooth necks of thrashing birds blossomed from its skin. Their orange swan beaks gargled in infected clusters and vomited tropical jet streams, beach foam, low-tide mud to accompany the flourish of a thousand bird trumpets and molted feathers that fluttered all around us.

The Angel screamed out in more pain than all of mankind could ever feel. Clutched its head. Roared as technicolor bands radiated from its face—a little like the emergency broadcast signal I watched on television for a whole night one time. The bands quivered and then erupted from the back of its skull.

Only one thing was left in the Angel's face cavity.

A storm of feathers swirling in an emerald whirlpool—suffocating that albino sea monster prince, causing its throat to rupture in a violent allergic reaction. Clogging its gills. Crumbling rows of teeth. Drowning the leviathan as its swollen belly blistered with pink sores that rose in sick, small cones like tiny raspberries.

Seven grabbed Sir Galileo out of the Angel puddle, picked me up, and dashed to the end of the caboose. The Halo sphere let go of our train car, and with the elegance of a bowling ball on stilts, cradled the gushing Angel as it frothed with pillars of steam inside the water spray. Even so, the gap between our train cars closed. I thought the Conductor might've slammed on the brakes, but no. The caboose was being rocket-boosted by the Angel's sprinkler plume, and we crashed into the rest of the train, speeding the whole locomotive up like a runaway jet ski on hot iron. Ocean from the Angel's broken pipes rained down in thick waterfalls to turn the whole meadow into a land of waterpark lagoons and lakes. Seven held me tight. He jumped off the roof through a wet, glassy sheet back to our train car platform. We landed hard. I felt pain in my nose run all the way down my back while I coughed up a lungful of the Angel's sea. Sevs had to be in way worse shape—I landed flat on top of him.

The Lone Ranger held onto us as a wave tried to sweep us away into the new-formed ocean. He pulled the scarf off his face and then called over his walkie-talkie. An explosion in the caboose car sent the whole train butt sideways off the tracks, totally derailed. The caboose rolled over and was swallowed by a foamy cave of sea with the Angel sputtering wild and loose as a feisty backyard hose.

Our train car plowed through the waterline with a final log-flume splash. We were back on dry land. Me and Seven slumped on the platform. Everything was back to normal. Fresh breeze and sunlight welcomed us into safety as we escaped the last bands of fine Angel rain. Seven looked more than a little beat up. He struggled to move and was bleeding from behind his ear. I pinched my nose and it hurt, but there wasn't that much blood coming out.

"That was legendary maneuvering," the Lone Ranger said. "You didn't have to run over there—we were just going to throw the bomb." Seven looked at me and handed over my wet monkey.

"Teach Galileo how to stay in the zoo. I'm not sure I'll be able to catch him the next time he escapes." He scratched his armpit, made an *Ooo Ooo* sound with a wince, and then collapsed on top a bunch of silverware and bullet casings.

I hugged my monkey tight.

87

"He doesn't scratch himself like that, he doesn't make that kind of noise, and that's not his name." I found a spoon and put it to my monkey's nose. "From now on, you'll address him as *Sir Tycho Brahe*."

CHAPTER FIVE

If the Mouth of God Spoke,
It'd Chirp Like a Sky Full of Birds

The fight didn't faze us for long. We milled around our train car for a minute, cleaning up gun magazines while sweeping out dirt and broken glass, and that was all the time it took for us to shake off death's cold fingers from our shoulders. But there was another problem. A strip of the Angel's front lawn infiltrated the train during our battle. Black grass and wild shadow plants clung to the wall along with an assortment of skittering, velvet-furred insects. Totally alien. Fluttering about in neon pollen. But friendly looking. Of course, our self-appointed imperial bug smasher, Seven, convinced the group it was time to abandon ship. We chugged uphill along the tracks until we came to a small alpine lake. The clear pond snuggled up against a set of mountains spotted with patches of rocks and snow frosting. All kinds of trees grew on the slopes, and I saw a few birds circling over the water. I knew we'd only been on the train for about a day, but I didn't mind disembarking into this postcard. The great outdoors and nature made everything seem okay. We were stopped and it was waiting, like it always had been.

89

We got our stuff off the train and Seven proceeded to water the flourishing Angel rainforest with a few canisters of gasoline. The Conductor patted his locomotive's belly and gave her one last *choo choo*. A puff of steam released the engine's soul so it could sleep with all the other white clouds. Then our Railroad Captain lit a makeshift torch and sent the rest of his train to heaven. While we watched the Angel jungle burn, I noticed the Conductor eyeing over a wrinkled map. He reached up to adjust his baseball cap that wasn't there, and when he remembered it was gone forever, he gave himself a solid pat on his bald spot and traced a path on the map.

"Have you been here before?" I asked the Conductor.

"Yes," he said, and took out a small velcro patch and combed his beard. "But every time there were thunderstorms or blizzards. Couldn't make out anything but faded trail-markers, and I guess there were a few times where I was with a pretty girl who knew a lot more about the wilderness and these mountain ranges than me."

"What was her name?" Allie asked.

"You kids ask a lot of questions," the Conductor said. He observed how Mackenzie wasn't paying attention to him and was instead gnawing on a stalk of grass. "I like it. Her name was Ryan."

"Isn't that a boy name?" Toby asked. Allie flicked some dirt at him to correct his rudeness.

"I'm all for girls having boy names," one of the Black Bandits said. She gave Toby a wink. For a second, Toby's cheeks lit up and he made a face like he'd pooped all over the Power Rangers on his underpants. The Black Bandit group from the caboose car had officially joined our party, and one of them was a proper lady. Her name was Ed, and she was gorgeous, with long black hair draped over one shoulder even though she had some of it tied in a high bun, just doing its own thing, partying with the sky and the wind on the top of her head. The scrapes on her face made her look like an adventurer who survived a decade-long journey through harsh deserts, uncovering the secrets of hidden temples, or maybe destroying them to hide their mysteries forever.

A spit of meadow at the lake's lip served as our temporary outpost and we formed up by a marker for the Continental Divide. Ed patched up Seven—said he had some bruised ribs, a few cuts, and perhaps a concussion. He'd unanimously earned the badass crown for the day. I left the newly dubbed Sir Tycho Brahe on his lap to keep an eye on him while I investigated the rest of the Black Bandits.

They were all dirty, but then again, so were we. Mike was the biggest Black Bandit and wore a blue bandanna around his paint-can neck. He looked like the gruff lumberjack mascot you see on the sides of paper towels, but a lumberjack that bare-knuckle boxed pine trees instead of wiping orange juice and baby vomit off tables. He smelled a little like beans, had stains on his shirt, and was missing one of his front teeth. Mike got on his knees beside Mackenzie, who'd made it her life's mission to taste every remaining blade of grass on the planet. She scrunched her one eye shut and asked, "What're you?" He pinched his thumbs and forefingers together and held them to his face to make silly glasses. Her eye stayed scrunched, not pleased with his answer, so he wiggled his fingers and made a noise.

Blooloolooolooloo!

Still no response. Mike put his hand to Mackenzie's head and then tugged her ear. A gold coin dropped out of her hearing hole right into his palm, a classic magic trick for sure, but Mackenzie thought he'd done it for real. She bit down on his hand and Mike gave an unsuspecting yelp.

Mackenzie pinched his arm and stopped biting. "I knews he was a leprechaun! Gimme yer gold err I'll bite cha' again." Mike cracked up and I could tell Mack-a-Doodle was in love.

Toby and the Lone Ranger, whose real name was Will, sat with their feet dipped in the lake. Will tied his red scarf around Toby's arm like they were starting a boy band. The two were in the middle of a drawing competition on Toby's handheld videogame system, passing the toy stylus back and forth and giggling a little more each time. I snuck behind them and peered at their masterpiece. Drawn on the screen was something like a cheetah mixed with a mountain lion, only it had two heads, one wearing a top hat, the other wearing maybe a baseball glove, and oh, it was pooping. Toby drew a pair of sunglasses on one of the lion thingy's heads and they both broke out laughing. Boys can be real dopes I tell ya, every last one of 'em.

I let those two continue their doodling session and ignored Mackenzie as she searched through all of Mike's pockets for precious metals. Ed sat on a tree stump and I plopped down beside her while she finished bandaging one of Seven's cuts. The Conductor watched his train leak smoke from a private spot at the end of the lake.

"Alright," I said loud and to everyone, "who's ready to play the question game?"

Mike raised his hand and Will followed his lead. Ed looked at me and sneezed. She tugged on one of her earrings—a tiny blue door—and whispered something to herself.

"So. My new friends," I said, "what the hell do you amigos think is going on around here?"

"Well, we don't think it's coincidental." Ed tickled me with the end of her hair. "The, what did you call them again?"

"Angels," I said. "Bad, dirty Angels with their curse-shaped Halos."

"Geometric foot soldiers from heaven then," Mike said, scooting closer to us—somehow managing to ignore Mackenzie as she pulled on his shoelaces. Will and Toby followed, trying to get rid of some leftover giggles from their drawing session.

Ed pinched some strands of my hair and brushed her face with them. "Yeah, so let's stick with Angels. Once the stars started going out we didn't hear much else. The news stations didn't air anything after the Angels showed up. Those things, they have to be connected to whatever is happening in the sky, right?"

"We've been calling that the Mouth of God," Allie said, "but we don't really think it's *God*. It's more of a joke, because we don't understand what it is yet, so we're doing what people used to when they didn't know what something was, and just call it God."

"Yep, yep," I said. "We're all top-notch truth seekers for sure." Mack-a-Doodle had her hand raised and waved it back and forth. I pointed at her.

"Yeah, yeah! Sevs is a professional telescoper and he's gonna figure it all out with the Great Seeker."

"An astronomer?" Mike asked.

Mackenzie shushed him and prodded his armpit for gold.

"With a godless gaggle of children," Ed said.

"Who seem to have held it together better than anyone else we've run into," Will added. Ed stopped playing with my hair and eyed Seven, who I could tell was pretending not to pay attention.

"What exactly have you been teaching these kids?" Ed asked him, but I didn't get it. She seemed upset.

"Easy, Doc," he replied. "I haven't taught these kids anything other than survival skills. That includes how to set up a tent, start a fire, and also how to load and fire high-powered rifles and grenade launchers and use the deadliest weapons at our disposal—their imaginations and their ability to think freely." Mack let out a toot, as she'd do when she was nervous. Tension started to agitate the dinosaur digestion parade in my tummy with black tarpit pools. Then the sight of an Angel insect crawling up Seven's arm turned my stomach into a prehistoric puking competition.

Before I could get a word out, Sevs cast the fuzzy fella into the Chasm of Eternal Solitude with a metal canteen. Glistening gold guts sputtered, popped, and vanished in a wisp of glitter.

"Seven!" I yelled. "If you murder any more bugs, we're going to have some serious friendship issues." He smeared its exoskeleton corpse on a dead root of the tree stump.

"These things could be relaying information back to the Angels, or explode your arm off, or who knows what. Infiltrate your dreams and make you wet the bed."

Ed gave the doorknob on her earring a small flick. "Oh, I wouldn't worry about them too much." She inspected the insect's squished head and thorax with a poke of her finger. "No mandibles for biting, no venom in its hairs unless your arm melts off in the next ten minutes. Probably harmless." She had the floor again and took the opportunity to pry into Seven. "So, Mr. Telescope. What exactly is your plan?" Seven twirled Allie's backup earphones like a lasso and tossed 'em to Ed.

"I'm trying to settle down in a giant hot tub full of rubber duckies and beer." Something told me that Seven being a butthole made it hard for him to have romantic courtships.

"Charming," she said, brushing off the lasso cord. "I'm actually quite familiar with the stars, so I'm dying to hear what you're searching for." Allie waved her hand for Ed's attention, then tapped on her Lord Bookworm glasses.

"We're going to find a telescope communication station, a big one in the Pacific Northwest, and make contact with the Great Seeker. Its real name is the Orbital Schwartzchild Gravitational-wave Observatory, OSGO for short. It's an array of ground telescopes and detectors that links up to the largest space telescope ever made, floating in low-Earth orbit. I know you've heard of it. Seven is going to use it to discover the source of the phenomenon. There are still astronauts onboard that need our help processing data with more powerful computers."

Insects buzzed and clicked as they searched for their newly dead friend.

"That has got to be the stupidest plan I've heard in the last six months," Ed said with a wide hand gesture to all of creation. All of a sudden I thought Ed was very ugly, well, except for her hair, and how her arm muscles were lean and strong like she could punch a hole through a bear's face.

"You," I said, almost shaking, "you're the stupidest plan I've heard in my entire life, which is six months times twenty-two. What's *your* genius idea? Where the hell were you heading?" Things were getting awkward turtle pretty fast.

"Mr. Seven, you should get your little girl in line before I have to spank her." Yes. The turtle had flipped upside down and was flapping its helpless little fins.

"You're gonna have to do way worse than spanking to shut me up, and don't bring him into this. It must be hard for you to understand, since you probably hung out with delinquent, uh, cookie-cutter Barbie girls your whole life—but I have what we call a brain, and I'm gonna use it to make you look stupid and feel bad about yourself. This is between you and me."

This catfight was a spectacle to behold, alright. Ed flushed as red as a clown's blood-soaked carnival balloon. She was about to use her big girl words on me, but Will spoke up. "Ed, admit it. We didn't even have a plan."

"I second that," Mike added, and he slipped the gold coin into Mackenzie's back pocket without her noticing. "We've only been thinking about ourselves. I'm done with that. If they're really trying to understand what's going on, well, that might be more important than anything else right now. They're onto something. I can feel it." He patted Mackenzie's head and she started to drool. "Can't you?"

"This is ridiculous," Ed said with a stuck-up adult head shake. "Mike, you've talked more in the last three minutes than you have in two weeks."

"Seven," Mike asked, "what do you know that we don't?" Sevs shifted himself more upright against the tree trunk and started turning his thought gears.

"Two theories formed after the Mouth opened. The first and most realistic, to me, anyway, was that the human race was undergoing a mass hallucination induced by an advanced species or consciousness. As batshit as that sounds, many skeptics found it more viable as a hypothesis than the alternative. The second theory was that the academic fields of omniversal realities, parallel universes, and multiverses were being proven correct right before our eyes. I was never a multiverse enthusiast—didn't much care for anything beyond our cosmic horizon. Poking at planets and stars I could fly a spaceship to was more my thing. But I've had to make some concessions due to the last observations we were able to make."

He held his hands together like an alligator mouth, and they chomped hard.

"We are being colonized, invaded, merged, synthesized, or eaten by something from outside the bounds of our universe. Probably."

"So, what was the global flash that made all the stars move around suddenly?" Mike asked. "That happened in an instant. It doesn't make sense."

"Before the Mouth opened, all of the stars we saw in the sky weren't really there. The light emitted from them was old. One year old to thousands of years old to billions of years old. We were always looking into the universe's past, at what it used to look like, instead of what it actually looked like. Now we are seeing the real stars. In their true position."

Seven wiggled the fingers on both his hands and then locked them together.

"There were two events that coalesced into the Mouth of God. First, something merged with all of our space in an instant. More than likely, it was the special fabric of a brane universe or bubble universe, since we know space can expand faster than light can travel. Researchers have been studying CMB radiation at the edge of our detectable universe, looking for patterns of an event like this in our cosmic past—a point where we may have brushed up against the boundary of another expanding universe. It seems that now we've run right smack into one, at least one. And just like light's speed can be slowed by traveling through another medium, like water, it has now sped up unfathomably by traveling through the merged membrane's vacuum, slipping instantly from point A to B as if a photon's destiny is predetermined, like it knows where it's going to end up and arrives at our upper atmosphere without traveling any distance at all. The consensus is that the flash we saw was billions of years of what's called extragalactic background light—starlight and exotic particles in transit through space, catching up to us in a moment of time so single and minute I doubt there is enough space in the universe to write down all the digits comprising its minuscule numerical equivalent.

"The Mouth of God is an echo of this event. Slower, too, likely because it's now interacting with all forms of matter instead of only space itself. You know, regular matter like what we're made of, plus dark matter—you get the picture. A lot of the intergalactic lightshow up there is theorized to be dark energy being excited by the MoG field, like how our atmosphere experiences aurora from solar wind particles. There are other theories as well. The Higgs field moving to a different energy state. Or a sort of spatial isostatic rebound, the fabric of space-time itself expanding so much that the universe's density got too low and a higher pressurized dimension blew through us. Maybe a second universe was born in ours and underwent rapid inflation. You could invent any theory about ultra-sentient unicorns or angry Calabi-Yau manifolds and it might hold some weight."

Sevs shrugged like he'd just made all of those words up.

"So. We lost all but one of our orbital telescopes in the initial flash. The particle onslaught was too much for most satellites' circuitry to handle. Some of the subatomic debris is so energetic we can *feel it,* even now. They can land with the force of a raindrop. But astronomers are a notoriously crafty bunch. Direct measurement of gravitational waves has been going on for a few decades, and we knew that they traveled at the speed of light. Well, guess what? Light is not the only thing that moves instantly anymore. The OSGO array had its sensors on black holes thirteen billion light-years away and closer, waiting for them to potentially merge and release measurable waves. Now it's measuring how the Mouth of God interacts with black holes, and the energy released is similar to that of a black hole merger. We were able to time two 'chirps' of these events in neighboring galaxies, showing us where the leading edge of the Mouth was, its direction, and also how long it took to pass through a known galactic cluster."

"So you should know how long it will take to reach Earth?" Will said.

Seven stared into the sky.

"That day we estimated that we had eight months, three weeks, and one day left before the leading edge of the Mouth of God would arrive. We have forty-six days left now." It got awfully quiet after he said that. Of course, me and the kids

99

knew how long our clocks had left to tick, but the Black Bandits didn't have a clue. The bugs would've shut up too if they were smart enough to know what we were talking about.

"And what are you going to do about it?" Ed asked. She didn't look mad anymore. She'd gotten her calm back and was smug as a dog sniffing its own poop, which only made me angrier.

"There is an underlying logic to all this. A math. A hidden nature with rules and laws. A heart beating with the blood of our universe. And like all hearts, it can be stopped. OSGO also serves as a node for observing gravitational waves through pulsar arrays, watching how they interact within our galaxy. Well, the Mouth of God's initial emergence through our space-time sloped our entire galaxy in a single direction. And not just ours, but every galaxy. We're all sitting still now, cosmic expansion has stopped."

Seven paused to frizz his hair up. "Einstein has finally gotten the static universe he always argued for. Gravity is for locals only, now. All matter is shifted toward a convergence at the center of our universe in a celestial-splitting spike. A tower of dark matter and gases and shredded galaxies forming a spire with a single peak. What's waiting there is responsible for all of this." Seven looked up with a grunt and pointed to the brightest star that could be seen through the big blue sky. "It's right there, waiting to feed off all this death. I am going to find out what it is, and *we* are going to stop it."

Ed wasn't impressed.

"So, you're going to find this—*this*—this what exactly? Angel disco ball at the center of the universe, which for all you know could be an interstellar garbage fire, and then somehow manage to travel the insane distance to it and stop the Mouth of God. How can you believe that's possible?"

"There is always a possibility, no matter how small. I believe we'll stop this with nothing but will power and random chance. With more truth and style than anything you suckers have ever seen."

Ed pulled up her hand, and I knew what was going to happen before it did. She wagged her finger. "It is wrong of you to give these children hope—that you can do anything about this."

"Wow, Robot is right." Seven made a finger gun and shot it at Ed. "You are stupid. Can't you see? I'm not giving these kids hope. These kids *are* the hope. I'm not the one who made the Angel fall to its knees and literally blow its mind out the back of its skull as the physical restrictions of its form broke down into exploding sea water and volatile shapes. I don't know about you, but I've never seen that happen before." He pointed straight to me, and I found my hand clenching the Ursa Minor pendant around my neck.

We all got quiet. Even most of the bugs shut up. Just a few probably shouting to each other that they'd found food or learned how to ride a super small bug unicycle from an escaped Angel insect. Ed caught an angry glance from me and let her eyes sink to the ground. Everyone suddenly became aware of it—got super heavy from those intergalactic raindrop particles crashing down on our tired bodies. I felt them splash off us, join forces, and turn into invisible sea lions climbing on our backs and heads. Mike slouched as he watched Mackenzie chew on his shoestring. Will shaded in extra detail on his and Tobes' mutated-cheetah masterpiece on the gamepad. Even

Seven's arm struggled under the weight as he held Allie's hand. I started to feel it, too, the cosmic sea lion fins slapping all over me, but I shrugged the blubbery bastard off. Tossed him back into the particle sea. Ed, on the other hand, was hunched and ready to break in half. We'd all seen so much. And I hated that I already didn't like one of the most confident girls I'd ever seen and would probably ever see. So. I helped her out. Got rid of whatever angry thoughts I had about her. Plopped 'em right out onto the dirt. I went to Ed and hugged her around the waist as tight as I could and tried picking her up with all my strength and against the heaviness of the universe smashing into us.

"You," I said, "I'm going to take you to the places you don't think we can go, even if you don't want to come along for the ride." I did my best to take all that weight for her.

Sometimes people need stuff like that.

I lost my balance, Ed squirmed, and we toppled over on -to the ground. I could feel her laughing through her belly, since my head was on her stomach, and of course this made me laugh, and our giggles spread to everyone else. Allie's headphone jack slipped out of her music player and the song she and Sevs were listening to started playing out of our portable speaker. A good rock song, Seven's favorite:

"Seven Years" by Saosin. Go figure.

Me and Al Pal rehearsed this one almost every night. I jumped up and grabbed an invisible microphone. It was *Imaginary Band Time*. I sang while Allie shredded on her air guitar.

O

.05   "*Get it off my chest, the story ends* . . . I will find a way without you!"

Allie mounted the tree trunk and threw her instrument's neck back. Mike twirled two sticks and started playing away on drums. Seven picked up the bass and Toby grabbed another guitar while Will pulled out a harmonica to sweep in on the chorus. Ed raised her hand, fist closed, pinky and index finger stuck out. I ditched my inviso-microphone and grabbed her hand to sing into. The world in her eyes was dim. Covered in an unsure and thick dust. I breathed in for the next line and blew it all away with my voice.

"That mistake was gold, but life without you, is something I could never do."

CHAPTER SIX

Don't Put Sea Anemones Down Your Pants, Stupid

I made a new friend before we set off on our mountain climb. Another bug from the Angel's garden had escaped the train fire and was on a grand adventure. All alone. Its cuteness bobbed back and forth on a dandelion—having a roller coaster ride or maybe transmitting top secret information with its antlers and hind-butt deep into the sky. About the size of my thumbnail, the exogrub had a coat of white hairs with a fuzzy bumble bee collar stained in a mysterious yellow sheen, sometimes green, sometimes hyper blue. An ant definitely not of this world. I watched it levitate a pebble with its mind.

I knew Seven would greet 'em with a stomp from his boot, which was ridiculous. Wasn't that what the Angels were doing to us? Couldn't he see that? So. I decided to keep my new friendship a secret. Tycho Brahe had a zipper running down his monkey spine, and I unzipped it to make the white fluff of his insides into a nest. My bug friend crawled inside. Sensed around a bit with its squiggle-tipped antlers. Then curled up and went to sleep. I knighted the little wiggler with a royal name: Nappy Sir Sleeps-a-Lot.

Ed made accusatory hand gestures at Seven while lecturing him about something. He came over to me afterward and apologized for squishing the other bug, and the spider, but I didn't totally buy it. I think she talked him into the sorry. He did let me carry the Dance Party though, and I thought it looked awesome sticking out the top of my backpack—a gunmetal middle-finger warning to any Angel circling above. I strapped Tycho to the gun barrel so he could take in the view with Nappy Sir Sleeps-a-Lot. We were all geared up for our mountain adventure, or surviving, or living, or however you wanted to look at it, really.

The grass tickled my knees and deposited tiny insects on my leggings, just hitching a ride. I was fast becoming the world's Queen Insect-Farm Exoskeleton Mama.

A swift breeze blushed the trees and carried soaring birds. Some fish played hopscotch in the lake. Bits of plant pollens and umbrella seeds drifted across the field in search of a place to grow, somewhere to call home, just like we were. And crowned above the trees, a large murder bird watched the lake from a branch. Careful and quiet. The hawk glided down to the water, skimming its ripples close, then landed on the bank. Pitter-pattering around in the mud. With a screech and a hop, the hawk *splooshed* into the water, where it flailed in mortal combat with a fish. After properly assaulting the innocent lake citizen, Mister Bird flew back to its perch and tore the gill-breather apart.

Nature. Beautiful and scary at the same time. The fish flopped frantically in the bird's talons, and I sort of felt sorry for the thing. No one wants to be eaten alive. Ripped from their home and forced to watch their life flake away into an unknown habitat.

"I don't think nature is on our side anymore," I said as we walked beneath the bird and funny-smelling scales that fluttered in the sun.

Will brushed some off his shoulder. "Nature has never been on anyone's side. Termites tear bark off trees. Trees fall on hikers. Is it the termite's fault for being hungry, the tree's for not being stronger, or gravity's fault for existing?"

"It's young," Ed said. "That hawk." She knelt to bury a spiny fin in the dirt, placing a small twig as a gravestone on the burial mound. "The immature red-tails hop around on the ground like that, eating things they aren't biologically designed to. Fish make up less than one percent of their diet. That hawk doesn't really know what it's doing."

The Conductor led our group, still reaching up every now and then to tug an invisible *choo choo* out of the air. We walked in pairs when our path took us uphill around the belly of a sharp mountain. It was still an easy hike, so everyone goofed off. Mackenzie rode on Mike's shoulders. He picked pinecones off the trees and handed them to Mack-a-Doodle, who'd become his personal shoulder-mounted cannon. She tossed them back down the hill, and at us, and at a squirrel chewing on its own tail. Me and Seven trekked together and watched the show from the back of the line. Allie held Will's hand—not the other way around, and Ed found two sticks and started twig-fighting Toby on top of a mythologically-large and fallen tree. Their sword fight was epic. Toby and Ed were silent in their battle, hopping and dodging and ducking as their sticks swooshed and clacked and stabbed. Tobes finally got his branch stuck in her hair and tried to fling her off the trunk.

Around that time, Mack-a-Doodle hit the Conductor in the back of the head with a pinecone. He looked up and shouted at a dumb squirrel like he'd hated them all his life and thought the mangy rascal had dropped the pine-bomb on his bald spot. The Conductor charged ahead, kicking rocks and sticks as he went. I jogged past everyone to catch up with him.

"Hey, Train Captain, what's going on?" He spat over the edge of the path and kept quiet. "Don't worry about that squirrel. I know he was being a genuine bundle of ass blanket, but I've eaten at least thirty members of his extended family." I raised my fist. "You hear that? You dumb-fuck furball! I ate your families, all of 'em—grandmammys, eggs, everything!"

The Conductor kept his sights on the path as it bent around a harsh corner of rock into the unknown. "I'm a little cranky. A geezer who doesn't want to accept the facts. No more squirrel eggs for this fellow. I don't deserve to get what I want—I'm not sure anyone ever deserves anything."

"Hold your horses. Or shove them off the cliff along with all your boo-hoos. This thing you don't think you deserve, are you talking about seeing your Big Blue Lady again?"

He nodded.

"I've been wondering about that. Are you talking about your girlfriend, or the beach?"

The Conductor smiled, probably because I sounded like a moron. "The Pacific Ocean. Raging, peaked, and endless. Maybe we'll make it to a shoreline before I'm tucked in for my everlasting dirt nap. Unlikely though."

107

I tugged on his arm until he stopped hiking. "Hold your seashells, old man." He stared at me and hunched his shoulders. "Hold them, dammit."

The Conductor opened his hand and pretended to clench a hefty conch shell.

"You're gonna want to grab your other one, too." He picked up a second imaginary seashell. "Good. You know, maybe you're right—no one deserves anything, not ever. But that doesn't mean the world gets to be a big bully and push you around. Sometimes the thing you're looking for hides from you with the whole universe helping out, every star and rock and cloud laughing at you because you're so sad and struggling in your search. But if you're careful and clever—patient as a dead llama—you can catch these things sneaking *right behind your back*, sticking their tongues out at you."

The Conductor turned around. Behind us was the valley we rode through on the train, and it was almost filled to the brim with water. Bright blue. Sparkly and beautiful. A new ocean was being formed from the destroyed Angel, broken and sunken at the valley bottom, still blowing entire lakes out its sprinkler spine. The water bubbled with smooth blooms in the way a hose does when you hold it underwater and point it at the sky. There were ripples and waves and the shiny sun reflecting on it all in a big, glittering streak. Everything you'd want in a real sea. The water finally climbed to the top of the valley wall and spilled over, making the lagoon look like it stretched out to another continent.

"Go ahead and give her a call," I said to the Conductor. "She's missed you."

He stared out at his Big Blue Lady. Added some salt to her

sea. Put both his imaginary seashells in one hand, and then held them to his ear.

I returned to the back of the line where Seven walked behind Al Pal and Will. Lord Bookworm and the Lone Ranger were in some sort of deep conversation. Will kept pointing out over the booming white clouds and mountain peaks. He pretended to smooth the rocky range with his hand and sweep it into the lake.

"Right," Allie said. "I bet the chocolate goat herds live in a cave down near the mud banks, and the gumdrop canaries live in those trees."

Will pointed to the lake. "Well, obviously the goats will die from drowning in their cave during the next flash flood. They'll float out, and the canaries will eat the herd and turn brown."

"Exactly. Their babies will be mutated from the chocolate and they won't be able to fly, which will increase the twizzler wolf population, since the deformed birds will be easy prey for them."

Oh yeah. That conversation was really overloading my dork meter. Seven grunted and fell back. He was too tough to wimp out on such an easy hike, so I figured he was pretending to be hurt so we could have a private conversation.

"Avery. Don't ever come after me like you did on the train roof. Okay?"

"I wouldn't have to come after ya if you lifted some weights every now and then and got a little stronger." I tried to wrap both my hands all the way around his arm, but he shrugged me off.

"I don't understand what happened."

"Neither do I."

"And you're okay with that?"

"Yes. No. I don't know. I saved you, didn't I?"

He tried not to smile.

"You sure did. Unless that Angel floods the entire planet and drowns us all."

I nudged him with my elbow. "The pancake you made was just too legendary for that Angel bozo to handle. I gave it the full breakfast incantation, too, like a proper witch." Seven nodded in agreement. "Anyway, it can be more fun sometimes not knowing everything."

"How so?"

"Because then you get to make up the reason. Whatever you want!" I jumped up and threw my arms out into the air. "*Twelve.* That's how I beat the Angel."

"I don't think a number you can punch into a calculator is going to help us."

"I'm telling you, Sevs, when I said the word 'twelve,' something in the Angel changed and made it interested. Or maybe afraid? I think it was the Angel's name."

"I guess if I traveled across vast gulfs of space and time to a realm of inferior beings—and then got called by name, and then had three slices of a curse-imbued dead animal thrown at me—I might undergo a violent acataleptic fit as well."

I giggled because it was funny, and because I didn't fully understand some of those words, but I thought as hard as my think-core could think about what he said. My stupid imagination gave birth to something that destroyed a being who should've been able to turn my circuits and gummy bears into a chewed up, peed-on wad of gum at the bottom of a broken toilet. There was meaning in that somewhere, but I was way too distracted to figure it out. The higher up we went, the more majestic the mountains became.

When you're short, everything else seems big. Trucks, houses, ceilings—they all can seem pretty huge. For adults, those things aren't so big to them. But up in those mountains, the cliffs were hundreds of feet tall. Even parents and fancy businessmen had to feel small looking at how they towered. They'd all toss their ironing boards and briefcases and beige neckties right off a peak into the sacred and wonderful air. For me, it was like staring at the edge of the world. As we climbed up and up, the whole mountain range didn't feel smaller, like a model toy set, and it didn't make me feel tiny, either. Instead, I could feel myself becoming a part of the whole thing. Its breath became mine and my little footsteps became the heartbeat of that place. Soft and wonderful.

Everyone else must've felt the same way. Ed and Tobes dropped their stick swords while Mackenzie called a truce with nature and paused her pinecone bombardment. Crisp air whispered through slats in the rock and wisps of red dust danced along the cliffside. Even the Mouth of God didn't seem so bad then. Its silver-yellow echo haunted the sky and not me for a change. Our path narrowed, and we fell into a single file line. Seven seemed to be doing alright even as we crossed a stream with slippery rocks and toppled trees. My left foot was killing me, but I was used to the pain. It was an on-purpose kind of hurt and mostly my fault anyway. We took breaks every now and then to eat a granola bar or use the water filter to fill up our bottles. We found a nice overlook on a big flat rock, so we decided to lie out in the sun for a while. Will gave his harmonica some spit shine and played it slow. Allie used our portable solar panel to charge her music player, and Toby doodled while waiting to charge his game system.

The Conductor sat with his legs dangling over the edge and ate an apple. No way you were going to catch me with my feet hanging off the tallest chair I'd ever seen. I sat and hugged my knees beside Sevs as Ed checked his cuts.

The Conductor pointed to the view. "Down there, it looks like the model train set I had as a kid. The mountains. Trees, lakes, the fins of rock and overhangs are a close match to my train set before it all got destroyed." He tossed his apple into the air and watched it fall.

"How'd it get broken?" I asked.

The Conductor tried to adjust his lost hat again, then gave up. "To this day it stands as the strangest mystery I've ever beheld. One of those unexplainable moments, like seeing a two-headed unicorn abducted by a UFO. Paranormal. That's what it was."

Mackenzie crouched into leaping position and swiped a claw at the Conductor. "Be nice to the *uni*-horns."

"Right. I was about nine years old, a determined little fella. I'd already made up my mind about being a train conductor. After working on the set for over a year, I got to watch my toy locomotive make its maiden voyage around the world my father and I created for it. A landscape of rolling green hills and stone tunnels with a rickety bridge spanning a glacial river. We painted it all by hand. Pieced it together rail by rail and boulder by boulder. Every detail down to the tiny glass of whiskey on the porch of a shack. Rams headbutting on the hillside. Passengers scolding their children or checking their watches on the platform. Our dream come true. Somewhere we could live where my father wouldn't have to leave for that damn war and never come back."

"Which war was that? Will asked.

"The one that blew up the most complete Quetzalcoatlus skeleton ever found. He went down in a museum in Beijing defending natural history and evolution—a true hero." A shaft of light swept across the ridge and painted the Conductor on the cliff's edge with artistic lighting for the briefest of seconds, just as his dad must've looked in that museum—grenade clenched in teeth, back up against fossil replicas, pistol firing down exhibit hallways as he protected one of Time's grandest memories.

"Accordingly," the Conductor continued, "I was by myself when the train made her maiden voyage through our miniature wonderland. She made it through the tunnel without a bump, rolled clean over the bridges, and was coming to the final curve. The home stretch to complete a long journey, passengers safely in tow. Nothing but sky and meadow waiting for 'em. But that's when the track switch was thrown. It was impossible, and I saw it happen. Out of nowhere, this heavy metal lever that took both of my hands to pull moved on its own. Pushed by the finger of something invisible. A poltergeist, my father, maybe both. Maybe it was a test, this force you all call the Mouth of God seeing what it felt like to ruin my life before coming back for everyone else's. The train and its cars got diverted around the town's lake to the edge of the set. Right where my brother had snuck in. Crawling on his belly wearing a dinosaur costume. He flopped his head down on the tracks. Bit my train. Thrashed like a lizard before proceeding

113

to kick the model trees against the wall, trample the bridge, and cave in the tunnels."

"I bet you fought him, right?" I asked. Boxing fists raised and circling. "Punch, punch, right? Left—right—*right*, right?" The Conductor threw a jab out at the scenery.

"I sure did. Took out one of his teeth. But I wasn't strong enough to bring him down in time."

Will made a sweeping *choo choo* with his harmonica. "I bet you're tough enough to take him down now. You could plow right over him with a real train."

"I didn't run over him. I left him behind in the train car, the one the Angel exploded. The one that rolled off through all those trees." A wind gust tugged at the Conductor's beard and filled the silence left by his words. "I guess he told you all his name was Captain Frumpy Butt. He was always stupid like that. Never serious. I couldn't stand him, not back then. Not now. So, I made him stay back in the coach car. Didn't want him messing with stuff up in the front cab."

The rest of the adults didn't know how to respond. Mackenzie forced her hands into Toby's pockets and sniffled. Words turned to bad oil in my mouth and I left them pooled there with helpless, malformed dinosaurs gargling tar and emotions. But Allie shuffled behind the Conductor. She sat down, huddled up, and planted her forehead on his back.

"Your train got its revenge today," Allie said to the Conductor. "The force that moved your toy train from back then is still here. You should blame it for everything, not yourself."

The Conductor nodded. Took a quiet, shaky breath. "I never forgave him for all of that back then. Not really. I didn't understand. But I guess all he wanted was to play with me and be my friend. Right up 'til the end. With all his big, stupid, gibbering heart, in his own special way. In a way that I've never deserved to be loved in all my life."

Allie took her glasses off and stretched the frame arms so they fit over the Conductor's face. "Captain Frumpy Butt didn't see you that way. Everything was magic and dreams to him. He thought you were the wizard up front making the whole train move with spells and old reptile blood." She spread her fingers wide, palms cupped to make a full set of antlers on his head. "His moose told me so."

"Sweater moose Randy was a real hero." I let out a loud half-moo, half-wildebeest snort because I had no clue what sound a moose actually made.

"Speaking of heroes." Will patted Sevs on the shoulder. "You jumped off the train to chat with the Angel that killed everyone in the coach between us. You were trying to reason with it, weren't you?"

Seven fidgeted with the elastic brace Ed had wrapped around his knee. "Yeah. I tried. Gave interdimensional diplomacy a shot for good old science and peace. I told it we were too dangerous, too volatile to be near each other. That if it came to a fight, we'd both lose."

The Conductor nodded and everyone else followed his lead, except me.

"Seven," I said, pointing my best finger at him. "They will kill us no matter what. Pop all our skulls like candy kittens, then snort up the dust, blow out some snot bubbles, and pop us some more. Next time you're face-to-face with one of those Alleluia Assholes, tell 'em to suck your fart and then blow a new hole in its brain for it to think through."

Seven fumbled through his pocket and pulled out a chess piece—the carved wooden horse head of a knight, and then he crushed something imaginary against his palm with it. Spider and Angel bug guts smeared across my memories. Nappy Sir Sleeps-a-Lot rustled at the thought, too. My own words were about to be spanked. Put in time out, and then used against me. *Killing.* I felt it then, that there was so much more to ending something's existence than my traumatized brain could make a proper think about. Luckily Mackenzie stood up and interrupted Seven, wiggling Mike's gold coin in her fingers.

"I think indjians used to sit here, like this. Eatin' stuffs. I can feel the ghosts, promise, promise. They're here rights now."

I believed her. Mack had a weird way of knowing things she shouldn't, like one time when she woke up and said we needed to honk our car horn for no reason. Seven didn't want to, but she went nuts on us until we did. So. Right as we honked, a mountain lion none of us knew was in the tree above our car got scared, and it dropped off the branch onto the hood. The killer cat just lay slumped on our car with a broken neck and a fat rabbit clenched in its teeth. All Mackenzie said was, "Dinners are served."

Mike looked around for any sign of *Native Americans.* "What are they doing?"

"Watchin' us. They're scared of the sky, but now not so muchies."

"Why?" he asked.

"Because we're not scared. They say we makes them feel stronger, like they used to feel, before being all dead and lonely.

The indjians are sayin' they wishes they were alive with us—true, I tell ya." Her one eye wasn't scrunched up like when she thought real hard. No way she was making this up.

"Mackenzie—stop calling them that." Allie put her hands on Mack's shoulders and nodded to Ed. "Ask them what their tribe name is if they are standing right beside you, please?"

Mackenzie ignored her. "They like Will's harmonickee. Their most precious mammoths made the same sounds."

Will laughed. "It's a little too far south for mammoths to have been hunted around here."

"Then why," Ed said, giving Will a smack on the butt, "were the remains of mastodons and mammoths found in a ski resort's retaining pond *three hundred miles* south of this montain range—with bone-tipped arrows lodged in their ribs?"

Will considered Mack-a-Doodle. How she stood with arms out to her sides, legs spread like a starfish, ready to accept a gold medal for some grand paleontology award that didn't exist. "Promise, promise," she said.

Will blew into his harmonica, playing slow notes that matched the strength of the wind. It looked like his song commanded the swaying of trees far below us. Their needles fell for him in a single, echo-hushed swoop.

"How'd you get so good at playing that?" Allie asked.

Will wiped his mouth. "I like to pretend it changes things. That the sounds I make become a part of places and help me learn more about them. Love them in a certain kind of way. Like we're both not alone for a short time, but sharing something."

The Conductor shushed all of us. "I hear thunder."

117

We got quiet, and I could hear it, too. Some unseen king-dom collapsing into ruin. Up in the sky a group of wide, black airplanes flew in a diamond pattern. We heard their engines rumble. Maybe it was just me, but I saw the white contrails they left behind bend from the Lone Ranger's harmonica notes.

Toby stood frozen. Windbreaker flapping free with the dork-horned kaiju on his t-shirt snarfing down a submarine. He pointed to a nearby mountain with bubble of tar expand-ing behind its peak. The disturbance ballooned with slick black drippings and speckled stars, taking the shape of a rott-en mega-squirrel egg. Sputtering from a hole, the membrane sack popped. Neon streamers spread their fingers through a cloud of steam and black gush. Something appeared behind the rock face, and it moved. Purring. Silver armor unfurled in long coils that lashed out and over the mountain. A sleek metal tail swished around to our side of the range, where the shiny tentacle-feeler set a whole slope of boulders avalanch-ing into the lake—cracking through trees and plowing up soil in bulldozer streaks. Everyone but the Conductor backed away from the outcrop. He sat right there on that cliff edge to have the best seat in the house.

Ed put her hand on my head. "Have any of you seen a phenomenon that large before?" Seven pulled Toby and Mack close to him. They held hands, and all three remembered something the rest of us didn't.

"We are not going to talk about Space Camp now," Seven said. He crouched down to Toby and Mack's level. "And *that* is not going to happen again."

A silver shape rose over the mountain peak like an enor-mous blimp taking flight. The sleek snout nosed through a low-hanging cloud and parted it. The creature looked like it sneezed out the cloud, so I decided to call it the Cloud Maker. Milky lines spread over its torpedo face and traced a pineapple-shaped pattern down to where the long feelers joined at its neck, or maybe its butt. Then the Cloud Maker split. Its face opened into a mouth lined with bands of flexing, pointed spines, transforming into a great silver pinecone balloon with an armored sea anemone trapped inside—sluggish, throbbing, and jellyfish tongued. Blue spit foamed as tentacles brushed over the mountain, dissolving a whole forest of trees caught in its chomper. A family of deer rained on a clear rock bluff. Tumbling with bright red splatters. Three black bears stood hind-legged on a mound of mulch and roots beholding the destroyer of their den—so massive it could've swallowed their star-chart ancestor, Ursa Major, in one bite. Constellation and all. The Cloud Maker stretched its mouth open and quivered with all its seed scales. Far below, birds flew from the trees as the sound hit in a roaring scream that shook pebbles loose from the rock walls. My skin prickled as a whole colony of ghosts killed themselves to flee my body. The Conductor finally stood, but only after puking over the outlook's edge.

"Is . . . is this a *Miracle* ?" Mackenzie asked.

"What?" Ed said.

Seven shook his head and pulled Mackenzie close to him and told her, "No."

The airplanes broke out of their diamond formation and white rings appeared under their bellies. Missiles streaked down with the glowing tips of cigarettes, promising to do a lot more damage than Mack-a-Doodle's pinecone grenades.

Launching those missiles was a mistake though.

I did a science report on sea anemones for Mrs. Graber's

119

class in school—got to go up to the front of the classroom and be a marine biologist for about ten minutes. It bored everyone to death. But I learned a lot about those slippery and colorful noodle creatures. If you didn't know, some sea anemones can sting you. So don't ever put one in your bathing suit to try and be funny, plus it's rude to the animal. They have tiny cells in their tentacles that will shoot out a toxic harpoon with a bolt of microscopic energy when disturbed. They're called nematocysts. Jellyfish have 'em, too, and you should *already know* not to put one of those down your pants. One second the cell is sleeping, its weapon stuff all coiled up and snug, and then next second—bam! Your whale gets harpooned. Thing is, you've gotta trigger the cell to make it explode. And that's just what those rockets did.

The blue anemone slug-tongue boiled with electricity, and sharp laser light pooled in the Cloud Maker's mouth before it whipped and spiraled skyward in zigzag tangles, erasing some of the missiles. Airplanes fizzled and poofed with orange explosion blossoms when the lance of color licked them. The jets smeared over the sky in a bleeding rainbow of static that must've blinded every animal within a hundred miles. The surviving rockets whooshed down on the mountain and detonated all over its peak. They impacted in bright yellow and red plumes of sparkling weaponry—blasted us with sounds that stopped my heart from beating—then started it again. The thousand-trunked howl of every mammoth spirit ever slaughtered in the valley trumpeted deep at extinction frequency as their woolly souls rose from the dirt.

The Cloud Maker wriggled itself into a face plant and carved a whole ridge to pieces with its mouth. The last lone jet fighter flared its engines and nosedived, flying faster and faster in a lazy spiral. With the Cloud Maker's silver mouth still open, the pilot flew straight into the monster's chomper, which made the mouth bulge and burst Hindenburg style. A crater opened up on the mountain range and erupted with fleshy strips of silver-ribboned monster meat. They tattered the landscape. Rolled over tall trees and snapped the mighty mud-suckers clean in half. Flocks of upset birds perched on the alien gore and skeletal aftermath to lick sludge off their feathers. Butts wiggling, the bears rolled on their backs in the forbidden blue honey leaking from an anemone appendage. Glitter from the Cloud Maker's skin turned the scene into a celebration of two Mother Natures annihilating one another, and the specks floated through the air to join fish scales from that hawk's meal. The fuzzy spores pollinated the whole valley and smelled like burned batteries or acid—something dangerous under the kitchen sink your parents would protect you from, if you still had parents, that is.

Mackenzie walked to the edge of the cliff and faced us. Behind her a low cloud was stained red from a mist of blood. The cherry-colored cloud floated over the extraterrestrial disaster zone as Mack spread her arms. "The canyon peoples have changed their minds."

"About what?" I asked.

"About wanting to be alive with us."

CHAPTER SEVEN

The World Never Takes
A Break From Trying to Kill You

Mackenzie pointed to a cliff down the path from our overlook. Two people stood on the edge of a rock high above the trail. They looked tiny, being so far away, but we could see them just fine. They stood still for a minute with their clothes flapping in the wind, and then they jumped off. We watched them fall hand in hand until they hit a bushy tree. One got tummy-stuck by a branch with their arms still reaching out for their friend. The other tumbled out onto the trail. It was a shame. The tree was a real looker, and the perfect size and shape for me and Allie's Super Ultimate Treehouse. Of course, it was sad we'd come across other survivors the moment they gave up on living, but I don't think it was very nice what those two did. The person stuck in the branches was right where the library was supposed to go—and who wants to read in a room with a dead person hanging from a chandelier? Serial frog smashers, that's who.

We gave the strangers a moment of silence as a snow of Cloud Maker scales coated the path in white spots. Ed and

Mike went to check the bodies, and after some whining from Toby, he caught up with them to help search the corpses. They didn't come back with much. Ed found tent stakes in one of their pockets, so we thought there may be a campsite on the ridge where the couple jumped. Tobes hijacked a sweater from one of their packs. It was red, black, and turquoise in one of those pretty tapestry patterns you find woven in museums. In the exhibits with people laid out on animal skins around a fire looking either happy or scared in their wax faces. He gave the sweater to Mackenzie, which slouched wide on her shoulders, but was fitting in the way it made her look like a psychic wizardess who hid potions and magic gummy frogs in oversized cloak pockets.

We ventured up the trail to the tree. Ed had hidden the body, but you could tell where the jumper hit the ground by the thin streaks of blood in the dirt and, of course, by the person's hand-holding friend still stuck up in a bunch of wet leaves. It looked like Ed tried to cover the blood by kicking dirt over it.

"Hey," I said to Ed. "We're used to the blood. No need to cover it up, silly." I wanted her to know we were all tougher than that. We had, after all, kept our cupcakes in our baskets after what we'd just seen, which was more than could be said for the two jumpers. Ed tipped an invisible hat to me and toss-ed it into the wind. Then she pretended like she wanted the hat back but it was too late and too far gone.

In order to get to the top of the ridge, we trekked a long way down the trail to where it doubled back to climb higher.

"I could climb up there." Will wedged his hand in a crack running up the tall cliff. Pulled it back out covered in Cloud

123

Maker spores. "But I wouldn't be able to get back without a rope."

"You know how to climb?" Allie asked. She examined his skinny arms and adjusted her glasses.

"Of course, everyone does. Some people don't practice it much, and some people get too scared with the whole staring death in the face thing when they're hundreds of feet off the ground." Will rolled up his sleeve and showed us a smooth scar. "One time I climbed a rock wall for two days and sent the last pitch with this gash in my arm."

I rubbed my hand over his old wound. "Two days? Where did you poop?"

"In bird nests, of course."

"Gross," Mackenzie said. "Mikey. Would you leave treasure in a bird home?"

"Most of it would end up on the ground from overflowing, but yes," he said. "I've gone to the bathroom in places much worse than a bird's nest."

Mack-a-Doodle held the golden coin Mike pulled out of her ear. Symbols from a language I couldn't recognize circled the treasure's edge. In the center was a tree worn smooth from a million thumbs. Pushed through the leaves were the heads of storks with something speared on all their beaks. But you couldn't tell what that something was—they'd all been scratched away. She inspected the gold closely and scrunched up her eye. "Where'd this come from? Better not be your butts."

Mike smoothed one of his eyebrows with a dirty thumb. "A whale gave it to me."

Mackenzie froze. Shocked with pure paralysis serum as her entire world was blown away. I could see it in her head—a world full of whale people falling in love, playing bubble soccer through kelp fields, going to underwater beaches, and taking their whale children to school. Her little reality always stayed so sweet even with all the nightmares exploding their brains out before our eyes.

"I was sailing across the ocean. The crew slept while I was alone on watch duty in the middle of the night. Nothing but blank waves. And thoughts of people. People I told I never wanted to see again, but for some reason couldn't stop thinking of. But the whale broke all that heartache just for me. She poked her head out of the surf with green microorganisms glowing on her face. Her blubber lifted from the waves like a space shuttle entering a new world. I waved to her, and she sprayed me with her blowhole. It was a small nod to each other, that we both existed. That we were the same. The coin glowed in a tiny barnacle cup under her eye, this moon crater crawling with a miniature sea kingdom under her rule. It was one of her secrets. A gift she gave to me because we could only spend that one moment together before we had to say goodbye forever. It still hurts me with a special kind of sadness —that I couldn't give her anything to remember me."

Mike teared up and Mackenzie took his hand. He was turning out to be a bigger softie than he looked.

"I'll be yer whale," Mack said, and made this horrible sound that made her cough. *Mmmoaaaaaawwwhhhh.* Mike patted her head and accepted the offer. *Eeooowhurrr,* he replied.

After a long session of whale call practice, we came across a giant shred of Cloud Maker skin, a whole red slope, a breeze-blown hillside with raised waves of noodled muscle. Ed got

125

up real close and took a sample to keep in her water bottle, a really cool one with a holographic orb sticker slapped on it.

"I've studied animal carcasses before, but this one seems more machine than lifeform. Like an organism infected with technology." She ran her hand across the Cloud Maker flesh, which was scaly and silvery, a bit like snakeskin. Under it was red pulpy stuff with hyperoptic bands shimmering through the muscle. Some rocks and pinecones and ferns were stuck in the flesh, but it was strange. The forest debris looked like it was growing out of the gunk, eating the blubbered slime-meat to grow. Consuming. Making something new.

Watching the dead chunk of Cloud Maker shimmy and twitch was a little unsettling. Kind of. It was interesting, too. I know old Sevs was dying to get a look at the stuff to see if he could find a better way to kill the Angels and their Halos and whatever the donkey diarrhea the Cloud Maker was. Everyone else left the slab of monster parts and headed up the ridge, but I waited a minute. I scooped up some of the Cloud Maker's goo with a small stick and offered it to Nappy Sir Sleeps-a-Lot. He uncurled from inside Tycho's stuffing and ran his head feelers over the snack. Light beams sizzled out of the flesh and Nappy absorbed them, setting his fur aglow with golden motes, the smell of cinnamon solar flare. The feeding stick burned and the food disappeared. I gave him a little pet and he curled back up for sleepy time. Take that, world. Kids *can* take care of pets.

I helped Seven as much as I could for the rest of the hike. Pointed out wobbly rocks and nasty roots waiting to trip him up. My left foot hurt something crazy, but that was alright. I learned to hide my limp long before I met Allie and the rest of the gang.

We found a forest friend coping with their injuries, too. Half of a deer crawled across the hiking path, dragging its tummy tubes behind in a sad tangle. Allie and Will tried to crouch-walk up to the poor animal. Give the deer some last comfort and pets. Maybe tell it about Randy, Captain Frump's sweater-moose, and how it was waiting for them in an afterlife nature preserve—one made especially for horned forest animals who witnessed extradimensional bioterrors engulf their habitats. But the deer saw 'em coming, snorted with a frantic, incomprehensible, *not-another-bad-thing-again* bleat, then scrabbled with its two legs in turbo mode all the way across the path, plummeting over the edge to meet death antler-first on the hardness far below. Will and Al Pal held each other as they came to terms with the collapse of the valley's ecosystem.

And then we did all we could do. We pressed forward. Placing purposeful footsteps in the tracks of deer-slush dividing the path.

After a while we were up as high as we could go. It was easy to see over the mountain where the Cloud Maker had appeared, and pretty clear why that couple jumped to their doom. There was so much blood in the gorge. Giant jellyfish tongues stuck out of burnt landslides. Shredded organs and mangled armor plastered the forest in such a way that you couldn't tell where the landscape began and the trauma ended. All the blood had swooped downhill to turn a whole lake red. Entire trees up to their tippy tops were painted the same color. No

127

way Ed was going to be able to kick enough dirt to cover up that much blood for us. Not in a million years and with a million boots. I knew that she'd try to do it anyway, even knowing that she couldn't make it all go away. That made me a little happy. But the monster was still moving, too. Chainsaw gumlines whirred and tentacle tangles shiver-wiggled in blue acid foam. It was the aftermath of a temple-toothed mega shark feeding on a royal sea slug princess. My cowgirl Ed looked none too pleased by the scenery—from the bile crater where the mouth had exploded—to the pulsing yellow-blister entrails boiling a river into steam. I nudged her at the edge of the cliff. She jerked, but I kept my hands steady.

"I wish I could make a joke about that thing over there," I told her. "Something that would cheer you up. But I don't think I can do it. It's pretty bad."

She crouched beside me and bit her lip. "Well, I'll give it a shot." She looked out at the big mess and thought hard.

"You know, I wasn't going to say anything, but it's my birthday today. That environmental meltdown out there sort of looks like a giant, smashed birthday cake, doesn't it? A red velvet cake with silver fondant icing."

"Then the bones are the candles!" I yelled, maybe a little too excited. Ed gave me a fake smile, but it was good enough. "Well, looks like you already blew 'em all out."

"Yep."

"Did you make a wish yet?" She shook her head, and I snapped my fingers at her. "Do you have any idea how many dreams were vaporized and destroyed just to give you that wish? All the lasers and souls evaporizing and wizard monkey wars?" Ed let out a small laugh and nodded, but it didn't cover up the sadness I felt leaking from her. "Listen. Don't even think about telling me what you wish for. Not until it comes *true*. I really want to know what it is, but if you tell me now, it might not manifest properly, and I don't want that on my conscience." She gave me a curious look with a scrunched-up question hiding in her wrinkles. I kissed her on the cheek. "There's your first present. Now get to wishing." She knelt there for a minute, no doubt thinking hard about that wish, and then blew a kiss to her smeared-to-shit birthday cake.

We traveled farther down the ridgeline trail and found the jumper's camp. It may've not seemed like much to people who think camping means driving a big RV into the woods so the adults can watch TV outside while their kids whisper demon-elf chants and sacrifice insects in a fire, but to real backpackers it was close to paradise. There was one tent full of supplies. Flashlights, stoves, maps, sleeping bags, and food, beautiful, eat-me—right-this-second—or-die food. Dried jerky and nuts and canned vegetables and soup. Sleeping pads surrounded a triangle-shaped fire pit full of ash and burnt sticks. More than two people had to have brought that stuff up there, but no one else was around.

Allie found binoculars on the rock the couple jumped from. She searched the area for anyone else. Smoke signals or trash or airplane parts. Maybe a parachute from a pilot we had all missed ejecting from their jet. Anything. But the mountains stood dead and we were alone.

Our new campsite sat in a little bowl protected from the wind by boulders. A perfect place for a sunset meal. The sun dipped down to hide from the Mouth of God so it could live another day, and the Conductor set to making dinner and starting a fire.

We ate canned corn and jerky and snacked on a dessert of berries Ed had picked along the trail. The stars shone in their bright deaths and cast shadows on us from the rocks watching over the valley. Mike and Toby practiced arm wrestling, and Ed and Seven danced around the fire while Mack beat on an empty can. I hung out with Allie and Will at the cliff edge.

"Looks like all the chocolate goats are definitely dead now," Allie said.

A flock of birds took flight from their tree homes in the valley. "The gumdrop canaries are leaving too," Will added. "Looks like the twizzler wolves will end up getting stronger from eating the drowned goats." They both looked sad that their predictions about the imaginary animals didn't quite come true. Toby walked up nursing his defeated arm.

"No reason to cry about it," he said. "Let's be strong like the wolves." He found where the moon was rising and howled as loud as he could. Even got down on all fours like a proper quadruped. Allie and Will howled in tune while I got down on my hands and knees so Toby didn't feel left out, and we sang our wolf song to the night. I couldn't be certain, but when I heard our echo, it sounded like *something else* howled back. Something broken and afraid.

After we finished goofing off it got quiet for a while. Just the roar of the wind every now and then with the sound of guitars and singing from Allie's headphones. The Conductor's map crinkled under his finger as he charted paths. A fork scraped the inside of a can. Our boots shuffled on the dirt and our clothes rustled as we sat closer together. It made our own beautiful song to make the cold go away. We turned into the wax people in all those museum exhibits sitting around their fake fires. Mackenzie yawned and Mike's face glowed a serious red with his arm around her. Ed still looked like she was thinking about her birthday wish and Toby gave a concerned prod to a hole in her jeans. I sat by Seven's side. He gave me a furry jacket to wear and its softness kept me warm up against him. Tycho Brahe's head poked out from under my neck so he could watch the fire. Mackenzie looked at my monkey and growled.

"What'll happen if a gorilla snatchies one of us up?" she asked. Mike flipped the hood of Mack's prophet sweater over her head.

Ed snorted. "I wouldn't worry about any gorillas up here, it's too cold for a great ape to be romping around these parts."

"Not a sasquatch," the Conductor said. Ed flicked a hot coal out of the fire into his lap.

"You mean a bigfoots?" Mackenzie opened her mouth in awe, then bit her fist.

Will looked over his shoulder. "Well, if anything, a bigfoot showing up would make more sense than anything else that happened today."

"What we need to be worried about is the mighty slumbering beast of the Rockies, a grizzly bear." Ed swiped her hand and grrr'd.

The Conductor pulled a big spray can out of his pack.

"This here spray will scare off most bears that come around, but if a grizzly showed up, this might as well be bear caffeine."

Mike held out his hands and the Conductor tossed the can to him. He twisted the cap back and forth, unable to take it off. "I've seen a pissed off bear before. Want to hear about it?"

131

The can tilted over sideways and Mike made it rise and dip on invisible waves. Then he pulled something out of his back pocket—a can koozie. It was shaped like the head of a black, world-ending bear.

"Land had become a distant memory. I kept count of the days by carving small notches on a smooth length of wood, a peg I found drifting at sea. It was the handhold from another sailboat's helm, and whether the vessel it belonged to was long lost, struggling to survive, or had made it home to port, I will never know. Living on water does something to a person. Not sure how to put it exactly. It makes you understand how hungry you are, and where you stand in line with all of the other things that are hungry. Sharks. Plankton. Trees. The ocean. I think that all things are hungry, maybe in different ways, but everything *longs* for something else. That kind of hunger."

Mike put his hand through the koozie and used it as a puppet, nudging a stick with its bear nose.

"Our boat was small. Only room for four of us in beds the size of sleeping bags. A squall passed in the night, left us with strong wind in the sails, towering waves. Tall and white-capped. It took all of us to reef the mainsail, so we were all awake when the first screams came. We steered toward rays of light hiding behind the storm, and as our ship crested a berm of wave . . . the bear was there."

Mackenzie gasped. "In the middles of the ocean?"

"No, in the *whole* ocean. Hibernating underneath every drop. A cargo ship listed over, almost capsized, with the lights of its small city dunked and flickering. Stacks of containers shifted to starboard and threw her off balance. Fire poured across the ship deck and turned the people falling from the boat into star-blessed embers, a cosmic baptism if I've ever seen one. Three orange life rafts picked up the survivors in dotted clusters, and that's when the oil caught fire. Fuel on the waves ignited in the outline of hunched shoulders and a roaring mouth. Wind whipped the waves to make bristling wisps of fur. The blackness of the water became a beast with split jaws spilling sea through jagged teeth. Rising with pure hatred. A hunger people aren't built to understand. That mouth spread unbelievable. Wide. Lined with fire, waves, the life rafts getting sucked inside, wet paws prying loose cargo containers until a final belch of air sprayed skyward as the ship cracked in two, bitten in half by a perfect upwelling of snout."

Mike held his palm to the fire. Deep burns or cuts traced across its softness, and they drew a fate that overrode the lines and creases from his birth. The bear koozie puppet gnawed at his flesh.

"I know. I know it doesn't make sense to see a bear in all of that, but it's what I thought at the time. It's what all of us on the boat thought. We all saw the bear. How it howled. Lifted its throat to bite at the moon. Slunk back into waves. The crew was lost with the wreckage, swallowed by the whole Atlantic as the monster became one with the ocean once more. I bore witness to the longing. The true desire of that ancient, graveyard tide sloshing souls in haunted currents over most of our world. The forces responsible for that disaster, they are more alive now than ever before. I hear them sing in drops of rain. Hum in dew on grass. Whisper from the water inside everything."

Toby's mouth was so wide open that a bug flew into it and he choked. Mackenzie reached out and grabbed Mike's pinky finger.

"Let's not give the kids nightmares," Ed said. Toby tickled her under the armpit.

"I never have nightmares," he said. "Well, maybe I've had one. In it Mackenzie turned into this weird, glowing bat thing and flew around trying to shove worms in my ears."

Allie slid her headphones down to her neck. "It's alright. Sometimes being scared can be fun. Once my dad woke me up by cranking on a leaf blower in my room and blowing the covers off my bed. I was so afraid I peed, but just a little."

"I know how that goes," Ed said. "At the start of our town's whaling festival every year, my mother would dress up in a narwhal costume with a long tooth-horn jutting out of its head. At first light I could smell her. Covered in dark kelp from the channel in our backyard. Peeking around my door frame, she'd take a moment to sense the environment of my bedroom with her horn. Then she'd be a curious aquatic mammal. Prod my laundry basket. Poke some stray earrings off my dresser. But once the horn detected me, the ceremony began. She bellowed and crashed into everything, trying to gore me with her head as seaweed plastered my face and my homework was tail-fluked off the desk. She forced me to fight her. And I never won, not once. She'd thrash and moan so loud with me pinned to the floor that all I could do was cry and scream."

The Conductor blew a spit bubble out of the corner of his mouth and didn't bother to wipe it away.

"She was a little—I don't know—eccentric. Teaching me

the horrors of whaling, or something like that. Well, when I was about sixteen, I put up my best fight by harpooning her with a broom I had kept hidden under my bed sheets for months, waiting for the occasion."

"Bonk!" Toby pretended to whack her. I noticed Seven was pretty quiet, maybe even a little troubled.

"Hey, Seven, what's wrong?" I asked. "You don't like being bonked?" I gave his head a solid thump and it caught him off guard. Everyone could tell he was a little surprised.

"Of course not. It's nothing."

Ed tossed a hot coal at 'em too. "You know, you can tell us stuff even if it's sad. That's the way campfire talk goes." It was nice to have someone else do my job for once. Seven shrugged off whatever he was holding back and relaxed.

"When all of this started," he said, pointing to the Mouth of God, "the first thing I lost was my dog, Merlin. He'd gotten old and had a hard time hearing and seeing with these grey thunderstorms building up in his eyes. His back legs didn't work well and he couldn't fetch anymore, but he still loved it when I threw a stick or a frisbee anyway. I wanted to bring him along after the Mouth opened, but there was no way he was going to last very long on the road. I couldn't stand the thought of leaving him by himself, either. Of scavengers finding him and eating his tired body. So, I went out into my backyard and dug a hole. Put his bed down at the bottom. Merlin sniffed some mushrooms while I tied a bandana around his neck, a wizard bandana with stars on it, and I put a stick in his mouth. He wagged his tail with that twig-wand clenched tight in his teeth as I launched a frisbee across my backyard—made it soar clear over the shed and a row of tall cypress trees—and he watched that disc with such magic in his eyes, like the frisbee would just keep going on forever."

Seven grabbed an imaginary shovel over his head, then brought the grave digger down.

It's amazing, really. How fast you can go from laughing to wanting to cry. From imagining a mama-sized unicorn whale trying to gouge your pajamas to the dull metal thud of a shovel on the soft skull of an old dog. A loyal longtime friend. Sadness peered out from behind every nook and cranny of our world, and sometimes you forgot how to ignore it.

I took Seven's hand in mine.

"Seven, I am so. So sorry. I promise, as long as I live, that I'll never bonk you on the head again. Real or fake. I don't want you to be sad about that, and if we ever find a dog, we'll name it Merlin, even if it's a girl, and we'll give all its babies other wizard names. I'll get Allie to draw stars on a bandana so they can have wizard powers too. We'll even tie a stick with some moss or fungus on it to their doggy head so they'll always have a wand nearby. And if shovels are making you remember and be sad, the next time I ever see a shovel—I will dig a hole with it while insulting its dirt-licking mommy, then light the handle splinters on fire and bury the hole-maker while it's still alive and you'll never have to see the shovel and think about bonking or Merlin's thunderstorm eyes or bad wobbly legs or all that stuff ever again."

"Whaddya know," the Conductor said. "Looks like robots *can* grow hearts."

"You really would beat up a shovel," Allie said.

"If Mackenzie turns into a bat with worms in her claws, will you beat her up for me?" Toby asked.

Mackenzie put her hood over her face and grabbed some noodles. "I have the ears of a bat and the nose of a Christmas tree!" She jumped up and flapped her arms while shrieking and hopping around. It may've been the funniest thing we'd seen in months. Not her noodle-bat transformation, but the face Toby made as his nightmare became a reality. I'd seen him watch a herd of people running down a hill all get lasered in half and melted into orange juice, and he was still more disturbed by Mack's cawing and flapping.

"Would ya'll like to hear some old man secret wisdom?" the Conductor asked. Our Train Captain combed his beard with the trusty square of velcro, and we nodded. "I think you've all figured it out, but you might not know you have. It was probably easier for the kiddos than the grownups, them being so young and seeing so much. Easier for 'em to adapt, I think." He took a moment and left the velcro stuck in his face hairs. "I've seen so many people bawling, torn up, and losing the remnants of their civility over all these horrors we've seen. It's so many I've lost count. People crawl around now like they've got nooses around their necks that string up to God's puppet fingers. And look, I'm not saying it's wrong to be sad or grieve. But this goes deeper for most everyone out there. There's an inherent lack of mental fortitude in these people. They've been deprived of the ability to handle and deal with the world as we've known it for the last year. I've been asked so many times how I pull off keeping my calm and sanity, and it makes me sick. None of you have asked me that. You never will because you get it. And do you know what *it* is?"

Silence across the board.

"It's this," he said, pointing first at Mike and Mack. "You

137

are as strong as you choose to be." His finger drifted to Allie and Will. "What you can handle has no limits," now Ed and Tobes, "except for the ones you choose to put on yourself." He brought his pointer to Seven. "I don't care if you look at a field of corpses and pretend their dead hands reaching for the sun make the prettiest flowers you ever saw. Believe what you must to stay the way you are." He dropped his hand but looked at me. "That imagination you have might be enough to put the stars back where they belong, but even if it isn't . . . "

Me and him were locked together. I saw steam rise into a clouded sky in the world behind his eyes, and I floated there. Turning like a rusty train wheel battling up hill, sparking and everything, barely able to get a grip. "You'll leave heaven weeping for the rest of time. Alone. Ashamed. And afraid until it drowns in its own tears."

"I got another way to drown the Angels," Toby said, and ran off to whizz behind a rock. If ever there were a classic Toby conversation transition, that'd be it. With everyone in a good mood it was easier to talk about the heavy stuff. To stay positive while looking at the spontaneous combustion of the universe above us, all the golden blood painting dreams that didn't belong to us.

Will pressed his harmonica against Allie's forehead. He let go, and the harmonica stuck to her skin for a few seconds before falling into her lap. "I can't help but be haunted by the *why* of all this. These things, they could wipe us out in an instant if they wanted to. No questions asked. Simply plow right over the whole solar system."

The Conductor remembered the velcro in his beard and removed it. "It's strange. How these Angels have machines that can level a city but choose to use melee weapons at the same time. Like they enjoy hand-to-hand combat. Reminds me of an emperor who became a gladiator so he could step into the arena. He wanted the blood of exotic animals to spray in his mouth. Thought he was a mythological creature re-incarnated."

"They can't destroy everything," Ed said. She crushed up a dirt clod in her hands. "That's not why they're here. What you've all said is all true—so *why* are they here?" She held up her dirtied finger to show the tiniest bit of crystal glinting in the firelight. "They are looking for something. Small and precious." I'll tell ya what, I loved that gal more and more every time she opened her mouth.

"They sure think the opposite of humans," the Conductor said. "They don't think we're much more precious than a germ in a petri dish. Why do you think they look like us then? Must be some kind of practical joke I'm too old or too tired to understand."

Seven drew in the dirt with a stick. "I think the Angels in human form don't resemble their true bodies at all. Not as a joke, but as a filter. Their base form is more than likely represented by their Halos, simple geometry and shapes. They're creating human bodies as a form of filter, like when you want to block extraneous light emitted from stars to study the kind of light that is more important to you. Narrow down your stimuli to focus on something specific. They're experiencing the world through the lens of our species and physical bodies in order to find what they want." He put the mouth of a water bottle to his eye and peered at the laser-shooting pyramid he drew in the dirt. "The human form is their microscope."

139

"That observation is a tad more profound than you make it out to be," Will said. "They must be searching for something they can't find anywhere else. Something they can't pinpoint with all their technology. Not anywhere else in our universe, and not anywhere they came from. What would that be, a feeling? An idea? If we could figure out what it was, and if it's really that important, we might be able to bring this fight to an end."

Allie twirled her headphone cable and broke into the adult's conversation. "I like that you said —*bring this fight to an end* and didn't say —*kill them all.* That's what the Angels are doing. It's what cavemen did to each other. Kill what you don't understand because it's easier that way. That's not how I want to win this. A real hero to me, a real legend would find a way to talk them out of it with reason and logic. With some truth."

"That's a noble way to look at it," the Conductor said. "What bothers me is you'd think the Angels would be closer to the truth than us. Being so smart and all. But they're here cutting us down anyway."

"They definitely know the truth. That's why this is happening," Toby said, coming back from his bathroom break. "They know it and are scared. They don't like the truth and they're here to try and change it. Pretty smart, right?"

Mike and Mackenzie dismissed Tobes' logic in unison with their snores. Toby looked at Mackenzie with suspicion, I guess to make sure she wasn't going to sprout wings and fly around again. I couldn't blame him. She did still have those cold noodles gripped in her fingers.

"What do you think, Robot?" Ed asked. I had to remember

to eye Seven accusingly for letting my nickname spread. Couldn't let him think I was starting to like it. "Sounds like you kids might have better insights than us."

"I'll turn up the volume on her," Sevs said, and prodded my belly. I put on my grumpy face and stared into the fire. Will played his harmonica, and I watched how the flames licked the wood, almost like they were in love.

"I know what it feels like to want to find something so bad you'd tear the world apart to get to it. Something you can't find anywhere else. But I keep that struggle to myself. No need to be dramatic about it and poke every amoeba in the petri dish until they explode their nuclei."

"What is it you're looking for?" Seven asked.

"A special thing I've felt. But I'm not sure exactly what it is, like I don't think the Angels know exactly what they're looking for either. They know where to look, but don't really know what they're looking for."

Sevs had anxious schools of fish swirling in his ocean eyes. "Where do you look for this most special thing?"

"Behind the closed doors inside my head. And all of you help give me the keys, one by one, to unlock them and step through. I've been through a lot of those doors, seen all kinds of worlds and people and things up in my imaginatorium, wonderful and scary, but I'm still looking for the place with this most special thing. It's hidden somewhere deep in my thoughts. But I know I'll find it when I put my hand on this doorknob, and it turns for me from the other side."

I looked at Ed's tiny doorway earrings and hugged my knees. "And this door opens and on the other side is you. All of you. In this place where we met before we were us, and the place we'll be when we are no longer. It's where the force is that makes me feel the way I do about you. What makes us best friends."

I squeezed my legs harder.

I knew it sounded a little weird, and I was afraid everyone would think I'd hit my head too hard jumping off the train. Seven put his arm around my shoulders and I could feel my heart expanding, invisible and huge. I could feel his too. We understood each other. There weren't words to be said about this. That wasn't the point. More hearts from around the fire expanded into ours, silent and warm, and we watched as they wove together and mixed in the only way they ever could. Beautiful and strange, twisting into the fire to light up the world. I leaned in and put my head on Seven's chest and closed my eyes.

"Can you tell us a story?" I asked.

A log in the fire cracked, and then Seven began.

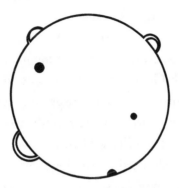

TO BEAR THE WEIGHT OF ALL SHED LIGHT

~A Campfire Story for Weary Adults and Sleepy Children~

Far away from here, casting its shadow on everything we know and see, is a garden. A garden so full of life and myth that all other gardens look like barren deserts and mirages in comparison. On the sprawl of its endless boundary is a tree that has been growing since before our world was ever made. But before that tree even sprouted a leaf, it was a seed. A seed that was planted in the grass by a child. A little girl. This child asked the two most revered and decorated warriors in all existence to become guardians of the plant because the child believed one day the tree's roots would spread to every universe, every star, every world, and every life so they could all become one. So nothing would have to be alone, as the child had been for so many years.

The White Guardian listened to the child and vowed to help the tree grow as strong as possible. The Black Guardian

143

shook the girl's hand and took an oath to give their life to the plant if that's what it took to keep it alive.

After the pact was made, the White Guardian gathered their instruments, sharpened their judgment, and left for the stars. The Black Guardian found a watering pail and helped the child nurture the plant. Every day when their hands were stained with dirt and their clothes were soaked with sweat, the girl and the Black Guardian would stretch out on the grass and watch the sky. Naming interstellar clouds. Telling tales of legendary beasts or discovering ancient tombs. They watched stilt-legged birds tiptoe careful and shy through streams and said prayers for the fish speared by their beaks. The Black Guardian educated her about death and she taught them about life. They learned each other's secrets, and together, charted paths through their hearts which were overgrown with sadness, vine and thorn.

When the Black Guardian was busy, the girl would pick up a wooden stick and pretend to fight off monsters. Whacking at trees and statues of long-forgotten animals. The girl held her stick sword high before an audience of lazy caterpillars to proclaim that she was the Black Guardian, fearless, the bravest warrior in all eternity.

One day during the child's training session, a white wolf appeared in the garden. Its mouth bloodied from a freshly mauled fawn. A steaming black mark burned along its side and smelled of wounded stars, of caustic void and blindness perpetual. The child wavered, stood uneasy as she pointed the pretend sword at the wolf, and the weapon quivered in her hand. The wolf circled her. Hunched low with raised fur. And in absolute silence, the wolf lunged at the girl. But her hand steadied—and with a confident thrust, she rammed her makeshift sword through the wolf's jaws and tackled it to the ground, prying the wolf's throat open until the wooden tip punctured through its fur.

By the time the Black Guardian arrived, the wolf had run away to find somewhere quiet to die. The girl wrapped its broken fangs in the roots of a flower and planted them in a tidy mound. It was then the bandaged soldiers poured in through the garden gates. Missing limbs and limping. These scouts found the Black Guardian and whispered to them.

The Guardian left the garden at once.

As the Black Guardian navigated between worlds and stellar clusters, they saw what the White Guardian had accomplished. Entire solar systems were laid to ruin. Whole planets wobbled cracked and broken with their moons shattered into drifting rings. Colonies of explorers floated in clouds of debris, their bodies pulverized and orbiting as monuments to fear and loss immortalized in hard vacuum. Transmission static echoed with screams. No communication could be established with the galaxy's outer rim, the hubs that connected them to every other system in the universe. The Black Guardian had seen enough and headed back to the garden.

Upon arriving, they found the White Guardian telling the child of all their accomplishments. They began to argue, the two Guardians—and the child listened.

"You are destroying all the things the tree needs to grow," the Black Guardian said. "How can you pretend what you are doing is right?"

The White Guardian laughed. "I'm simply pulling weeds. Only the strong will be touched by the tree and lend it the strength it deserves."

"Well then you should kill me too," the child said.

Defiant, but trembling.

The White Guardian showed her a familiar mark on the armor of their breastplate. Singed black and smelling of malformed space. They stroked the deer-hide fringe of their collar and told the girl quietly, "*I already tried.*"

The White Guardian left in their ship and the girl fell by a mound of dirt, the one which housed the tree's seed.

The Black Guardian handed the child a watering pail. "I will leave here," they said, "but I cannot save those among the stars anymore." They stuck their sword in the ground and leaned upon it, gazing toward the heavens to bear the weight of all shed light. "To kill the White Guardian I will have to sacrifice them all, and it is my duty to follow them into the grave and beyond."

The child threw the pail across the garden. "I don't care about everyone else. I don't care about the worlds and suns and this sleeping, stunted seed. Why can't you stay with me here and be my friend? Why don't I get to be brave like you and follow everything and everyone into the grave?"

The Black Guardian laid a hand on the girl's shoulder. "You wanted this tree to bring all life together, and it will. Just not in the way you wanted. Through death we'll all become one, and for that I am sorry. You will have to care for this garden and return to existence a life more beautiful than anything we've ever known. Out of everyone left alive, it is you who should enjoy the birds in its canopy and learn the wisdom whispered by its leaves. We will all be hiding there, somewhere beneath the grass. Sleeping in the folded wings of a butterfly."

The Black Guardian hugged the child but could not look at her. "Brave like me, you say? I will soon wage war against armadas and titans of such enormity that the stories can only be told by you—by connecting the never-ending vastness between the stars with your imagination. I will wade through death and blood for so long that I will become nothing but a long, black smear rivaling space itself. And I will do it all, take every lonely step, swing every cold and cracked sword, so I can live forever inside your heart—where you'll learn its soft and steady beating was the only thing that ever made me brave."

The Black Guardian left and never returned. The child never got to see them fight. Never got to follow the red trail of footprints they left on their journey. Her nights were spent looking into space, watching stars brighten sharply before dimming to a cold black. In her mind whole armies were formed, the Black and the White, and they fought through every corner of every galaxy. They started out on foot. Running across the sands and snows and grasses of worlds and moons with their swords raised and rifles aimed. She pictured the Black Guardian bandaging a lone survivor atop a ruined skyscraper, the whole city swept away by a wave of blood, the frail bodies of all those the tree was meant to shade flowing and bending against the corners of buildings and park statues.

The war moved to space. Massive ships melted each other's hulls and sent smoldering vessels crashing into frightened crowds huddled on fewer and fewer planets. Suns were depleted of their energy to fuel weapons of immeasurable power, and the worlds surrounding them became forgotten.

147

Dead and cold with all those on them left to sleep in ever-lasting winter. And each time, emerging from mountains of corpses and disaster, was the Black Guardian. Still alive.

One midnight she saw a hopeful glimmer—a ship returning to the garden. But the hurtled bulk of wreckage only grazed the garden's atmosphere, its long tail of dead astronauts reflecting sunlight from their visors in frenzied twinkles.

Her imaginings only grew stronger as the seasons changed. She spent long days in the grass letting insects find warm spots on her skin to call home. An occasional owl or fox would find its way into her garden, seeming to come out of nowhere, like the souls of those lost in battle returned to her as animals. The garden flourished with life even as her tree struggled to sprout, only managing a single leaf on its small length of sapling. Even so, she watered it every day. To pass the time she gathered caterpillars and worms to watch them play and wiggle with one another. She carved a length of branch into a fine wooden sword which she practiced with, slashing at stars and the ghosts of generals from the White Guardian's army.

Finally, a night came where her sword practice ran for hours, her muscles spent and tired, her movements slick and graceful in the starlight. She imagined the war's climax—a crossing of blades in the garden's meadow with the White Guardian and the Black Guardian trading blows and cuts.

Punches and bruises.

With a final great swing, the Black Guardian pierced the White Guardian's armor at the neck, splintering their crooked spine into a sharp flower with its petals fluttering away as a fine, pink mist.

She traced the Black Guardian's movements with the tip

of her sword, and as she made her final swing she collapsed to the lawn, exhausted. She smiled into the universe, and for the first time, it smiled back. The remaining stars burst with light, each one beaming out to one another with brilliant lines of traced gold. Every battle, every story she had imagined played out overhead in a single moment of wonder and awe as myths were slain, kings were burned, and the whole of heaven ascended into oblivion right before her eyes. And then all was gone. Only her garden and the lonely sun which gave it life remained.

Time continued its single-file parade with the girl dragging her feet at its front. Instead of imagining valiant battles, she recorded the flight patterns of exotic birds. Measured the hoofprints of deer to keep track of how the fawns aged. She knew everyone was gone, that all their struggles, their loves, and their dreams were lost somewhere in the ash that sometimes rained from the sky. But it was this soot, this scorched snow of bone and flesh and planetary cores that finally let her tree grow. Slow at first, one plank of bark at a time. But as more star debris drifted upon the garden the tree grew faster. Sprouting branches and whorls of bark for woodpeckers to dig into. Squirrels began to nest in its leaves. Animals came in the night to eat the fruit that dropped from its canopy and piled in tall pyramids. The girl watched as the tree drank up the dead hope of the universe and began to make a new one.

As the tree continued to soar higher, through clouds, through atmosphere and space, the girl began to tell a story—a tale which she carved into its bark.

It started in a desert. Capped with frozen hills of sand. Motionless. Empty of all life. Then, a hole. An opening from *somewhere else*. And through this gaping fault a grand

149

creature emerged—multiarmed, whale-throated, the size of a whole moon. The queen of all seas. The girl detailed the eco-systems of all this monster's parts. Barnacles on its flesh which housed unique tide pools of near indescribable wonder and complexity. Arcs of reef rife with algae and reptiles, the crustaceans which cleaned the brows of its many eyes, and the bacteria in its gut which could give life to any world it pooled upon. But something else emerged from the desert hole as well. A man. A whaler. *The* Whaler.

The Whaler hunted the sea monster across the sandscape. This formed a new ocean, because as the Whaler hunted the sea monster across the desert, the sea monster cried the whole time—spouting tears that washed away each and every dune—all the soundless valleys—filling the desert with the salt and wet of unknowable sadness. The Whaler waged battle through storm and wave and calm sea. Bomb lances snared in baleen plates. Masts punctured and cracked. Javelin volleys struck brow and blowhole and blubber ridgelines with so many harpoons lodged in flank and flipper and fin. Magnificent pink flag banners trailed from their spiked shafts to make the sea monster the sole survivor of some confused and forever-lost parade. And at long last, the Whaler pierced the bow of his boat into that perfect animal one final time, and the sea monster died.

Nameless children spilled from the sea monster's heart where the bow slashed its chest open. Knowing why the creature's heart was made of children, the Whaler began to cry, too.

He had finally become the sea monster.

As the nameless children woke, they saw what the new sea

monster had done. But they would not hunt him like he had hunted them. Instead, they told the new sea monster stories to keep it crying. So its tears could flow and soak through all of time. Memories. Dreams. Imagination. The children's stories migrated through these rivers and surging plumes of sea, their meaning swollen in every drop of shame and heartache, and they flooded throughout the hierarchy of creation to birth an endless ocean. A boundless nursery of surf to grow the saddest story ever told, the story to drown all the sorrow ever felt with a single message sunk to the core of all emotion.

The way the tide moves unseen to a lone jellyfish beached upon the shore, one wave at time, to bring it back home.

The fire died down and the night was cold. Toby sat in Ed's lap holding her hand. Allie leaned her head on Will. The Conductor looked skyward to the moon and Mackenzie and Mike were still conked out. Coals went from black to red to orange in a slow dance that made me sleepy. I stared into the heat until my face was warm and then rounded everybody up and herded them into the tents and sleeping bags. They were so tired they didn't even notice I stayed outside and zipped them in, except Mackenzie, who flailed her arm through the flap, hyperventilating, fighting both me and her claustrophobia. An offering of Sir Tycho Brahe, an old gummy worm, and a compromise of half-zipped tent flap got her to go to bed.

I walked to the ledge where the couple jumped and looked out at the gorge covered in the yellow shadow of the sky.

"Hello again my orbital oracles up there," I said into my walkie-talkie. "Make sure to cast your telescope vision to the stars. Whatever you do, don't look back down here [blip] All you'll see is a blood stain. One I'll never be able to clean up for you. Emotion level for the day: Lonely Porcupine on a Pool Float. Robot out [blip]"

I toed some dirt off the cliff edge. White scales from the Cloud Maker still pollinated through the valley gore. Reflecting light, drifting mischievous beyond the cold ridgeline in sparkled mists. I could almost hear them humming. Calculating some secret work. The world never takes a break from trying to kill you sometimes. That was alright though. I had secret work of my own to do.

PART TWO

—— × ——

ONTOLOGY'S END

CHAPTER EIGHT

*I Know Where All the Sheep You
Count to Sleep Become Rainbows and Lava*

After Seven's epic campfire story on the Cloud Maker's graveyard ridgetop, an hour or two before dawn, I snuck back into the tent and curled up in my sleeping bag. Then the *Late Night Robot Picture Show* started playing in my head. I'm talking about dreams. They never really let me sleep, so I guess I *really* am a robot in that kind of way. Every time I started snoozing my mind hit the hyperdrive button and blasted off. Before I could even count to one little, headless sheep—I'd teleport to a petting zoo and be feeding animals that were just big tangles of human arms, their little bird-mouth-hands pecking at my toes. Or I could be on a soft hill by the ocean watching statues of giants crumble into the sea. Dreamworlds unfurled through hypnogulfs of cloudscape and pumped me into their weird and beating nervous systems, making me an ambassador for humankind among the grandest wastelands of reality.

155

I found whole deserted civilizations for me to explore. Eyeless, pelican-beaked seabirds carried me across the aftermath of long-ended parades. I rode on six-legged anvil steeds through crater playgrounds with colorful cloth reins flapping like streamers. Bumbling robots led me through alien aquariums filled with turbosharks that inhaled disco jellyfish and exploded them into crystals for their friends to eat. Danger lurked in some of the domains, too. I proudly bushwhacked my way as a calm, cool badass through illegal party gatherings in backwater dimensions—nudging past hologram figures, molten starfish herds, and street fights between noodle werewolves and pissed off pyramid-squids until the strobe light geometry police whooshed in and melted the crowds with lasers that smelled like neon pine trees.

There were so many secrets in those places calling out to me. Whispers telling me to open a closet or peer around the next corner—maybe turn a dinosaur egg upside down in a museum. When I followed those voices, I was led to gateways that brought me to a single world. A joint hub between all those realities. A place I called the Sculpture Garden.

The Sculpture Garden's interior was kept in a constant state of sunset. All the hedges and fountains and flower beds stained in warm pinks and twilight purples from a pair of suns snuggled up on the horizon—a horizon that curved all the way around to make a circle, a ring. The whole structure floated inside a planetarium with unrecognizable constellations crinkled along its ceiling.

Constellations that weren't exploding, I might add.

Of course, I named this world the Sculpture Garden because of the sculptures. Stuff like broken ocean buoys stuck in sea-creature fossil beds. Huge hands made of marbled wood poked their fingers through dense fruit groves. Ponds and marshland and cubes of rainforest populated the ring in thick stacks, mostly connected by wooden bridges, catwalks, aqueduct paths, tramways, and the occasional hidden waterfall access—my personal favorite because those passageways always had glow-in-the-dark cave paintings. Sometimes the Garden's vegetation formed tombs or plant archives lined with slick, carved boulder gates. All these sculpture exhibits formed a massive and winding garden walk around the whole ring. Constructed in half-buried greenhouses. Poised on columns in shimmering emerald pools and catacomb algae pits. Galleries rose atop ivory temples draped with treasure and the limbs of broken mega-beings, ancient gods of long dreamt dreams. The sculptures were tremendous or tiny, quiet or noisy, but always alone and in need of repair, which was my job. I was the Curator of the Sculpture Garden. Always had been for as long as the hamster spinning the wheel in my memory core could remember.

Time slowed down when I was in the Sculpture Garden, so a single snooze session felt like being there for weeks. This gave me time to learn the different controls and puzzles to fix the sculptures. I pushed and pulled levers on cone buoys until their colors chirped in rising bands, bird-song sweet, to make confetti shoot from their tips. Geometry ornaments needed to be placed in marble beehives so insects could pollinate flower-sulked castle walls. Bath shrines connected waterways where gondola boats carried amethyst databanks purring with pure archaeological mystery, and I had to canal-paddle them into the right fountain slips so squirt-gun-headed iguanas could hose off their sensor ports. Some sculptures came with controllers, almost like they were made for extra-terrestrial videogame consoles, and I could use them to change the environment and shift the structures. So. I might raise a statue's broken arms on a lopsided pyramid until their hands cupped the double suns in the distance, powering the whole structure, letting trapped water flow down its steps and refill the surrounding coral reef ponds—which would then cause a bright pink urchin queen to rise and reveal a new seaweed-draped ecosystem in need of pruning and irrigation. Each time I repaired an exhibit, the Sculpture Garden bloomed with more art for the strange garden life to feed on.

Every night was different though. When I entered the Sculpture Garden it was always in an alternate time period, a whole different geological era. There was the Scorch era where those double suns were so close that all the sculptures were baked white and steaming and I could only move through heavy shade and tunnel ductwork. The Monsoon epoch flooded swamplands and caused chaos when creatures floated from their natural habitat into foreign sculpture areas. You ever try evicting a snorkel leech from the skull-trumpet of a spotted barnacle bison flailing all its tube grazers? If you do—bring band-aids, a boomerang, and the biggest pool float you can find. Trust me.

Sometimes I could only repair an exhibit through multiple eras. I'd place armfuls of glow snails at the bottom of a broken lighthouse during the Twilight period, then wake up, have a normal day, and fall asleep again so I could hike up a sand dune in the Desert age to the migrated snail colony at the lighthouse peak and use their light to focus a crystal beam.

I watched whirlpool lagoons evaporate and leave skeleton graveyards. Saw amphibian mammoths get stuck in gulches where—a million years later—their spine bones became a well-walked animal bridge.

And once, just one single time, I saw the monster that broke all the sculptures in the Garden. Caught a glimpse of its blubbered ridge of forehead and frantic arms plowing through jungle outcrops before I hid in an underground moth nursery. Had my tears licked away by soft ropes of insect tongue to feed their dreaming babies.

Traces of battle were easy to find in the Sculpture Garden. Chiseled claw marks on pillar ruins. Bodies plaster-casted from lava flows either in mid-crawl or with spears raised against a long gone enemy. Pathways often formed the shape of gigantic, stumbling footprints sunk into meadows—evidence of a void-cursed beast's final steps before dying. Before merging with the Garden forever. Leaving nothing but pointed ribs to be swarmed with whispering fungus and singing tendrils of moss.

So. I had questions about this. Why did the Sculpture Garden exist in the first place? Of all the derp-brained beings in eternity, why was I allowed to enter the Sculpture Garden? It was clearly a sacred, hard-to-find spot that even the most seasoned dream travelers couldn't access. I saw them explode every now and then. Dream astronauts who tried to enter from other sleepscapes. A figure might crawl out of some floam-oyster in one of the coral gardens, a big floofy hat brimmed over their masked face, robes flapping, arms flailing like anemone tentacles as they celebrated their arrival—only to get laser-beamed by a defense system that dissolved the party wizard into streaks of acid. They looked like glitter meteorites when they pierced the sky, and when a whole expedition of trespassers showed up they rainbowed in full-blown meteor showers.

This took me a while to understand, but I figured it out. What was going on. The Sculpture Garden was the home and birth nest of a device. A device of such enormity my little sprinkle brain could barely comprehend its ageless splendor. The Sculpture Garden was its soul made into plant and statue. Smooth curves of a gleaming ark peered from the bright white moon which orbited in loops through the Garden ring. Swirled decorations on its metal whale throat cooed as a magic beacon. The machine's bow peeked out of its moon tomb and jet-spurted with tropical waterpark streams every time I repaired a sculpture, watering the Garden, saluting me in aquamarine glory. Skeletons piled thick around the object. Praising, blessing, worshiping its holy ornaments and polish.

I called it the Fountain Heart.

I was able to find it in every dream if I dug deep enough and braved the howling unknowns rampaging through my brain-maze. The Fountain Heart called to me with an irresistible hum, one that guided me through entry-level dream worlds that connected to the Sculpture Garden. Past wounded rainbows bleeding on salt flats, through playcrowns in crashed spaceships, and monster skull archways tunneling beyond the fifteenth marvel of the universe. Tucked away in the Sculpture Garden were pieces of the Fountain Heart's sacred gearwork. Its hurt organs and injured machinery. Investigating these sad, sunken control panels in bogs and studying corroded moss-stuffed turbine exhibits became my ultimate secret project. Flashing cylinders wedged in cave walls whimpered until I reprogrammed their weird shape-math. Amoebasized gerbil wigglers needed to be microscoped and herded into delicate cellular Ferris wheels to unlock gates for depowered aquariums. I was given tests to make sure I understood all these components. How they worked together and needed to be arranged. And believe me, none of the quizzes made any sense.

I'm so stupid, obviously red squishy diode number three million one hundred and ten actually needs to be a spiny golden pyramid. Of course! No. The tests were bogus, and if I wanted to unlock new areas in the Sculpture Garden I had to pass them, which took an understandably long amount of time.

As I tended to pinball gazebos and goo-covered microphone arrays in treetop laboratories, I felt the Fountain Heart analyzing me. Connecting with me. Feeling how *I felt* about the sculptures and what they meant to me. Giant eyes swiveled in wall cracks to watch my fingers work. Rare figures wearing funny hats watched on from a cold distance, ones that didn't get annihilated by the Sculpture Garden's defense system. I shouted to them, *Why me? What am I doing here?* The only response I got rattled from the Sculpture Garden itself. Gargled, shaky, and scared. The answers were imprinted on my being in a language I couldn't understand, but I felt 'em alright. Licking my skin with their frenzy and worry.

This world, the ones it connected to—they all tried to speak to me. They needed my help. They needed me to curate this reality and give it purpose, give it meaning, so that when the goliathan that broke the Sculpture Garden returned, the Fountain Heart could fight back.

That night on the ridgetop was no different. I put my head down on a bundled jacket and despite trying to stay awake, I stumbled headfirst into wonderland. All was normalish at first. Totally boring. Just a nighttime street with houses and porch lights and big yards with sugar-scented flowers vined in and out of white fences. A stoplight hung low in the street and flashed red over and over again. When I finished scouting for emotionally damaged zoo animals with severe cases of head-butting syndrome, I came across an iron gate. It was black and studded with the heads of roaring lions. Heavy door knockers hung below their throats and quivered.

Yep, that thing was definitely haunted.

Something smelled bad, which is a weird thing to happen in a dream, and my sniffer led me to pine needles lining the gate fence. In the needles was a small, dead mouse wearing a life jacket. She was soaking wet like she'd just drowned. I don't know why, but I pet her a little. Tried to cast a *good-night-sleep-tight* spell on the silent squeaker with a twig so she'd have good dreams. Then, feeling a little stupid about my witch-power abilities, I picked up the limp furball sailor and placed her in one of the lion mouths. The gate cracked itself open and waited.

I walked through and teleported to an area of the Sculpture Garden, one I'd seen before but never been to. A section I called the Dream Core. This section was elevated on a mound of moss and shrub bulbs which made a lookout where you could see the whole ring. In a way, it was the center of the Sculpture Garden, made even more clear since it was surrounded by a tall hedge maze. The Dream Core stayed lush and vibrant through all the Sculpture Garden eras, pretty much the only constant exhibit in the ring. A cool, misted, everlasting tower fort of green. The Fountain Heart had never coaxed me into the Garden with a dead animal before, so I imagined the small sacrifice was why I showed up in the ultimate off-limits district. No way around it though— I was lost. In new territory in dangerous times. I took off my shoes to show my respect, wiggled my toes in the grass to say hello.

The Dream Core's protective hedge was only knee high at its peak, a ceremonial maze. Glowing through bends and elbow turns along the bushy path was a mosaic art walk. Chopped up tiles sunk into dimpled rock that puckered around the gold-specked crater rim of a tide pool. I investigated with my best art-museum posture and deduced the images to be a creation story played out in chronological hieroglyphy along the path.

Proud, balloon-throated and wet, a four-armed whale god burst from the center of a desert to flood its orange dunes. This was the *story* at the end of Seven's story—the one the girl carved into the bark of that enormous tree in her garden. I wandered around the path to make sure. The artwork depicted the sea monster and the Whaler, that mysterious person who hunted the beautiful beast. There were ocean pantheons and magical blowholes and lots of harpoons and sunken ships and blood and sad children. At a certain point I felt like I was one of the children that came out of the sea monster's heart. Or, to be a little weirder, I felt like I was in a story *told* by one of those children, a story to keep the new sea monster crying for all of time. And with that thought, I

163

skipped ahead through the story, stepping over the maze walls to make my own path. Spank my own destiny.

I paraded in a straight line, crunching plant barriers, pretending I was a genuine beer-bellied barnacle sniffer stomping through sandcastles and sphinxes at the beach with a towel cape flapped by the wind. I imagined a squeaky giraffe inner tube bulging around my waist, a baby hammerhead shark wriggling in my hands as I raised 'em proud and firm to the sun with tattooed waves, endless and sharp, curled across my arms, my shovel-feet plowing through shallow moats, kicking the shell-studded towers of make-believe kingdoms into the eyes of children, into the flimsy plastic cups of their fumbling, sunburnt parents, all while screaming a sacred proclamation to the foamy surf, to the shiny blood-stained beaks of seagulls—a motto as mysterious and deep as any ocean ever crossed, one that surged with monster shadows to a frothy crest beyond the understanding of little girls, ancient humans and Angels, but one I could find a never-ending undertow of secrets inside of.

The Tide Will Erase All!
The Tide Will Erase All!

As I stopped my imaginary beachside rampage, waves from this phrase churned against the front of my brain with a curled pull. To be clear—totally tropical breeze—I wasn't the same Robot I was before. *Reprogrammed*, that's the word for it. This chant. This feeling. Somehow these words contained the whole meaning of the maze's mosaic path, the purpose of the four-armed whale legend. It was the ocean-genesis prayer meant to honor the holy blubber queen and all she created. No. More than that—the *Tide*. This was prophecy of a never-before-seen flood. An eternal-abyss sea punishment. A celebration of endless drowning.

I peered inside the tide pool at the Dream Core's center. Manatees nibbled on lazy starfish that lined the inner walls of the hole where thin eels ribbon-darted through arcs of coral and yellow seagrass. The tide pool was deep. At its bottom, a massive crystal plugged the hole. No telling how far the aqua tunnel burrowed down below it. The gem was easily five stories tall and surrounded by crystal ruins. Just the corner of *maybe* a marble building. Steps of a wooden rope bridge that *perhaps* lay between the sunken lip of a swimming pool and a cracked pillar. Bubbles rose from the bottom along with an object, a controller for fixing the Fountain Heart, and on that controller—beaming his antlers into dream space—Nappy Sir Sleeps-a-Lot.

"What in the insect hell are you doing here? Get off of that!"

Nappy shook his thorax fanny on top of the Fountain Heart's control box. Buttons, knobs, and sliders covered the controller's U-shaped face, which was a little bit like a video game controller. I'd rewired it a few years before so the controls made more sense to me, and stringy electroguts poked out of the casing that I'd never gotten to shut quite right. Nappy licked some of the wires with a thin tongue that whipped around like a party blower horn. He sparkled again, only this time the motes of glitter rose above his white fur to form a hologram. Soundwaves wiggled silver in its light and his antennae perked up, maybe to receive some sort of transmission. So. This is why his bug butt was always taking naps. He was patrolling dream worlds. I wasn't sure if that was a good or bad thing, but then he crawled through a gap in the casing and made the whole controller buzz. Great.

The presence of this Sculpture Garden controller meant the tide pool ruins were an environmental shape-shifter puzzle, no different from others I'd solved a hundred times before. The joysticks and switches were used to move things in the landscape until they slid into their proper positions. But first came a kind of weird handshake between me and the Fountain Heart. An opening ceremony. I punched in a sequence of buttons to bring the main control panel to life.

"If this shocks you to death in there, you wiggler. Don't say I didn't ask you to get out first."

The screen flickered on and asked me in its weird symbol language if I wanted to activate the puzzle. I closed my eyes and pressed my palm flat on its surface. Flashes of what I could only guess were the Fountain Heart's memories infiltrated my mind, implanting visions from its memory core into mine. My thinky-thinky parts merged with these strange moments, and I felt everything they'd felt. I became an ocean creature. Lurched straight out of the water so I could see the full moon spread across the waves. Then something cruel and heartless clawed through one of my eyes, and a gash tore open in my side as hundreds of flexible fingers invaded my organs. I jumped to another memory where I was the head of a heron mounted on a cabin wall as it burned at dusk. Then I flapped wings to fly over a jungle pit, the steaming slosh of huge reptiles. Next, I was a rocking chair frozen in place as a train choo-chooed by. A magnolia catching sunlight. A dolphin in a swimming pool. And finally, a lone door stuck in the shallow surf of a sunset beach, blue, on the verge of creaking open.

With the mental handshake complete, my consciousness returned to the Sculpture Garden. Symbols appeared on all the controller buttons. Pink ones that glowed and lime green dials with markings like silly string and a slippery orange slider. There was one red button sunk deep under a flap that took pressing two buttons at once to open, but I'd never been brave enough to test it out.

It probably would've just made my head fall off, nothing serious.

First, I balanced on the edge of the tide pool. Jiggling the joysticks showed that I could control the underwater bushes poking out of the diamond plug. With a few good clicks and thrusts, I commanded the leaf tendrils to grip the well walls and climb. Water gushed over my feet and bubbled. Wrapped in kelp and pink egg sacks, the crystal tip emerged. Shards splintered and fell as I waddled the diamond away from the tide pool rim and sat it down with an earthquake thud. The bush tentacles rose as towering kudzu creatures growing out of the crystal. They bobbed back and forth like elephants trapped in a cage dreaming of killing themselves. I pushed two blue rectangles and rotated the night sky around me. Billowed and huge, the Fountain Heart's moon orbited to perfectly align the shadows cast by the hedge-maze creatures. The shades of their heads merged into a soft circle on the tide pool and turned the water black.

Then the Sculpture Garden started to tremble.

A bulge of white feathers welled up from far below where

167

the crystal plug had been. Swans floated to the surface, many of them dead, their loose necks piled on top one another. Others took flight to circle the Dream Core—all of them in various stages of honking, diving, and puking up black water. During my midnight session of the Unseen World game with Seven back on the train, I'd imagined these birds being up-side down under the water. But in this place they floated above the surface, which put me beneath the world of my own imagination. The swans were all still crying. Even the dead ones.

So. My imagination blew a hole right through the Sculpture Garden, and it didn't take long to figure out that was a bad thing. Swans sputtered with a gasp that flung limp birds in a cloud across the entire Dream Core. A royal column of slender ivory feathers erupted from the tide pool. Enormous —a terrible bird head on a pillar of rocketing pure whiteness. A shiny orange beak hissed as it craned into the sky, eyes wild and scanning the habitat, tongue lance probing for prey. She was the Empress Swan. The bird who survives by drinking the tears of all beings across worlds known and unknown. I clicked controller dials and slid all the sliders to full capacity, which spun and multiplied the hedge maze in a thick circle, closing me and the Empress Swan inside like a giant leaf egg.

This was *it*.

The goddess of the Chasm of Eternal Solitude. And my dream hole had unleashed her upon the Sculpture Garden. Deep below the tide pool, out of sight, the sound of drums and trumpets and underwater mammoth breaths rose in a burb-led swell. A parade marching out of the Chasm to spread its confetti and desolation and despair.

Thousands of smaller swan necks bristled in full-blown infection streaks along the Empress Swan's tower of throat— weeping, sobbing, spewing tears in firehose streams. Kudzu shredded and bowed as the Empress Swan pressed her dino-saur-sized bird beak hard into the garden shell to make an escape. The plants parted. Light spilled through leaves. Some-where far away, a jellyfish beached upon a cold shore and there was no way to tell if it wanted to die or if it wanted to be saved.

CHAPTER NINE

Downstream Paddle Apocalypse Part I

I woke up with the Empress Swan's roar fading away in an echo of pulses on my skin. An underwear check showed that I wasn't quite pee-my-pants terrified. With the tent flap open, I could see everyone packing up our campsite and eating breakfast. I dug a finger into my ear and put my shoes on. No need to get worked up over a dream. It was just the same regurgitated bananas I saw every time I closed my eyes, pretty much. It couldn't mean anything. Because if it did, it wasn't going to mean anything good. Ed popped her head in the tent and her hair dangled in my lap. She handed me a steaming cup of oatmeal with a chocolate smiley face on its froth. Her tiny door earrings swung back and forth.

"I'm sorry to tell ya," I said, "those doors hangin' on your ears might lead to bad hallways. There might be whole worlds on the other side, and I can't promise there are nice things waiting." Ed gave one of them a concerned tug. "Don't worry though. I'll open and peek inside for you first. I'll peek inside all of 'em."

We went through all the stuff the campsite had to offer one more time and traded out old sleeping pads for new ones and got more stove fuel. There were some extra-fluffy jackets for the Black Bandits, Tobes, and Allie, but the Conductor didn't want one. His coat was rough and beat up, a little like him, and you could tell it was special. Made for the most kickass Train Captain around. Seven loaded up his shirt pockets with ammo and strapped a knife to his chest. I didn't want anything except for a big, folded, blue tarp. Everyone thought I was weird for wanting it, but I bundled it up nice with some rope and tied it to my pack anyway. We said our goodbyes to the nice folks that left all the equipment, wherever they were, and journeyed onwards.

The Conductor led us on a trail that swished back and forth down the backside of the mountain. A river snaked at its bottom with clean rapids. Rocks were loose on this path, and our Train Captain tread careful as he checked his footing for us to follow. He shoved a large rock off the side and we watched it tumble down and break apart through dead trees.

"Don't let that be you!" the Conductor shouted and poked us with a stick. It was a little scary, but there were plenty of holds on the cliff wall if you felt real fall-to-your-death queasy. I liked that feeling though. It made our adventure seem dangerous, and since we kept on going forward, it meant what we tried to do was worth doing, even if it meant risking a fall like the cliff-jumper friends. Having our hands speared by leafy branches as we reached out. Watching love itself land neck-first on a lonesome mountain trail.

Toby tried to be brave by walking as close as he could to the edge. It was pretty easy to tell he had a little boy crush on

171

Ed and was trying to impress her. His attempt failed when a rock gave out below him and he had to grab onto the Conductor's poking stick to stop from tumbling down into the river. Ed thought it was cute though, and she made sure he walked beside her on the inside of the trail. Tobes kept kicking rocks all over the place. Probably because he felt a little stupid for almost dying, but that didn't stop him from trying to be a hero.

"Don't worry. If a rock falls from up top, I'll make sure to catch it before it knocks you unconscious," he told Ed. "Even if it's a boulder or the whole cliff collapses."

Seven tossed a few pebbles at the rock wall to simulate an avalanche, and Toby lost his freaking cupcakes. He shrieked, and I mean *shrieked*, like a koala having its molars removed by a tiny lawnmower, and he pulled Ed to the ground to protect her with his sweaty boy body while the rest of us shoveled handfuls of small stones and dirt on top of them.

We took a break for a while and gazed upon a highway bridge arched over the river. I told Seven I had to go number two and ran off to set up something special. It took a little longer than I'd hoped because in the spot I picked out I found a dead body—and I mean *dead* dead. Basically a skeleton with some bad burns and a chewed up red cape. Classic superhero style. I put my finger in the skull wound that looked like it killed the brave fella. I respected this girl, or guy. It took guts to wear a cape at the end of the world. It meant you weren't afraid—which is the hardest lie of all to pull off, since everyone, no matter who you are, even your dear, Angel-murdering Robot, gets scared when the sky implodes into an astroclastic flow of drooled star saliva. I held the hero's hand for a while. Put their wallet in their lap and stared into the multicolored sphere printed on their shirt, an orb that looked like the intelligent, transdimensional soul of a starship.

Before I regrouped, I let Nappy out for a bit. His white-fur insect parts didn't look changed at all, no different from when I first found him. Or when he was in my dream. Nappy Sir Sleeps-a-Lot walked in a woozy circle on the caped hero's skull, still waking up.

I decided to trust him, Nappy. So. I asked the critter something I'd never asked anyone before.

"Nappy . . . do you think it was really *him*? Was it Seven?" My Angel bug-pet rested back on his butt and cleaned those majestic antennae with his two front legs. Spores rose from his hairs and formed a hologram again, this time a wispy red boulder that sank into a lawn. Photon helicopters circling overhead. "Ugh, you're no help at all."

See, my earliest memory—the first thing I can ever remember in my hamster-wheel memory bank—is a dream. A dream where I was placed on my unsteady two feet inside the Sculpture Garden as a spit-bubbled toddler. And the face of the one who put me there, the first face my brain can recall —yep, it was Seven's. Frizz-mess curls of hair, broad shoulders, simple, plaid long-sleeve shirt, and his shaded, smiling face. He set me down. Nipped my nose with his hand shaped like a wolf. Then disappeared into green leaves, slinking backward into a bush. So. When I met Seven for the first time at my school, I almost threw up in my binder. I *had* to befriend him, which was something that noticeably annoyed him at first. Astronomers spend most of their time talking with stars, not interacting with people. Especially kiddos. But I forced my-self into his life and made him tell me about the cosmoverse.

I won him over with cuteness, spunk, and the occasional kick to the shin and witty insult. The bond was sealed when he gave me the Ursa Minor pendant, leaning down to loop it around my neck, his face as close to mine as it was in my dream. We'd both been to the same world. I knew it. It had to be him. It had to mean something, mean everything.

The whole group made fun of me for being constipated when I got back. Except Allie. I gave her a big old wink and thanked her for not being a meanie. We hiked a while longer and finally got to the bottom of the mountain and followed the river downstream. The river stones were smooth and when we got bored we'd throw a few into the water. Ed picked up a super-heavy rock and heaved it into the river so it splashed Allie.

"Why are we walking by the river?" Al Pal asked while she sucked out drops from her sweater.

The Conductor rolled his jeans up to piddle-paddle his feet in the water. "See across the way? Up the embankment? Those are the rails I was going to take us along. Would've been a real pretty ride."

"Also, following water will almost always lead you to civilization," Will said.

"Not so likely anymore," Allie said. "We're probably all that's left of civilization now." She looked around at all of us, sizing up the human race's chances of survival. I stuck my tongue out at her and she nodded, pleased with our odds.

Seven looked skyward. "I don't know about that, Al Pal.

Those planes yesterday probably mean there's something left somewhere, even if it's military."

"Mysterious mysteries everywhere," Mack said. She was real serious, staring off into the water. "Squeaky mysteries. Very squeaky, indeedy." Mike pinched his nose and honked, but it couldn't stop Mackenzie from losing herself in the water's flow.

Downstream we came across some abandoned rafts.

They were red and scuffed and smelled of old, wet, rubber mold. There were paddles though, and we all got excited that we weren't going to have to walk for a while. Mack shed her overalls—completely butt naked—and jumped in the water to chase after a fish while we loaded everything into the floats. Tobes and Allie looked on all adult-like, shaking their heads at the goofball splashing about, but I felt like goofing off too. That's what kids are best at. I left my underwear and tank on and snuck into the water. It was cold, but I went under anyway and crept up on Mack, found her foot, and clamped down like a baby alligator. She didn't budge. Mackenzie grabbed both my ears and pulled my head up out of the water. Patted my hair and put a *starfish* on my head. All its tube feet curled and wiggling. Then she licked my cheek.

"Robots, why is the river salty?" Her scrunched eye stayed on me while I confirmed her observation with a suck of my finger, a stroke of the sea star's rough orange skin.

"Well Mack-a-Doodle doo, the ocean sputterin' out of that Angel has probably leaked into the river. I hope the normal freshwater fish don't get contaminated." I thought of the Empress Swan, all her children infected and weeping along her neck, and how I didn't want that to be the reason why it was salty. Mackenzie gave a small goose honk and flexed her non-existent muscles, and I noticed she'd drawn more rabbit heads on herself, covering her legs from knee to ankle. "Hey doofus, stop stealing Seven's pen to tattoo yourself. What's up with all your bunny buddies, anyway?"

Mack held her face and spoke through her fingers. "Robots, are you having *a serious* with me? Right now?"

"Yes, we're having *a serious*."

"He's not my buddy!" She grrr'd and gave me one hell of a spank. "He's my number one enemy, Robots. My mortal combat." Looking off in the distance, she placed a hand over her forehead and let out a breath.

"The Velvet-Eared Magician King. I must destroy hims."

I pinched one of the rabbit faces on her knee. "I see. Keep your friends close, and your mortal combat doodled all over your legs." Mackenzie squeaked and gave me a wet, naked hug, along with a gentle fanny rub to soothe my stinging butt cheek.

No one paid attention to us though. They were looking back at the trail we'd hiked down, past the lookout where we'd all taken a break. On a feeble nose of rock was my big blue tarp strung up with rope off the side of a cliff. Painted on it in yellow was *The Tide Will Erase All* over top a robot head impaled by a harpoon and peeking out from behind waves. The dead hero sat beside it to drive home the point. The tarp flapped as a huge flag and could be clearly seen from the highway bridge with its few abandoned and scorched-black cars. That'd been my special project for the night. I used up almost all the coloring paint in Mackenzie's little toy bag on just the robot head. I spent all night trying to think of a message to write on the tarp, but that message didn't come to me until I was asleep though. In another world. One that swelled inside my head with foam and wave and depth.

Strangeness hung heavy on the riverbank. See. Our group seemed to *understand* its meaning as they stared up at the banner, fists clenched, heads held high. Seven adjusted the sword slung to his back and thought hard.

"Boop beep?" he asked.

My answer for him came in the only way it could. From the ankle-deep water I kicked into his face.

CHAPTER TEN

Eat Asphalt & Shit Band-Aids

We boarded the rafts and barely had to paddle. The water carried us on its wet yawn of current and trickled in moist squeaks on the rubber of our raft. We passed underneath the bridge where curse words I'd never seen before were spray painted on its arch supports. Of course Toby shouted them as loud as he could to hear the profanity echo through the damp concrete and steel. After we drifted past, I looked back and saw a cool painting someone made on the side of the bridge. It was of a girl astronaut jumping from a spaceship while ripping her helmet off in a big hurry. A massive rainbow eye shone on the helmet's visor—the same as that multicolored sphere on the dead hero's shirt up by my tarp banner. Maybe the caped crusader graffitied it right before taking their dirt nap, leaving one last mark on the world. The technicolor peeper beamed on the astronaut lady's face as she screamed out through all the hypersonic colors, hair blowing in the void, spaceship in a nosedive below a black hole. I gave the brave space explorer a salute because I knew she must've had crazy dreams like me. I wanted to tell her to hang in there. Getting sucked into forever while nightmare geometry infiltrated your mind was the new cool thing to do, if you asked me, anyway.

Toby and the Conductor manned the oars, but while our Train Captain paddled us with expert river strokes, Toby got easily distracted by the water tornadoes that peeled off his oar. Yeah, we kinda spun around in circles for a bit. Ed and Seven tossed a moldy tennis ball back and forth while Will showed Allie how to play the harmonica. Mack-a-Doodle stood behind Mike and sniffed wild and snotty at something down river. She sneezed on my elbow without an apology.

"No no no no no no no no no," she said, then flopped over the raft edge and punched at the water with both her hands, letting out a very unflattering power shriek.

Mike picked her up like she was a sack of wet pajamas. "Calm down. Whales don't panic."

"No!" she shouted to the Conductor. "We haves to go back now. Now. *Now*, now. Turney us around."

The Conductor checked the gully, the shrubs, the slopes of erosion and the timeworn bands of geology striped around us as the wind tugged his beard. He gave Seven a *what-the-flippin'-hedgehog* look and shrugged his shoulders.

"Maybe she heard a twizzler wolf howling," Allie said.

Mike patted Mack-a-Doodle on the head. "How about I tell you where all my leprechaun gold is?"

"I saw its. I saw the water's bear. It's here." Mackenzie dove into Mike's arms and cried loud enough to pop an ear-mite. "I punched it for you. I tried."

179

Mike pulled out his bear koozie again and turned it into a hand puppet, trailing it through the water to make the bear head prowl for prey. "I know it is. Of course it is. Some days I wake up and can feel wet holes in my neck from where I've been bitten in my dreams. It scares me. It really does. But if I turned back every time I saw its shadow or heard its roar, then I would have never met you." He took her small hand in his big one and traced a smooth scar on his palm with her finger. Outlining the strange trails through the map of his wound. Showing her the path to something secret and old and hidden. "Thinking about not meeting you scares me more than any deep-sea bear king. I'll do whatever it takes to stop it from getting us, because if you're gone, there won't be anyone else left to hold onto the treasure I've been hoarding. You have to be my whale, okay?"

Will killed the silence that followed with his harmonica. "We've changed an awful lot in the past two days, haven't we?" He looked at Ed and she gave him a nod.

"Well, if we're going to be together for a while, I guess we might as well be honest with one another," she said. Mike held onto Mack-a-Doodle and Will messed up Allie's hair. Ed pulled a cigarette out of her shirt pocket and smoked it. "Before the Angel attack on the train we were going to hijack all the cabins. Your seats, your stuff, and your lives if it came down to it."

No one said anything. I looked over the side of the raft where white Cloud Maker scales drifted alongside us and smooth rocks glimmered. The only sound I could hear were the flippers of an imaginary school of awkward turtles churning current below our float. What Ed said should've made me feel angry. That they were so close to eliminating the last scraps of kindness and milkshakes and humankind they'd happened upon in exchange for whatever was in our backpacks. I'd been right to think of them as the Black Bandits when we first hopped on the train. But Will was right. They'd changed in the short time we'd been together. I wanted them to tell me why. Seven reached over and flicked Ed's smoking stick into the water.

"No shit, cowgirl. And don't smoke around the kids." Seven pulled out a gutted walkie-talkie from his bag. "Missing one of your detonators, right?"

Ed's eyebrows arched with so much surprise I was impressed that they didn't jump in the river and swim away.

"I was ready to derail your caboose with your own gym-bag bomb about ten minutes after we got onboard. Your group was the only one armed on that choo-choo train. It was more than a little apparent. I could've blown out all the candles on your birthday cakes with one click, and even made a wish on it. Probably for that hot tub full of rubber duckies and beer. You're lucky Robot here doesn't have more channels on her walkie—or she might've popped your weasel on accident." He made a lame explosion sound along with an amateur-grade wizard spell gesture. "I would've triggered my little party popper to get rid of that Angel, but Robot's monkey tried to escape from the zoo, and we couldn't have that." Seven blew Ed a kiss and then tossed the walkie over his shoulder into the river.

Allie shied away from Will and smacked the harmonica out of his hands. He took her glasses off to wipe their lenses.

"It's been easier to kill people than to get to know them.

181

Like you said last night, it's what cavemen did to each other, and I agree. I've been very caveman for a while now. Understanding other people can get you hurt. It's been easier to not even try." Will leaned down so Allie had to see him. "It can make you feel like you're all alone, kneeling down before some great unknown creature. A beast that could tear into you. Into the way you think or act, sort of like a twizzler wolf might sink its teeth into a deformed chocolate gumdrop canary and shake its brains out. But I can't pretend everybody's a wolf anymore. I'm the thing I should've been afraid of this whole time."

Ed reached out and pinched Toby. "Sometimes that great unknown creature would give up its own life to stop a boulder from crashing down on you." Toby retaliated by holding the oar handle to his head to make a gleaming horn.

"Your mom's a great unknown creature—and she's gonna spear you narwhal style!" He thrashed, jabbing Ed with his new horn-tooth, making what I can only guess were sounds he thought the magic animals made while smooth tongues of rapids flowed us in dips and bobs. Laughter and cheers rang out against the slab layers of sediment rock as Toby battled Ed around the raft, smacking her a good and proper punishment.

Everyone seemed pretty okay even though we'd learned our new friends were thinking about killing us and robbing our toy boxes. It was alright somehow. Like when you accidentally start going down a hill on rollerblades too fast for you to stop without falling, but then you decide to be okay with falling and spread your arms. Feel the wind take you as far as it can before you eat asphalt and shit band-aids.

Allie brushed off Will's harmonica and played some notes

for us. I scooted over to the Conductor and put my arm around him. "What a crew we have," I said, eyeing the group. "Looks like no one has been torn into emotional confetti yet, so I think we'll get along just fine."

"I'll give you some emotional confetti out of my wrinkled backside," he said. "If I sense funny business from anyone, I'll beat them open like a piñata and eat their candy all by my lonesome." He nudged me in the tummy with the end of the oar and I pretended to vomit up lollipops and bubblegum. No one seemed to get what I was doing though, except Seven. He picked up an imaginary piece of my candy-barf, unwrapped it, and tossed the invisible treat into his mouth. Our Train Captain observed. Then he picked up a piece of my imagination candy, too. He put it in his jacket pocket and said, "I'm saving this baby for later."

Somewhere in the unseen bonds forming between us was a waking mystery. One breathing so quiet I could barely hear it, gentle and low like birds hugging one another. The shushed sound of fluttering wings grew as we came around a horseshoe bend in the river, and the mystery disappeared against hard sunlight on rock.

The cliff beside us was hurt. It had a boo boo so huge no band-aid was ever going to make it feel better. Even if you fell on your rollerblades and pooped one out the size of a school bus. A giant crater sank into the stone with exploded boat parts and shiny orange life vests all glued around its edge. Hundreds of black birds cawed and flapped and pecked all over the inside of the hole, so we couldn't see what was at its center. Toby and the Conductor paddled us to the riverbank to get a closer look.

I smelled sundried death stirred by the birds as they hopped and hovered over one another. Toby searched through his backpack and pulled out a red bundle of fireworks. He flicked his lighter, lit the fuse, then threw them into the bird party. Bangs and crackles thunder-shocked through the whole bend, and the birds canceled their buffet meeting to fly away down river. Seven drew his sword. The Black Bandits readied their rifles. We all jumped out of the raft.

Half buried in the rock—a massive iron gate gleamed heavy, hot, and black. Tar-plastered heads of lions were forged into the metalwork. At least six people, snug in their life jackets, hung from the lion mouths where they'd been chomped. Although it was hard to tell for sure, since so much shredded skin mangled in with the flotation preservers. There was a big dent in one side of the gate where a boat had rammed it at high speed. Rusty stains ran down from the lion mouths and fanned over the ground to match the red dust. Seven and the Bandits investigated the scene, banging on the metal with their boots and checking the bird-pecked bodies.

I couldn't move. Couldn't stop staring at the lion mouth where I'd placed the brave, soggy mouse sailor in my dream. And I fully understood my *good-night-sleep-tight* witch spell hadn't worked. Because the one-armed, no-legged, life-jacketed girl inside the metal mouth was still twitching.

We called these Miracles.

They were evidence Angels had been near. On our journey we ran into them over and over again. Sagging in the middle of pretty farms or exploding out of skyscrapers and mini malls. Strange billowing smoke as hard as marble floated on one lake we'd passed, screaming out in pain every time someone looked at it. A purple jungle gym of twisted shapes wiggled and pulsed through a whole forest canopy—spewing neon acid on the exposed bones and spilt organs of a lumbering, aquarium-sized animal a bit like a deformed crystal hippopotamus. Sometimes cars or boulders floated in midair, cut up and stacked together the wrong way. It was like the Angels were making Earth their own personal Sculpture Garden. Terraforming it with dreams and nightmares from another universe.

Sometimes we came across other people kneeling in front of a Miracle. Sobbing or praying to it. I met Allie at one, too, that guillotine-tower that spat out refrigerators full of oranges as its method of execution. Always oranges. Every time. I never understood why people were drawn to Miracles—not until I stared into the eyes of all those Duke Ellingtons with prey dangling from their mouths.

The Miracles meant something to those people.

This one meant something to me.

Seven and the Bandits hopped back in the raft after they put my twitching sailor out of her misery. The iron gate disappeared around the next gooseneck bend, but I couldn't stop staring back upstream. The Conductor turned me around and handed me a shiny flake of mica.

"We can't have our team robot malfunctioning on us. I know you've seen worse than that. Those people haven't been dead for long, but you shouldn't worry. I bet the Angel is long gone by now."

Will didn't look so sure. He adjusted the scope on his rifle and kept it pointed ahead, clicking the little focus knob on the tiny telescope back and forth. "I've gotten up close and studied every one of those things we've come across. Some aren't formed as well as others. If they're less symmetrical or broken up, it means the Angel is struggling or gone. But if they're solidly built, then the Angel is alive and well. Strong. Just like that gate."

Mike cupped some water from the river and splashed it on his face. "I've thought those structures are a sort of byproduct. That the Angel's presence in our world causes them."

A bright light shone in my eyes and I tried to bat it away. Seven had his sword partially unsheathed, angled perfect so it reflected sunlight into my eyes.

"Agreed," Sevs said. "I believe the Angels have to constantly perform calculations to maintain their physical shape in our universe, or else they'll slip through the fabric of our reality. It's possible they need anchors to tangible objects here in order to stay in place. When they are distracted, or the algorithms become too complex for them to handle, their thoughts interact with matter and cause them to take on other forms. But the Angels could also be making them on purpose. We've been calling them Miracles."

Toby splashed everyone in the boat with his paddle. "I don't think there's anything special about them. So what if they're made of holy particles or extradimensional whatevers? They're in our home now. Which means they're still stuck with our rules. And if their thoughts can change things, then what about ours? Seven, didn't you say when the Angels came the laws of science changed some? Doesn't that mean we can probably do things we couldn't do before?" Ed wrapped her arm around Toby's neck and knuckled the top of his head until his hair looked like a bird nest.

"I think the Angels have given you wee ones thoughts that

kids aren't supposed to have." She kissed him on the top of his hurricane hair. "And I think you're right. I know it doesn't make sense, especially after everything I said yesterday. But this hope you all have, it almost seems like I could reach out and touch it, bring it to my mouth and make a little snack."

"I'm not sure what to think anymore," Allie said. "You grow up believing everything's fine and okay. Safe. Then the sky peels back and things that were always there that nobody knew about come crashing down. You learn your parents don't have all the answers. That death is waiting behind every tree in the forest and cloud in the sky. They are things we always chose to ignore but now have to face. I'm still learning how to do that. How to be strong."

Al Pal looked over at me for a hand, but mine was shaking. What Seven and Toby said about thoughts changing our world, it meant those people were eaten by that gate because of my dream. How was I supposed to fight that? Everyone in the raft looked to me. *Me.* The Angel killer with no pancake in hand. I still didn't know how it happened, but I could tell they were looking to me for an answer—the way they ignored the sweat dripping in their eyes, their hands nervous, ready to clench onto whatever words I was about to offer. But I felt so weak. So powerless against the forces of my imagination and the world poking holes in its playdough. What was there to say? *Sorry guys, I can't do it anymore.* Pretend to be tough when all I wanted to do was huddle into a ball and go to sleep. That was the safe way out. The easy way. But I *hated* the easy way. Doing the hard thing led me to who I was, even if that me was a psychotic, universe-ending, cupcake-annihilator robot. I knew I needed to share whatever sprinkles I had if we were gonna survive.

187

I stood and put on my gritty *fucking-around-time-is-over* face. My hands turned into fists and I was angry. At myself for wanting to give up. Because when I looked at Seven, I knew that's how he'd die—by me giving up on myself and trying to keep him alive like he'd kept me alive. He smiled at me and I knew I could do better, knew I could make fate and physics crap their pants.

"I'm going to save you all." I hacked up some snot and spit into the river. "Even if I'm scared and if I don't really know how. I'm keeping my weapons out, even if I only have a stupid flapjack. I'll use whatever I can. I'll stand before all the Mouths of God. Its Angels and Miracles. I'll make them go away like they're making us go away. Even if it kills me and I turn into nothing forever or everything for never. This hand will always be the one stretching out to hold yours. No matter the distance. The blackness and dead stars between them." I reached out to Seven. "The thing that connects me to you, I'll use that to tear heaven open so you can hack it violently to pieces."

That seemed to get to 'em. It must've been weird—seeing a kid standing in a rubber raft barking about how she was going to rip universes apart with her larval-infant imagination. Who would believe me? That my sprinkle-sized mind could put a dent in the coldness of reality-flavored ice cream?

As I stood there in an icky puddle of doubt, a hundred-million-year-long rumble growled through the basin. Fossils harmonized inside all the dusty bedrock bands as dinosaur bones sang from the depths of extinction. Up ahead, rocks crashed down the slope and a soft roar echoed along the canyon. Toby immediately tackled Ed to the raft bottom even though the boulders were nowhere near us. We gave the event a nervous laugh, but then it appeared.

Steep cliffs buckled as crystal water gushed into the river gulley, spurting with a shockwave of foam and dry pebbles. It was an ocean. The sea that spilt from Twelve's Angel spine. Mist fizzed with the glare of a rainbow as the new water-fall spat something massive down its glossy surge. Something pink, broken-backed, and inflamed. A creature the size of a hospital slapped fins and a thick neck against the canyon wall, rolling its fat triangle jaws in the torrent of water. With a wet flop, the sea-monster prince from Twelve's eyes dunked its infected blubber snout-first into the river. Birds descended upon the exposed ribs and blistered wounds of the Drowned Leviathan, its whole body clogging up the rapids.

Dead. Decaying.

Reminding me that the Tide rose not to give life, but to curse it.

CHAPTER ELEVEN

The Grand Laramidian Gulch

We paddled through a pod of dolphins fleeing the miracle scene, bottlenoses porpoising in leaps and breaches through the rapids—sleek and shiny and unbelievable. The Conductor's map showed that there was a small state park ahead of us, brand spanking new. So we abandoned ship. Our team checked their weapons and secured supplies on the riverbank. Will tied his scarf around his neck to become the Lone Ranger once again. Mike stripped his gun and cleaned it while Ed and the Conductor pumped us some clean water. Allie and Mackenzie split up our food so everyone had enough to eat, and Seven dunked his head in the river and wrung out his hair. I noticed Toby lounging by our packs with his feet kicked up on my bag. He was playing on his hand-held videogame, concentrating super hard, his dumb tongue stuck out of his mouth while he mashed on the buttons and miniature keyboard.

I licked my finger and jammed it in his ear. "Just so you know, we are trying to save the actual universe over here. Maybe you should help us out?" He glanced up but continued to deliver salvation to his digital world by pressing the "A" button over and over again.

"In this game you type in a word, anything at all, and it'll pop up in the level. You can type in:

'A CUTE PAIR OF GIRL SHOES'

—and poof! They appear and you can have a little girly giggle fit over 'em and then have some tea afterwards."

Toby flipped his handheld around and showed me a blurry pair of ballerina shoes sitting on some grass. A random pixel penguin waddled over and put the shoes on, making hearts appear around its beak.

"See? That's easy. But I think shoes are dumb. So I'm going to type in . . .

'GASOLINE' and 'MATCH.'"

A digital gas can appeared on screen and he dumped it onto the ballerina penguin. Then he dragged the match over to set their pixels on fire.

"Well, that was rude," I said.

"Destroying a pretty penguin isn't very challenging. So I'm going full hero over here. I typed in something that is super hard to kill because I want to get stronger, even if it is in a stupid game. I typed in:

'NUCLEAR-POWERED DINOSAUR,'

I'm close to beating it."

He looked up at me like he was the bravest knight you ever saw. I took my dirty, tattered, dead-animal-skin of a shoe off and smacked him with it.

"One," I said, "does it look like I care about ballerina slippers and tea?" When Toby didn't answer, I forced him to smell the inside of my sneaker. He wiggled around and slapped it from my hand.

"No! Okay, I'm sorry."

"No. You're not. Not yet, anyway." I took his game away from him and examined the buttons. He tried to grab it back, but I stepped on his chest and held him down. I typed away on the tiny keyboard until Tobes broke free and snatched the system out of my hands.

In the game level was exactly what I'd typed:

HOLY IMMORTAL ICE DRAGON WITH LASER ANTLERS AND TELEKINESIS MIND CONTROL POWERS

I'm pretty sure Toby didn't even understand what *telekinesis* meant, because I barely did. It was just stuff I'd heard Seven talk about. But the game sure knew what I meant. On the screen, winter's sacred abomination slithered through a city and leveled anything in its path. The holy ice maker wove its long, albino dragon body through buildings, levitating cars, freezing bullets, cutting innocent dogs in half with lasers shining from its pink antlers. A flying serpent most certainly named Summer's Final Goodbye.

"Good luck beating that with your cute shoes and tea party, ya moron. Leave the penguins alone." I made a little waddle, squawked a little *wenk wenk*.

Tobes hit a button on the game and then closed it. "I saved your monster to the memory stick. It's going to wait there in its tiny prison until the day I tear its icy head off and force you to eat it like a popsicle." He pointed to his head. "This imagination is gonna make you blow your poo hole, baby." There were a lot of crude gestures I could've made, and a lot of grosser things I could've said, but I decided to just shake my head and walk away, which probably put a dent in his self-esteem. I felt a smidge bad about it.

Our team circled around Will and Seven. The two stood across from each other in their fighting stances. I stopped beside Allie and Mackenzie. No one said anything. An orange ring of metal neon-sunset floated around Will's wrist, sizzling with solar-flare vapor, and Seven's sword was drawn a little bit out of its sheath. The only sound I heard was the rubber squeaking of an awkward turtle having an anxiety attack as it floundered around in our discarded raft. But then I heard something real, too. A choir sang low on the wind, whispering from tiny mouths on the ring that popped open and closed while dripping a kind of steaming lava.

Seven stared at a lonely cloud. "The kids are coming with us. Our chances of survival are greatly increased when they're close by."

"Yeah, right," Will said. He held out his arm and the ring followed, spinning in midair around his hand. Still drooling orange tang. It was that floating circular piece from the Halo we'd battled during the train fight, what I thought was maybe its mouth, if that even made any sense. One of the Angel's blind maidens must've survived, still *OoOoOo*'ing that opera finale even with a column-crushed body. "There's no way I'm letting them tag along before we clear the area. A goddamn *sea monster* just showed up out of nowhere. It's not safe."

Allie tapped on the rifle hanging from Will's back with the Page Master, a flat dagger she kept hidden in one of her books.

"It's okay. We've been by Seven's side ever since he found us. Kid's have all five senses, if you didn't know, and most of them are probably better than yours. We can help. I know it's dangerous, but it's worked. Not like a good luck charm either." Will wasn't buying it. He nodded back to the raft and nudged Allie's shoulder. She nudged back. "You three were about to kill us on the train anyway. How is that any more dangerous than an Angel?" Will closed his eyes and his hijacked Angel equipment wobbled.

"She's got a point." Ed waved Toby over to the circle. "It won't hurt to bring them along. If there was any real threat up ahead it would have already come after us." She was right. The sea monster was passed out in the pool, so to speak. One of its pimple-domed eyes was eaten up and pecked to hell, now just a soggy black bowl filled with hovering birds pulling at long strands of nerves. The jaw drooped slack, totally derped up, sideways, and sifting rapids through cracked molars. The Drowned Leviathan wouldn't be gasping anytime soon, even with fresh water raking over its slick gills and broad paddle-flippers.

The Angel ring around Will's hand hummed hard enough to shake the pebbles around my shoes. He pointed to a boulder beside him. Air vaporized around the ring as the lone opera maiden shoved rubble in her eye sockets, snapped her fingers backwards, and burst her lungs with a shrine-obliterating shriek. Some invisible force punched a lava-hot hole clean through the massive rock, which split with a steaming crack. Boys, I tell ya. Always flexing those muscles of theirs trying to be the baddest beetle on the farm.

"That's a cute balloon popper you have there," Sevs said,

pushing his sword back down into its home. "Sometime we should chat about how you managed to activate that thing. Very clever though, looting technology from an Angel. It's pretty neat. Perfect for classroom show-and-tell. I think I'll skip my turn though. Not sure I'm ready to show you what my toys can do yet."

That made me feel pretty relieved. Every day I saw Seven's sword sleeping in its cage, and I wondered what the blade dreamed of. Because I'd seen what it could do. Once, from far away. While I crouched behind a tractor and some hay bales. All I saw was a sparkled blood fountain splash against a white windmill, its turbine catch fire, its propeller twang apart in a catastrophic salvo of metal dismemberment. He had the sword before the Mouth yawned open, but most of the time it hung over the fireplace in his house, unless he wanted to cut a pineapple in half during a party. After the Angels descended it changed though. Sevs said he fused Angel technologies with the blade, and it had a limited power source, so he didn't use its magic tricks unless he absolutely had to. But I'd seen the sword perform on stage. So. I knew that when the curtain parted and the spotlight flickered on, a lot more than a rabbit was going to be pulled out of his top hat. It was going to be thousands of the furry bastards, and their heads weren't going to be attached to their bodies.

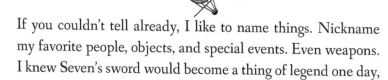

If you couldn't tell already, I like to name things. Nickname my favorite people, objects, and special events. Even weapons. I knew Seven's sword would become a thing of legend one day, and I wanted it to have a name that'd echo through all of time's exploded organ tracts.

One night, while we were hunkered down in a house shivering our buns off, I read through a whole dictionary. It was smaller than your average dictionary—a pocket dictionary of philosophy. As I turned the pages, I could tell the sword's name was there. I felt it seep up through the paper. It took a long time to read each page because there were a lot of big words on each one—I had to look them up, and then *look up* the words in the definitions too. The way they were put together made it hard to understand, and I spent a long time with each one in my imagination so I could make sense of everything.

After a while I started to figure it out, or really, figure out that a lot of philosophy was talking about whether or not you could *even* figure at all. I released each letter I read in my mind and they bonded into a single word that floated up to the ink on the pages. It rose after so many eons asleep on the bone-covered sea floor of existence. Nestled in sound hibernation. The word showed itself to me, and I paired it with the only other word that'd let the universe keep expanding to give us our night sky back.

Half-frozen and shaky, I unzipped myself from my sleeping-bag-cocoon and crawled to the sword. I ran my thumb across the blade's edge to cut myself and pressed my blood into the black Angel battery. It was a hypermetallic sea slug —a shape-shifting cylindrical organ connected at the hilt to heavy wires. Covered in mystic rune language. Some exouniverse fuel capsule that might explode or scream or melt a hole in your eyeballs at any second. My thumb glided through the dark battery membrane with its slippery anemone hairs blessing my skin. The bravest apposable finger left alive plunged into a full sea of unknown organisms swirling around with tube-feeler appendages. I felt it. The battery's insides were much, *much* larger than its outsides. Total spatial discombobulation. I became the tiny drop of blood leaking from my thumb. A cellular submarine. The battery's amoeba critters sucked on my life, my thoughts, my dreams as they pulled my heart through the sword's black wound.

Inside, I floated in pitch dark water that towered for endless leagues. Steep and haunted. This was an ocean hidden inside Seven. A secret sea deep below the beaches where my rowboat was tied up to a palm tree. Warm waves brushed against me as I drifted above a dead sea floor, a pool of pure midnight. Only one thing lived here among the paleness of crushed aquatic dinosaur skulls.

A blunt frisbee of blubber emerged from a palace of rib bones—the plateau of head completely capable of crunching a thousand-strong pod of Drowned Leviathans with a single chomp. Its snout curved smooth, like that interstellar spaceship from *Star Trek*, only smattered with barnacles, coral, and deep scars. The tube-feeler creatures left my body in tangles and glowed in patterns to communicate my most cherished secrets. They draped themselves over the sea monster's head as a sharp crowned helmet, a diamond starfish temple of living armor to protect the monster from threats in the deepness I couldn't see. Bubbles escaped my mouth as I poured myself, my true Robot core into the sword's name—gave birth to it in a moment that would last forever at the bottom of all oceans —spoken soft, whispered gently while my body was scissor-

197

mouth swallowed by the beast, the behemoth whose gill-pumped breathing created the Tide:

Ontology's End.

It's the biggest word in my vocabulary, or anyone else's really. Ontology is the search for truth, the study of reality and our existences. Wherever, whenever, however, and why-ever were of no concern to the sword. If an entity was blessed with the edge of Ontology's End, that entity was made known. Its purpose for existence observed by Seven and made final. Nature's truth got ripped from its home when the blade sliced open those things that reality did its best to hide from us.

I'm pretty much talking about the source of all being.

The path Seven made under his feet was the path that led to ultimate truth. Ontology's End was the tool that gave him safe passage to it—the instrument that would behead the mysterious interdimensional rabbit, Mackenzie's mortal combat—the *Velvet Eared Magician King,* lopping off its royal snow-kissed head to spill our partially digested universe out from its furry white throat.

During a stupid argument on the riverbank was not the time for Ontology's End to wake up. Another cranky abyss monster wasn't going to fix anything. So. Will's body parts stayed attached to him. Seven's chest didn't suddenly obtain a blistering magma hole. Ed made the two gentlemen shake hands and that was that.

We strapped up our gear and walked closer to the Drowned Leviathan. Mike led in front and whistled while loading heavy silver shells into his grenade launcher. The rest of us held our noses. We slipped into the rotting monster's shadow and walked underneath the arch of its flipper. Of all the Miracles we'd seen, this was definitely the smelliest. Pure neglected aquarium sick-snail barf. Tycho Brahe sniffed the dead sea monster prince and then gave an imaginary growl.

"Easy buddy," I whispered into his chewed-up monkey ear.

Once we were out from under the flipper we came to a corner of rock covered in starfish and seaweed, and after burrowing through curtains of kelp and climbing over a chipped barnacle the size of an above-ground swimming pool, we were free of the mysterious carcass.

A natural history park gleamed before us with mini pavilions, canopy walks, coral reef playgrounds, and open plazas full of plaster-cast skeletons and ancient habitat replicas. Absolute premium-grade fieldtrip fuel. Hidden behind the trees and gardens were glass-walled buildings with granite roofs, marine caves, and spiral staircases. Only one walkway ran through the preserve with a silver geological time scale sunk into the stone. We stood on the Precambrian part of the path which lead to four large exhibit halls scattered about in overgrown patches of lawn. Very modern, indeed. A parade float of sorts was tied to a streetlamp. The inflatable kite soared with slow wiggles, black and tentacled, a primeval octopus gazing upon the village with a single pouted peeper.

A banner trailed from the kite, too.

It read: *Grand Laramidian Gulch.*

"Oh my mopishmo," Mackenzie said, wandering ahead of us into the neighborhood.

"We need to clear the area first." Will held Allie's shoulder, but she was being drawn to a koi pond circled around what I can only call a giant land sloth. Golden-furred with spots of algae, posed taxidermy style with a curious sloth paw and cocked head, which had a cone-shaped party hat strapped to it.

Evidence of people living there was scarce, but findable. Cluttered, primitive gardening tools like spades and stone hammers—clearly a part of the natural history exhibits. But there was also a basketball in the ash of a long-dead campfire. A tricycle upside down by some vending machines. Three collapsed tents free of any blood stains. An ammonite stuffed animal from the gift shop dangled from a rope, and judging by the fluff bursting out of its seams, someone had been smacking the mollusk plushie with a Wiffle ball bat for fun. People must've been living there at some point after the Mouth of God appeared.

Toby kicked the basketball through some bushes and activated a host of animatronic dinosaurs that whirred to life.

Reptile necks prodded through thin strands of willow trees. Wings spread from rooftop perches. One Cretaceous lizard craned its bright red head crest and surfboard-length beak from a circle of rubber mushrooms, chittering. Captain Frumpy Butt's dreamed up pterodactyl queen gave a loud, magnificent *skchhhhhhhrrrrppppp* before retreating into the fungus with an electric hum.

Mack-a-Doodle hooted with her arm loose and noodled, imitating the replica of an ultra-sized woolly mammoth reared on its hind legs, hairy trunk held to the sky, trumpeting in prehistoric praise of the titanic oval bush at the end of the park.

Enormous kudzu pillars hugged clusters of shrub and dense fronds. Leaves layered over one another in tight, impenetrable fans. Bulbs and brambles and briars wove through sheets of green, misted, breathing. It was the hedge egg from my dream —the bush enclosure I created to contain the Swan Empress that crawled out from the Sculpture Garden. Only the bush was hatched now. Cracked. A leafy gash torn in its side. Clear evidence of an unstoppable inter-reality birth.

"Guys, don't even think—"

Will was too late. Allie, Mack, and Toby couldn't hold rank with the paleo-paradise laid out before them. They bolted. Almost on all fours like a squad of kittens gunning after a herd of laser pointers. My sweet gang of unaccompanied flames ran loose upon the world and the Black Bandits chased after them, shouting, cursing, kicking through flower-beds and sprinkler hoses. Toby ran into a glass-walled building labeled *Cryptozoology* and stared in awe at a bristly Bigfoot easily twelve feet high. Camping equipment was strewn through the lobby, and after rifling through the belongings, he ran back out yelling "Fuck yeah, *fuck* yeah," pumping a much-upgraded videogame system over his head.

Mackenzie was on a different kind of mission. She crawled through the mouth of a giant clam mailbox. Mike grabbed Mack-a-Doodle by the feet and pulled her out, letting her hang upside down while he tried to discipline her. She smacked him in the belly with the clam's tongue and squealed.

Something incredible must've been in there to override Mackenzie's claustrophobia.

We waded into the museumscape, peering cautious a- round fences, fossil arrangements, and tremendous bird dens.

Solar-powered speakers played soft jazz music along with nature sounds, but nature from several million years ago. Of all the post Mouth of God hideouts we'd seen, this was for sure the coolest.

Allie shrieked.

Bullet casings clattered out of a pickup truck parked underneath an iguanodon jungle-gym skeleton. Then spellbound, shy, and tail wagging, a grey dog made a wiggle scooch over to her. It kissed all over Allie's face as Will walked over, rifle aimed at the dog. Ed smacked the rifle barrel down, pointed to a lifetime supply of dog food bags stacked under a coral fan in the playground. Allie held the dog in her lap and immediately began trying to teach 'em wizard spells.

I clenched my fists to stop from crying. A happy dog. Why did it make me feel sad? Why did it feel like something was my fault?

The Conductor hunched over on the tiny tricycle. His knees bent up to his chest as he pedaled over to Will and spanked him on his way by.

"Attention, passengers," he said. "Merlin has returned to us."

"Were you not programmed to play with dogs, or does goofing around go against your prime directive now?" Seven patted my head. I stood there and stared at the botanical-bush-echo of the Sculpture Garden as it infiltrated our world. I was scared of what it all meant. I didn't want to go through the preserve, but I knew a missing component of the Fountain Heart might be waiting inside the bush egg and need my repair expertise. Plus, Seven would've been worried if I fell flat on my face and booted up my boo-hoo protocols. After declaring war on all of creation, I couldn't let anyone see me weirded out at the threshold of a low-key Miracle site—if it was a Miracle at all.

"I'm just happy to see everyone having fun," I said, and forced a smile. "Boop beep." Seven squinted. He was onto me.

We walked into the Grand Laramidian Gulch and watched our friends scout for danger and play with Merlin Two-Point-Oh. Seven picked up a green water gun from a patch of discarded toys and pointed it into the sky. I wondered where all the children and adults were. If they were like us. Camping. Hopeful. About to be annihilated. Or already dead in the mouths of iron lions. Seven pulled the trigger and squirted at the sun.

"All of this looks man made, not Miracle stuff. Seems like some people holed up here for a while, maybe the boat crew we found earlier." Seven watched the Conductor pedal his trike around the mammoth statue. Spears and arrows stuck out of the elder fur elephant's back and tummy.

"It's dedicated to Paleo-American megafauna hunters. Big-game, like mastodons, giant sloths, glyptodonts." Ed kicked the statue's plaque. "A bunch of spear heads and bones were found in this basin." She whistled at Will and threw a pretend mammoth harpoon at him while he fed New Merlin dogfood out of his hand. Mackenzie let the doggo's tail paintbrush-smack her in the face. Our new teammate was fitting right in.

"Sorry, Ed, I don't see any unicorn whales around here." Toby picked up a small traffic cone and put it on his head. "Guess your mom isn't lurking nearby."

"If she was around now . . . " Ed said trailing off. Reliving the weird trauma of fight-for-her-life bedroom battles with her narwhal-costumed mom. How it felt to be attacked by an adult

209

pretending to be an animal, pretending to teach her some hidden clue about nature and people's place within its blood-bath hierarchy. "I think she would kill me. She'd be more sea monster than toothed whale. She'd gore me with a gleaming tusk. Pin me to the ground. And eat me alive, heart first."

The Conductor stopped his tricycle by us, out of breath.

"Know what my brother said once? He told me that unicorns actually existed, much like ancient wolves. Their ancestors crawled out of prehistoric seas, tasted the sins of land, then retreated. The wolves became the giants, the hump-back, wright, and blue whales—the filter feeders. The unicorns kept their teeth, and only a select, royal few, their horns—the narwhals."

Toby held his chin high, cone-horn pointing skyward, feeling some sort of nobility he didn't deserve at all.

The Conductor sneezed at the massive bush. "This pre-serve is pristine real estate bought by a bunch of herbal drug enthusiasts. Committed six thousand acres to wildlife conser-vation and this outdoor nature museum. Heard about it in the news. Construction wasn't supposed to be finished until next year. Nothing about a giant bush, either. Might be some illegally-altered genetic breed the owners cooked up."

"As long as it's not spliced with Venus flytrap genes, I think we'll be alright." Will gnawed on a who-knows-how-old churro, then chucked it as far as he could.

We all wandered toward the hedge monolith at the end of the park, but we didn't even talk about it. The oval of trees and vines was pushed and pulled by a breeze that wasn't there, meaning the leaf shell was probably hypnotizing us. Luring us in for a reverse birth. A ceremony where we'd all be vaporized into primordial amoeba colonies that teamed up and made a new super organism, something with a million eyes and the head of a shark and sporting hyperchainsaws for arms. It made my heart beat horrified. But it beat excited too. The edge of dream we walked on was too fuzzy, too shifting for me to feel one way or the other all the way.

I wasn't convinced we were safe. Sure, the park's weirdness could be the result of being owned by ultrarich paleontology nerds. But the bush egg. The bush was an artifact from the Sculpture Garden. I felt like the preserve knew this. Allie led Merlin by his tattered leash through a row of flowers. They all bobbed on strong sunflower stems, but instead of having petals and a nectar core, they had round display screens that giggled with pixelated faces. I waved at the plants and their screens flashed me with smiles. Very strange ones. Smiles that said, *We don't really like you. Every time you look the other way we make mean faces with our tongues stuck out, but you will never see them.*

You will never know.

"Do you ever think about dying?" Seven asked me while toeing over a rock in a Zen garden. Lazy worms wriggled up out of the dirt.

"Of course." I nudged a few of the gummed-up grubs. "It's hard not to nowadays."

"Well, what do you think about it?"

"Lots of stuff. Maybe it's not so bad. Maybe death is the best thing that could ever happen and that's what the Angels are doing here. Setting us free by bursting apart our happy faces one at a time."

"I've thought the same thing. I don't think that's the case

though. It's not noble, the way they do it. If there is a greater purpose behind their methods, I haven't figured it out yet."

I huffed a little. I didn't want Seven to get bored with my thoughts if he'd already thought them.

"Well, maybe it's special for each person. The Angels could've wrapped up everyone's death in their favorite wrapping paper to make it easier for them to open."

"Death as a present. That's absolutely beautiful." Seven spun the water pistol around his finger.

"I think it might be like in your story. With the Guardians." I picked up a cracked tree branch and held it at the ready to attack any wolf bold enough to cross my path. "Maybe death is the thing that connects us all and there's no stopping it."

We both noticed at the same time—a white wolf the size of a jeep curled up by a mini forest of bonsai trees. The sculpture was made with real hairs, making it look like a giant sleeping wolf. Tiny stone golems were placed in the sand around it, some praying, some running and climbing away. If this was the White Guardian's wolf from Seven's story, the girl in the garden was far braver than I'd ever be.

Sevs joined my pose with his water toy aimed at the White Guardian's wolf. "Did you like it? The story, I mean." I nodded, and he squirted the snoozing forest-god. "I know it sounds like impossible fairytale stuff, but it might be true. It could've really happened, or be happening now, or even happen in the future."

I poked him in the knee. "How?"

"Well. There's this theory that if the universe is infinite, that if it goes on forever, so far beyond what we can detect, then anything that could ever happen will happen, over and over again, for all of time. There are countless other universes just like this one, where you and I are having this same conversation and you're holding the same branch. Even stranger are the universes that would be sort of like this one, but instead of holding that stick, you're holding a pool noodle. Some realities wouldn't look like this at all and some would, but with different rules and laws of nature. It's pretty clear now that there is *something* else out there, the place the Angels and the Mouth of God came from. So, if that theory is true, it means the story I told you might've actually happened."

"You mean we might all be inside the tree?" I asked.

"Mmmmhmmmm."

"Well, where's all the sap then?" Seven burst his gut laughing and I blushed. I was so embarrassed I snapped the twig without meaning to. I whacked him with half the stick to shut him up. "It's not cute. I was being serious."

He bit his hand where I hit him and thought. "The sap, I think some of it was in the maple syrup on the pancake you threw at the Angel back there on the train. It was so delicious the Angel couldn't stay focused and accidentally teleported an ocean out of its back—probably the Cretaceous seaway that used to divide this continent right here where we're standing."

He squirted me square in my face with the water gun and took off around the exhibit building. I chased Seven around the corner and caught him wiping out on a slip 'n slide. The Zen garden's backyard brushed right up against the hedge egg where a small tunnel burrowed into the leaf-shell embryo. Something probably made by a pack of wild dogs galloping

207

through the bushes. I found a pink megaphone and activated its speaker.

"Attention all Black Bandits, conductors, and Lost Star Children. We've found the path that will take us outta here. Pull up your underwear, sniff somebody's armpit, and form up." Seven pulled the gun on himself and watered his mess of hair.

"It wasn't a dino-age seaway that poured out of the Angel," I told him.

"What ocean was it then?" He sent a few sprays into his mouth, swished, and then spat.

"Yours." He squatted down and stared hard into my seeing holes. Curious. "It was the ocean you lost the other night, when you told me we were in the story all fiction stems from. It spilled right out of the world inside you onto the train car carpet. I wanted to give it back to you somehow, and I did. Those were tears that exploded out of the Angel. All the tears from all the Sevens in every reality, living in all the universes you just talked about. They were from you and Seven Point One through Seven Point Infinity. I know because the water in that lake the Angel made—all that wet still pouring out into the river canyon right now—it sparkles the same as yours. I wanted to give that water back to you, to all of the yous."

Seven didn't budge. Didn't even crack a smile. I squirmed around a little and he contemplated the end of his water pistol.

"What could I ever give you? What could I ever do to thank you enough for that? What would be good enough?" He was so serious that all I could do was shrug. "I'm not kidding—anything you want." I wiped my foot on the ground and accidentally smeared half a worm on the grass.

"Well, I did it for you, you don't have to give me anything back. But maybe if that ocean keeps growing, I want you to tell me about it. About why the ocean you cry is so deep."

He looked at my chest, and I noticed I was clutching my Ursa Minor necklace again. I let go and could see the stars shine in his eyes as they dangled. Perfectly aligned, just like they should be.

The moment was interrupted as our crew filed in. Toby sat on Ed's shoulders and brandished her rifle high in the air. Allie popped a green ball out of a plastic tube toy and shot Tobes clean in the eye. The ball bounced away into the bush for Merlin 2.0 to chase after. Mike and Will tugged on jump ropes tied around the mailbox Mack-a-Doodle had climbed into. She rode on its back, spanking the clam shell in victory.

"She insisted on bringing it with us," Will said with a nod to Mike. "So was he."

"This is good luck. Promise promise." Mackenzie clam-clamped her hands on an envelope. "Oh, umm, someone had a mail inside."

"Where's the Conductor?" Ed asked.

A bright-green beast stepped around the corner. Our beloved Train Captain was wearing a dinosaur costume—the park's mascot. White triangle spikes ran from the tail dragging on the ground all the way up his back. Teeth around the hood pretty much hid his face, and two eye domes poked out from the sides of his head. The outfit slouched baggy on 'em, sorta like a dinosaur onesie pajama suit—the dead childhood skin of his toy-train-destroying brother, our dearly departed, one-and-only Captain Frumpy Butt. The Conductor lifted his arm and waved at me with a soft claw.

Ed bent over and set Toby on the ground. "Alrighty there, Robot," she said while bending her arm in a mechanical fashion. "Lead the way."

"I'll save everyone the speech where I tell ya this mega bush was in my dream last night, and that I made it to trap a terrible feather muncher, and that it clearly hatched anyway, and that you'll never believe me." I had our crew's full attention, but I wasn't sure if they were ready to sign up for my Piku Bo-Bebop Tucan Maru.

"I think all of this is dangerous, Miracle or not. So be on your tippy toes. Believe me, I know there is something important behind these bushes. Something that will help us. Something that *means* something, even though I don't know what it is yet. It's there and I can fix it. I can fix everything." I gave Seven a serious nod and he returned it, then pulled the Dance Party from my bag and slung it to his back.

"All in favor of following Robot, *boop beep*," he said. I crossed my arms as the group booped and beeped in unison. So. I marched down the trail and into the bushes, parting scratchy branches and pushing through clumps of leaves. After fighting through tangles of twigs and vines for what seemed like forever, Merlin 2.0 showed up. Sitting trained-dog perfect in a small clearing. Tail wagging. Ears twitching. Head cocked, wondering why I hadn't given him a proper hello after my campfire speech about what'd happen if we ever found another doggo. I kneeled. Planted my palm against his flat, furry head, but not in a petting way.

"I want to love you, Merlin. So bad. But . . . I'm scared right now. Scared of this museum park, this bush, this everything, myself included."

Merlin, like all dogs, didn't really care what I said. He licked my face anyway. Just doing what all dogs do best.

Loving you no matter what.

"Okay, you tail wagger. I get it. But listen. You have to stay alive forever now, ya hear me? For Seven, and especially Allie. Yeah. I've seen you sneaking around. Licking her gross feet. Stealing her heart away already. That means you're gonna have to snack on eternity and grow ancient so you can protect her and all the Allies that'll ever be."

Merlin sat up straighter, shuffled his butt a little. He gave a single bark of confirmation.

"It's settled then." I clicked my tongue and licked his mouth. Gave him an ear scratch. "We'll get you a wizard bandana soon, I promise. Just show me how the hell to get outta here." Merlin tail-swiped me in the face before bolting out of sight. I tripped over a root, smacked my forehead on a branch, and tore my leggings on a thorn—hoping I wouldn't be trapped in the shrub fortress so long that the flowers on my dress became real and absorbed me into the bush. And then I stepped out onto a mowed lawn. The others ran out in front of me and checked out the hedge egg's interior.

A botanical paradise bloomed with bright splendor inside the bush. The garden core was a horticultural wonderland cradled by breezy ferns, broad banana leaves, overgrown hedge creatures, and spiny aloe plants with leaves the size of playground slides. They all embraced a tropical jungle bungalow, one trapped inside a massive, five-story tall crystal gem, a clear and fat diamond draped in lush vines of lilac, orchid, and lily springing from catwalks, decks, breakfast nooks, crow's nest lookouts, and secluded greenhouse palace

211

chambers—making what was clearly a sacrificial temple belonging to a cult society of insane florists.

Toby was the first to enter. He walked over to the middle of the garden where the dead, sad swan pond from my nightmares wept in full force. Only now the birds were fossilized. Frozen in white marble. Their tears still filling the pool.

A decaying whale rested beside a waterfall coursing down a bamboo grove. Plucked fresh from the sea. Mack-a-Doodle and Mike were careful as they made their way to the ginormous blubber queen, and they made ocean moos at her to see if she was still alive. It was doubtful though. The whale's side was torn open by teeth marks where piles of golden treasure and jewels poured out onto the lawn, a whole pirate chest flipped over and spilled.

The Conductor stood atop a miniature green mountain in his dinosaur suit. A train set weaved in and out of grassy tunnels all around him. It *choo-chooed* through steep, frigid mountains and desert plains and seaside hills in a multi-biome toyscape around the entire bush rim.

I gazed upon the great crystal at the yard's center, a master landscaper's final boss, for sure. These were the ruins buried beneath the Sculpture Garden's Dream Core—and the gem-fortress was the crystal plug I'd pulled out.

"You did it, Avery, you really did it!" Allie shook me by the shoulders. She ran off to a flock of brown and goofy-looking ostrich birds pecking their beaks into gummy worms squirming out of the ground. Seven knelt beside me as I tried not to cry.

See. At the center of the yard was *my* gemstone, a beautiful crystal tower, the one sunk beneath the core of the

Sculpture Garden. But the ruins were excavated now, re-assembled—and the tower *wasn't a tower*. This was the Super Ultimate Treehouse. The one me and Allie dreamed of building someday. The place where everyone I loved had a room and could live happily with all their shenanigans and arguments and feelings, good and bad, forever and ever as long as the sun still shone. It was a home for our new family. The tree's trunk was surrounded by smooth boulders and a stone path that led up to the house's lobby. A zebra wearing a top hat clomped by the revolving door. Most of the tree was covered in a clear crystal which cracked here and there where wild jungle leaves sprouted. Through the windows on the second floor I could see the crazy-cat wallpaper Allie wanted in her bedroom, the holographic game system in Toby's boy cave, the never-ending spin of stars on the ceiling of Seven's master bedroom. Gumdrop canaries pooped candy seeds onto the rope bridges that connected the living rooms to the toy rooms and library on the third and fourth floors. All the decks were freshly painted and stocked with chairs and tables with colorful umbrellas sticking out of them. There was even a popsicle stand, and I knew all of the treats inside were gonna be lion shaped.

I clutched the struggling buds printed on my dress. A glaring white cylinder beamed from the crystal peak of the treehouse's lookout underneath a magnolia tree. A magnolia with all its flowers in full, magnificent bloom. The Fountain Heart had broken into our reality and left something for me there, waiting patiently, and it wasn't a device that needed fixing or a panel with loose wires. It was a present. My dad's ultimate telescope. The one I'd dreamed up for him before he

213

died—a scientific instrument of untold zoom, bewildering magnification, gravity-wave sensors, and god-tier spectral analysis functions with a lens that would let him see anything in the whole flipping cosmoverse. The Greatest Seeker had finally been found. Decorated with yellow trumpets of sweet-smelling honeysuckle vine.

I took Seven's hand. "We're home."

CHAPTER TWELVE

*Making it Easier for the
Dream to Swallow the Dreamer*

Our crew of Lost Star Children and Black Bandits plowed into the garden dreamscape in a total gallivant, lemur-swooshing between plants, teaching Merlin how to herd the chocolate emu birds, baying at a dead whale, and thrashing Godzilla-style through toy trains.

"This is bad," Seven said and tossed the squirt gun over his shoulder.

Ed's hand found Seven's and she squeezed it. "Stop that. I think something very, very *special* is about to happen."

Goo dripped out of Ed's backpack. She spilled its contents, and the water bottle with her sample of Cloud Maker monster muscle rolled around on the ground by itself. That weird multicolored sphere sticker had sunk through the plastic and was floating around inside. Slime pressure popped the bottle's lid and oozed on the grass. She put her hand in the gunk and pulled something metal out, then hugged it to her chest. Her back heaved up and down a bit. She didn't try to hide it at all when she walked over to me and Seven, her arms cradling some long-lost secret.

Ed knelt down and looked right at me. She was so happy, tasting those tears of hers. "Robot, you really are special." My heart fluttered. "The *wish*—the wish you made me make on my giant, dead birthday cake. It's going to come true."

She twisted her treasure and held it out to me. The four-armed whale god from the Sculpture Garden's mosaic maze sat in her hands, perched atop a golden music box. That same creature from Seven's campfire story with a heart made of children full of sad stories.

Gears clanked with tomb-carved teeth of sonic clockwork, and a single note played. The first note of a lullaby that sounded pretty, but was really about lions killing baby antelope, or having your feet dangle off the sides of a chair. The whale deity turned a little bit, curious, and waited. Echoes of the metal ting faded away and merged into the everlasting fizz you can hear when everything is quiet and still. There was no stopping this, whatever *this* was. Not anymore. Everyone heard the note play, the way it stilled the bush leaves, perked Merlin's ears, and how an air of lurking terror activated turbofan engines around the treehouse base, humming the turbine ring to life with unknown magics.

The Conductor stood in a pile of debris from the miniature town he destroyed. Shingled roofs and stop signs and trees he kicked up were scattered about the lawn while the still choo-chooing train dangled from his mouth. The dinosaur mascot's eye twitched. Swiveled on its own.

Allie yelled, "Whoooah buddy," from atop one of the spooked chocolate birds.

Mike was busy rolling in more pirate coins than he could've ever pulled outta Mackenzie's ear—an entire sunken city's worth of whale-guarded doubloons. Water seeped from the gold and the mass of treasure booty shifted and churned.

Toby shook out one of his hands like he'd hurt it on his new game system. He pinched the memory stick in his fingers and dropped the handheld toy. The screen was frozen over. Ice spread out from the console on the ground and tiny mouths opened on its slick, cold face and started to sing. Snowflakes drifted up from the screen as the choir gained volume.

Ed didn't understand our worry. She bit down on the question she wanted to ask. But answers came screaming into our world anyway.

Pretend you're a passenger on a train. Fresh green skirt, clean blazer, a cup of coffee on your table. Through the window green hills dip and wind along a calm and sparkled sea. A wayward sheep is spanked by a shepherd. Ducks bob with quiet quacks on a long creek. In the distance, a crystal mountain looms and bewitches all the other passengers with its kaleidoscopic wonders.

Then a tool shack falls from the sky and explodes in the dirt. Cattle rain across a field and splatter the hillside. A choked creek floods with mud and stiff bodies. A green foot derails the train cars in front of you, kicks them hundreds of feet in the air, suitcases and passengers spread like dandelion seeds. Next, teeth. A jawline rakes the hills and plains, clamps down on your train car, lifts you high above the world, your fingers clinging to the window, slipping, your body tumbling out to behold a lizard creature of prehuman myth with claws powered by fate and ghosts and despair.

And inside that monster, a person. Being devoured as sure as you will become a death pancake upon impact with the ground. Just a smear that monster will bend down, sniff, and lick.

I was the only one watching the Conductor try to take off his mascot costume. Desperately. The buttons on his monster belly kept sliding back in through their holes after he undid them. Our Train Captain was losing it, totally frantic, pulling at the baggy sleeves and stomping around on the ruined town. The costume's tail swished back and forth, up and down. I felt it strumming through the air—that invisible, imaginary force that derailed the Conductor's childhood toy train into the jaws of his brother, Captain Frumpy Butt. That force was now digesting him alive. I ran to help, but his dinosaur tail swatted me straight in the head, knocked me hard on my ass. The tail swoosh gave the Conductor an opening and he lurched halfway out of the mascot's mouth. I saw sparks flying inside his head as he witnessed the world he'd destroyed, clearly against his own will. The mountain goats perched on high boulders were buried. Whiskey spilling off a porch table would never be put back in the bottle.

The costume lizard sunk its teeth into the Conductor's waist and his red syrup poured out onto the ground. He looked at me. Brought his hand up to wave goodbye. There was so much sad between us, and I don't know if it came from him or me, but he covered his heart with a hand to try and hold it in, to save me from the impossible force that punched through time and space to haunt his soul forever. He opened his mouth, I thought to scream, but all he did was undo the button of his jacket pocket and pull out a blue strand of wrapped taffy. The sad floating in the air drifted away with the wax wrapper. He popped the sticky stuff into his mouth, staining his lips a paradise shade of sugar-ocean blue, and held an imaginary seashell to his ear.

Then the dinosaur costume sucked him back inside. Well, all of him except his arms. The lizard gulped our Train Captain down and smiled big. I stared at the Conductor's arms hugging the ground. At all the fake passengers of the choo-choo train held gentle and dead by his last embrace. I hoped that comforted the Conductor somehow, thinking that his severed limbs might someday sink through his destroyed train town and—powered by the random chance of the Mouth of God—slip back decades in time to snug up a blanket around his childhood self, brush his own hair out of his eyes while he dreamed of iron wheels that'd never stop turning.

But a different dream made itself known, and it didn't belong to the Conductor.

Sharp and silent, a shadow swooped over me. Then the goddess of all pterodactyls pounced from the sky in a million-year-long prehistoric dive-bomb. This reptile bird was the size of a full-blooded giraffe. Her wings were covered in shredded organs, and I smelled the sharp scent of turtle blood and snake pee. Her crested head shone with reflective purple colors that ran in a zigzag all the way down her surfboard beak, where it speared the pajama iguana that swallowed the Conductor.

Like a bird with a grub, the giant pterodactyloid thwacked the lizard mascot into the ground over and over again. Faster and faster—until blue guts mixed with the dangled moss and specs of pond scum covering the behemoth bird beast's beak.

The Quetzalcoatlus stooped low and smeared the fabric dinosaur corpse on the ground. I looked her hard in one eye, but not the other, because she was missing one of her peepers.

A fat propeller plane flew over us and rumbled the ground. Totally real, not from my imagination, a dream, or a nightmare. A slower cargo plane followed it and little parachutes pooped out its back hatch above the wiggling octopus kite. So. The jet fighters that killed the Cloud Maker called for backup, and that backup had arrived. My flying dinosaur savior spotted the parachute troops and took flight with mascot prey clenched in her talons.

I realized that, in a way, the Conductor and Captain Frumpy Butt were reunited in her reptile toes. They were both consumed by the forever unknown thing the other had been searching for. Found now, they could rest. Held by one another in a conversation no one but them would ever be able to understand as they soared into that hollow pit you end up in after you solve your own secrets. Well, until the Quetzalcoatlus speared one of the paratroopers in midair, anyway.

Then I noticed the howling.

In one of the infinite universes Seven talked about is none other than Allie. Another version of Al Pal that survived this whole Mouth of God ordeal—the grand cosmic fire extinguished, in part, by her hands. She is in her early thirties. Straight black hair. Houndstooth dress over black stockings with sensible shoes, standing on a polished marble floor in the world's most prestigious post-reality collapse museum. A group of school children sit before her, the teachers absent, gone to pee.

She taps her glasses, then points to the backlit exhibit behind her.

"Superorganisms exist. Ones that stretch through the membrane of our locality into countless other existences. Their neural networks are made of intertwined galactic systems, stars, how they orbit, the trajectory of their coronal mass ejections. They encode their memories on physics itself. Altering basic laws such as the speed of light and the volume required for different quantities of matter to condense into a black hole. Their organs are entire worlds. Their tissues composed of grassy plain, dense jungle, and frozen tundra, even architecture itself—angles, sky doors, and bridges—acting as pathways and blood vessels."

One child gazes at an air vent. Another picks their nose.

Allie swipes a laser pointer over the crowd. With their attention regained, she gestures to the exhibit behind her. The backdrop is a garden. At its center, red wolves clamber and paw over one another in a tall spike, wide at the bottom and curved upwards to a single fox at its tip, snout closed and pointed to a double moon.

"If you don't listen now, you will not know when you're in the presence of a superorganism. It might eat you slowly, like a star fish kissing a sea urchin to death in a tide pool. Your atoms dissolving over the entire course of your life to fuel its purpose."

Allie pauses, resisting the nervous urge to suck the top of her dress.

"Or the superorganism comes for you all at once, deeming you a protozoan, microbial threat to its survival. One of its cells will appear as a phagocyte that can consume you with jaws, suction spears, or inverted stomachs. While molecular when compared to the whole of the organism, they will be monsters to you. Often taking the form of things you've loved and hoped for. Making it easier for the dream to swallow the dreamer."

Sleek animals rushed out of the bush wall in a four-legged sprint toward Allie, Will, and the brown birds. The red blurs bolted left and right in zigzags as Will shouldered his rifle. He fired a shot that took out one of the creature's knees and made it face-plant into a heap of chocolate bird dump. The animal was a twizzler wolf. A predator made of thick corded candy muscle that flexed and bulged with feelers of loose sugar noodling through the dirt. The flightless cocoa herd stampeded away with Allie clinging to one of their long emu necks. Seven released a round from the Dance Party, and a rogue wolf jumping for Ed shredded into thin strands of red licorice. She knelt there. Staring at her birthday wish come true through the spaghettied candy splattered on her face.

I slapped the music box out of her hand.

"Help us," I said to her. Not angry or upset, but calm and sure so she'd know I didn't blame her for what was happening. She didn't move though. Seven took off after the National Geographic showdown of the century, and I followed.

Another wolf head split open from Will's rifle bullet, and then he flipped the gun around, grabbed its barrel with a scarf-wrapped hand, and uppercutted a leaping candy carnivore under the jaw to send it into a spin. He kicked another sugar dingo in midair. Right in the ribs. So hard that the wolf vomited out a pumping twizzler-heart with all the veins still attached. The Lone Ranger stomped on the blood pumper as the wolf whimpered and tried to crawl away. Al Pal was in trouble though. Her chocolate steed was singled out by two drooling wolves, and the bird didn't know where to go, so it wailed out in confusion. Spun in circles as chocolate spittle bubbled around its chipped beak. One wolf attacked the bird's leg and toppled it over. Will tried to run to her, but he was intercepted by the rest of the brown herd as they stampeded back across the lawn.

Allie made a run for it. She was chased. Her hypothesized top-of-the-food-chain predator pounced and tried to eat her face, but, in a heroic bound, Merlin 2.0 jumped in front of her. The wolf clamped down on our wizard dog's leg and flung him away. Allie screamed. The wolf snarled. Towered over her. Mouth open. Twizzler tongues lashing wild.

Lord Bookworm dodged being devoured. Executed a summersaulting power roll she must've learned at a gymnastic camp and plunged her Page Master dagger perfectly through its chest, which hurt the wolf, but didn't stop it from snapping at her. So. Allie snapped back. She bit into the candy canine's throat and thrashed her head back and forth until she found a major artery throbbing through her teeth. With a solid chomp the wolf dropped dead. Allie stood, dripping in the life of her own imagination. Glasses tilted and smeared with it, arms still and loose, not twitchy and shaky like they

223

normally were when she was scared. She climbed atop the twizzler corpse as the freshly baptized queen of the food chain.

For a second, only a tiny sliver of clock hand, I rested my head on the grass. I was already tired of all this. Too much blood had watered the lawn. Too many realities were popping up in this small garden of broken dreams. And I knew this circus was just warming up. That the ringleader had lost her whip and a whole top hat full of hope.

Fire circled the swan fountain and the marble birds cried harder than ever. Toby stood in a cluster of ice crystals with a flamethrower strapped to his back, spewing molten-hot fuel into the wide open and hissing mouths of ice. Seven hacked away at frozen spikes as they reached out for Tobes from a nipple of glacier, an iceberg summit emerging from the new game system he looted from the park. The *old* handheld system was hooked to the flamethrower. Or, really, the weapon was *coming out* of the game. He'd typed in the weapon name and the weapon became real. Toby was serious. He'd become stronger in a stupid game, and it was going to save us all, now that our hopes and desires had come to life, grown solid. That fire was the only thing holding back the frigid evil birthing itself into our world.

Golden coins rained from the sky.

Mike pumped the dead whale full of weaponized party poppers from his grenade launcher and pirate booty exploded over the lawn in hot showers of arcade metal. Mackenzie latched onto Mike's trousers and wouldn't let go. Then the whale rolled over onto its stomach, and the gentle plankton grazer was lifted by the treasure. Gold with a mind of its own rose as a soggy pillar—the whale crowned at its top as an offering to the sky. The coins slugged across the lawn, surfing the whale through tall, thin bamboo, casting a shadow over me, the Black Bandits, and even Allie as she tended to Merlin's wounded leg.

The disaster was almost on pause, and it gave me a moment to think.

The telescope. The Great Seeker.

I nearly tackled Seven to the ground. When he tried to talk, I smacked him and gave the biggest shush I'd ever shushed.

"Seven—if this is my treehouse, and it is, then that telescope on the top is for my dad. I imagined it just for him. But I'm giving it to you now, Sevs. It has a mirror of dark matter that traps photons and recreates their entire life's journey in a hologram, all the things the light has ever touched, interacted with, and come from, all the way back to the birth of time and forward to its eternal-fire coffin. I made it so you can see everything you ever wanted to see. Whatever you want to find will be in its lens." Above him the white scope waited atop the crystal lookout, wet from an involuntary spurt out of the dead whale's blowhole.

Seven whacked at an icicle forming by my feet. "Robot, I can't get up there. I have to help."

"This is what we've been looking for. We can find the source of the Mouth right here. We don't have to keep searching for a telescope because—"

"Avery, stop!" Blood rushed to my ears. I couldn't hear anything. Not the sounds of the flamethrower, of dying candy wolves, or of the shifting pile of whale treasure. Seven *never* yelled at me.

Absolutely never.

My heart imploded in the same way as when your first-grade crush kisses your best friend during recess right in front of you by a slide that ends in a dark, still puddle.

He let out a shaky sigh and tried to hold something back, but I stomped on his toes. Punched him in the gut. Pulled on his shirt like a five-year-old freaking out that they had to eat waffles instead of cereal for breakfast. Seven pushed me away. Bit his tongue. Then he caved.

"That plan was never going to work, Avery. I just told you we were looking for a telescope so you wouldn't be scared." He looked at me with the sea I'd given back to him, flat and clear, so I could watch a school of sharks feast on the rotting carcass of a lie.

"You don't mean it," I said, clutching Ursa Minor around my neck. Its stars were sticky with the blood of a twizzler wolf.

"There was never anything I could do by observing the sky with OSGO. The orbital crew manning the Great Seeker ran out of food months ago. With their remaining fuel they deboosted and dropped altitude. They all died. Burned the whole observatory up in the atmosphere." He shook his head with that high and mighty look he got when he thought I couldn't understand something. "We're all going to die and there's nothing we can do about it."

Sharks nuzzled the lie-carcass and nosed into its rib cavity —but found no heart there to close their teeth around.

CHAPTER THIRTEEN

*The Tide Will Erase All :: The Tide
Will Erase All :: The Tide Will Erase All*

When Seven found Allie and me after the Mouth of God opened, we were on a hill at night. Watching someone try to take flight in a hot air balloon from a city park. Watching stars explode. Watching the world without making a single peep. Seven walked through the swings of a playground with Toby and Mack at his side, and I thought it might be a dream. They came and sat down beside me and Al Pal, not saying a thing. Just watching this person inflate their balloon with a flicker of flame far away. The nylon bulb swelled with gasps of heat, ruffling out in a white bulge with a long and wrinkly neck. An orange-beaked bird head rose above the park's tree tops, the wicker basket parting leaves as stubby white wings blobbed over branches.

It was then the shooting star appeared.

A streak of pink and silver glitter high in the night sky that cut a line through exploded starlight. The comet was slow.

227

Thoughtful. Breaking up into smaller pieces with purpose. Maybe seeding the planet with new lifeforms.

Hopeful, that's how I felt finding Seven's hand in the grass, holding it, making sure he was real and I hadn't lost all my cupcakes. We watched the lazy meteor and I made a wish. A wish to end all wishes. While I sat there full of promises of bubblegum and celestial wonder, the object arcing through our atmosphere was full of malnourished astronomers. Their skin on fire. Their hearts exploding through their mouths and their eyes depressurizing out of their sockets to watch projectile blood vomited onto control panels, levers, and blinking siren lights as hexagon mirrors turned molten and leaked through the space station's hull, drowning the astronaut gazers in splashes of liquid gold while habitat modules broke apart, heat shields failed, and the tremendous mechanical eye-core of the Great Seeker screamed through high altitude clouds completely on fire. Spewing lava coolant. Weeping solar panel squares. Adding another contender for the most horrific re-entry ever known to the chronicles of space flight.

I breathed the scene in with lungs full of clean night wind. Child fingers squeezing safe and sure. Then that hot air balloon shaped as a royal, pond-paddling swan ran into a web of power cables invisible against the horizon. Blue static hums volted across the swan wings, dancing. Sparks firework-boomed in orange tantrums of artificial lightning. The balloon engine burners rocket-belched flames that rippled the bird's skin, turned its nylon feathers into ash with powerlines thrumming in smoke and thunder current. Electrocuted, burnt, and quivering, the swan head lifted to sky.

Hissing. Plastic smolder-tears dripping from its eyes.

"You're saved," Seven said. Unblinking to take in the Great Seeker's twilight plunge into the Chasm of Eternal Solitude. "There's nothing left to be afraid of."

"You, you—I hate you." I covered my face with a hand, dug my fingernails into my skin. "Why did you stand up for me back when I fought with Ed? Huh? Why do you let me talk to dead astronomers every night!"

Seven checked his sword. "I don't have time for your feelings right now, okay Avery?"

My insides turned hollow and my heart fell alone into some kind of empty mouth that felt like it had been closing for thousands of years, from before I was born, and all of a sudden decided to close teeth from all directions clean down the middle of my blood pumper. Tycho Brahe clung to my chest and I punched Seven as hard as I could with my other hand right in his stomach.

"And you're too old to be carrying around a stuffed animal," he told me.

Seven waved over the rest of the group. That empty mouth split apart again, and the two halves of my heart drifted away from each other. It felt like they were never going to meet again.

Will, Mackenzie, Mike, and Ed interrupted my comeback. Everyone looked to Seven, worried and confused, and he stood tall like he knew what to do next.

"I'm running out of fuel," Tobes shouted from the igloo shrine forming around him. Ice spurs closed around his flamethrower pack, crushing it, and he was barely able to rip his game system from the freeze and jump out onto the scorched lawn.

"Guys, this isn't good," Toby said, brushing off the device. "Most of the buttons are screwed up. I can barely type anything. I can't make another weapon." He held out the game and buttons dangled from its casing.

I imagined this place to be the center of my life. The center of the whole dying universe where everyone belonged and could be happy together and not worry about ever-looming death. But there we were, being torn apart relationship by relationship and body part by body part. My wish for the Super Ultimate Treehouse came true, but I didn't make that wish upon a star. I made it upon a burning orbital observatory full of blood-soaked astronomers, and the consequences were now making themselves known, upside down, psychotic, and distorted as the constellations.

Fountain water washed ashes over my feet—the swan pond overflowing with bird tears—and then I figured it out. Why they'd been crying all this time. It was because we couldn't cry anymore. We'd all forgotten how. The part of the treehouse I spent the most time imagining glimmered atop its crystal canopy. Gazing up to heaven. My dad's telescope, the one I gifted to Seven, gleamed from the star deck and begged to be looked through, but I made it based on a lie. I felt its lens start to crack inside my chest.

Mike stood before his betrothed whale as it rotted and surfed atop the scattered pirate fortune. Water sprayed in a fine mist from between the coins, and a whole waterfall poured out of the whale's broken-blimp mouth. The motion of

it all was like a wave. Pulsing. Taking shape. Something growing hungry. Mike had seen this before.

"Get inside," he said. The treasure convulsed and swirled
to form something shaped like a head, and it crunched down
on the whale's spine bones. Ed grabbed Mackenzie as she
lunged for Mike, and Mack-a-Doodle flailed, grunted, bit as
any true-blooded wiggler would, but Ed was more seasoned,
more finely trained from the battles with her narwhal mom.

Mike saw Toby struggle to type something into his game
that'd give us a chance at surviving, and he took the handheld
away from Tobes to study what letters were left.

"This is easy enough," he said, and typed some words
in. From the game's screen Mike pulled out a sea-weathered
length of wood the size of a spear. The metal tip was wound
with rope and tied off to a small wooden keg with a fuse hissing from the barrel. It was a harpoon. A *Boom Harpoon.*

Mike watched Mackenzie struggle to escape from Ed's
grip, and that was all he could take. He pulled out the bear-
head koozie from his back pocket and poked the harpoon tip
through it. Then Mike took a breath and hummed deep and
loud, an underwater song that only sleek-tailed ocean giants
knew.

"*Uuuoooooooaaaahhhhhmmmmm.*"

I couldn't hear Mackenzie's reply because of the roar.
A bear manifested shape in the gold. Half water and half
cursed pirate coin, it bit the tortured whale clean in two.
With a seething, wet hunch, the bear launched the blowhole
carcass clean over the Super Ultimate Treehouse, staining the
magnolia flowers at its peak with blood. Mike's ocean trauma
had returned. Surfaced from the depths of his memory as a

231

carnivorous, sparkled-yellow submarine with a single treasure chest glowing at its heart. Its muzzle was nervous. Quivering open and closed. Drooling sea water and whale tummy tubes. Ed took off with Mackenzie under her arm for the downstairs lobby as Mack cried out whale calls, and we all followed with heads turned to watch Mike reclaim his hidden treasure lost at the bottom of the sea.

The sea bear lurched in the same way a storm wave crashes upon a lighthouse, and with a clap of foam, swiped Mike into the air along with a cloud of arcade prize tokens. The cursed ursine wave chomped down on his waist and gnashed. Bent-double, the ocean bear shook him apart so violently through the treasure I would've sworn Mike was turning into gold, except I saw one of his legs crash through a window. Mike had just enough body and just enough strength left to cradle his harpoon as he slid into the wave-crest mouth. The bear reared up with its neck stretched to the sun. Gargling. So we could see the lump in its waterfall throat as our friend was swallowed. I saw half a body tumble down the belly pool of coins to that pirate chest pulsing with a warm glow.

I didn't watch the Boom Harpoon detonate, but I watched Mackenzie watch.

I imagine the scene unfolded like a kindergarten school play inside her brain. Curtains pinned with paper starfish part to reveal the stage. The backdrop is of a lonesome nighttime ocean. An albatross puppet dangles from a string. Little kids in whale costumes hold up long cardboard cutouts of black waves, swaying back and forth to slosh the sea while one tardy and two-legged pufferfish runs out with a flat buoy, almost trips, then takes their place to complete the *mise-en-scène*.

In the center of the stage—a spit of island. A tiny hump of sand with a big bleeding paper mâché whale on top. Mike is perched on the whale's back wearing a captain's yellow rain-coat that's beaten and tattered from the passing of a recent storm. Kids dressed as deep-sea anglerfish run out holding two enormous bear arms that extend off both sides of the stage. They kneel and paw at the shore. More kindergarteners wearing angry bear masks swarm around the crinkly whale. Penetrating. Gnawing. Prying white cardboard-tube ribs from her thin butcher-paper blubber. Mike waits patiently on her barnacled eyebrow. Petting her smooth whale head in the special kind of way you do when the greatest love of your whole life is about to say goodbye, walk onto an airplane in the middle of a runway, and go on a long vacation without you.

Speakers hiss to life with surf and rumbled aquatic calls. Moaning in pain, the whale pouts her swollen blowhole. A trio of students move a pole up and down to fan her broad tail fluke. The bear-masked children crawl through her torn and bloated belly and pick up her flippers to flap them, laugh-ing, making fun of her plight, raking her sea flesh into ribbons.

Mike reaches into the blowhole as the children flip over their cutout waves and maneuver into a V. They form the massive snout of a bear. Sleek and black with lips of pointy sharp waves and domes of eye that glow red like Chinese lant-erns. The mouth opens wide to swallow the island, and some chemistry students inside the whale mix barrels of vinegar and baking soda, which erupts science-fair-volcano style to flood

233

salty blood over Mike's legs and the sandy island. But at long last, Mike finds something to give back to his beloved whale: a daughter.

He pulls a baby Mackenzie from the blowhole. Gives her a single kiss on her sea-slick belly. Then, as the jaws of that midnight beast close around them, he lifts her high into the air toward a magnificent moon that lowers from the catwalk. A spotlight flashes on and Mike gives her to a moonbeam. Mackenzie's plump, wet body is pulled up into the pale ray of light as the bear mouth snaps shut, grinds and chews, then flips over, becomes nothing but a blanket of waves again. Baby Mackenzie floats above the ocean and the children turn on fans that swirl her with silver glitter. The barnacle moon dangles quiet, unblinking, the center of a constellation that forms as the costumed children are pulled up on cables where they use tiny flashlights to make the stars. The constellation is large and gaping. A cosmic whale with tail fluke raised tall and proud and twinkling. The children bay open-mouthed, blimp-throated, bellowing below all possible hearing. They sing a song so lonely only the gaps between the stars can listen—and real Mackenzie—the sole member of the audience, strapped to a chair in the front row, tries to sing with them. Tries as hard as she can to harmonize with their deep and soundless good-bye. But she can't.

I know she can't. Because I can hear her screaming.

Pulverized treasure bear parts scattered all over the lawn. Ping-ed off the sad swans. Plastered the Super Ultimate Treehouse from crystal trunk to top-floor branches. A loose paw of shore-break slapped the deck clean of beach chairs, party lights, and the refrigerator cart, which spilled lion-shaped popsicles as the sea bear showered the whole bush lair with blood-tinged spray.

"I'll be . . . I'll be," Mack sucked in, choking, "*Mmmoaaaaa-awwwhhhh.*" She ended her call with a heartbroke squeak and pulled her hood down.

Seven fired a shotgun round to break through the revolving door into the main lobby. He was greeted by the alligator doorman, who was only trying to do his job, but Will didn't know that and activated his ring weapon stolen from the Angel, his *Balloon Popper.* An orange tunnel blasted through the gator and tossed the tuxedoed reptile's backbone into the lobby's chandelier, which fell right onto the zebra receptionist, who'd come out from behind the counter to see what all the fuss was about. Everyone ran in but me. I brushed away some vines beside the entrance and found an escape ladder, one I imagined in as a safety measure. I climbed up to the second-story deck and hopped off so I could be alone.

Snowflakes settled on the lawn's carnage. Mutilated bear-gold stained the grass. Candy wolves hissed and popped with split backs in patches of flame, and Ed's ocean-god music box glinted as a brilliant speck in the middle of it all. I could feel its note humming in the air, in my shirt, and even in the wooden handrail. A splinter poked my palm, and I pried it from the rail in hopes that the whole deck would collapse once it was removed. I pulled off a needled piece and found something white and shiny underneath. An emergency hypothesis flared in my brain, and I proceeded to tear all the wood from the

235

railing. The slivers were a familiar color. Milky. Leaking blue sparkles that made me look like an unsupervised toddler in a closet full of glitter. I finally figured it out, the material being familiar and all.

The inside of the railing was full of Cloud Maker scales.

Blue acid dripped from the otherworldly muscle-skin as it rebuilt the handrail, atom by atom. I knew those tiny specs were up to no good. The handrail was just like those pine-cones and ferns and rocks reforming out of the hunk of Cloud Maker flesh we inspected on the ridge. These motes hummed their secret code into the ground, and air, and into my dream the night before—analyzing all my electrical patterns while I slept. The scales recorded every single thought as it flowed from brain part to brain part, probably even messed with some of them, so it knew what presents we all wanted at our death-day party. It was my fault for falling asleep that night. I didn't protect my friends. The Cloud Maker scales that pollinated the ridgeline and drifted down river had been busy building the Super Ultimate Treehouse while I snoozed away our lives.

More lives were about to end, too. Camouflaged soldiers that'd parachuted from the airplane crept out of the hedges with their guns drawn. They surrounded the shrine of ice with Toby's newfound videogame system at its center. Cold pillars grew from the ground. They supported an ice dome carved with scenes of icebergs tossing ships into the air and glaciers plowing over villages, the farmers frozen stiff before they could hug one another. Toby's ultimate videogame boss, the one I created for him, emerged from a plume of sleet with a choir singing praises:

HOLY IMMORTAL ICE DRAGON WITH LASER ANTLERS AND TELEKINESIS MIND CONTROL POWERS

Summer's Final Goodbye awoke.

The dragon was serpentish. A furry albino snake with clusters of ice crystals and electric amethyst shards clinging to its pelt. Its head was soft, sloped like a deer god to a rounded snout. Legs tucked beneath frosty belly scales as pink antlers on its head pulsed beams of forbidden light—ornamental horns carved from the core of the steepest mountain ever known. I shuddered as a telekinetic field expanded in a wave of zero gravity, levitating me, and everything else in sight, a few inches off the ground. Then, as if that wasn't enough, a holy golden halo appeared as a crown over Summer's Final Goodbye, allowing it to properly judge all the badness hiding in our souls.

The soldiers opened fire. But their bullets evaporated before they hit because of the stupid laser defenses I'd given the dragon. With a twitch of its head, Summer's Final Goodbye levitated chunks of flaming lawn, dead bodies, and an oasis of palm trees into the air along with my whole gaggle of crying marble swans, forming a full barrage it hurled at the paratroopers. The riflemen—the ones that weren't crushed instantly by tree trunks, bird sculptures, and corpses, that is —retreated back through the bushes. With a forsaken blizzard roar, the dragon snaked its way through the bush and into the natural history park, precipitating hail and violent snow drifts as it went.

Ed ran to my side at the edge of the deck. A soldier rose above the hedges held out by a long, invisible arm, and a stone swan flew through him. She contemplated the G.I. Joe as his halves kicked and squirmed on top of the bushes for a few seconds.

"My wish did this," she said.

"No," I replied. "I don't think it was yours."

I left her and took off across the rickety rope bridge leading to the library. A few candles at the reading desk had set fire to a stack of notebooks inside the study. The moose head mounted on the wall slobbered and rammed its antlers into a bookshelf. I climbed the ladder, huffed myself over the last rung, and crossed another bridge back to the house. The third-floor catwalk looked down at the pool. Dolphin swim coaches with whistles dangling around their necks eeked at me, maybe complaining that they were in a chlorinated pool instead of a saltwater enclosure, but more likely because they were eating a finely dressed monkey wearing a top hat, gasping for air, losing its body parts one at a time to hungry dolphin beaks as a tray of mints sank to the pool bottom.

I headed into the main room on the floor, the science room. Missile streaks whooshed overhead and faded across the skylights. The sound rattled a plesiosaur skeleton dangling from the ceiling. Like I imagined, the science room was full of bones and shells in jars and insects pinned in boxes and old telescopes and rusty shovels and beakers. The aquarium built into the bookshelf teemed with bubble-mouthed corals and a disco-flashing nautilus. A curved bug farm hugged the wall and hummed with rare beetles and armored worms making tunnels and small mud towers, awaiting a true insect ruler like Nappy Sir Sleeps-a-Lot.

I passed an open door that led to the amphitheater room

Allie wanted for putting on theatre plays. An audience of stuffed animals faced the stage, dripping wet from part of the ocean bear that crashed through the ceiling. Costumes from the wardrobe littered the floor. Robes, witch hats, animals like sharks and squirrels and dinosaurs all strewn about in the aftermath of an epic tragedy that left the audience speechless, dumb, and unbreathing.

That tragedy started again. Reels spun on an old movie projector at the back of the room. A crooked screen on stage showed a film as dust passed through the beam of projector light.

Cut to green. A shot of grass blowing in steady breeze. Then feet. One of them crisscrossed with white scars on its sole. Blood drips thick and black from offscreen. The camera pulls out and shows a girl on the edge of a sea cliff. Me. Me holding the freshly severed head of a lion and staring far across the ocean. White credits flash the screen:

The Tide Will Erase All

A single, eerie chord of ghost haunting wavers as the music. Seven walks up beside me sporting a half-open Hawaiian shirt and a golf club slung over his shoulder. We conversate, but the audience cannot hear what we're saying. There's no sound. Opening credits flash and scroll under the white title. Just more sentences of *The Tide Will Erase All*, one after the other in smaller font. Over and over again.

On the horizon, an enormous palace rises from the waves. Mossy. Barnacle-covered. In polished white marble, it surfaces

239

between Seven and me right in the center of the frame. We're ignoring it. Not looking at the tower columns and carved statues. The fountain water spilling in waterfalls. Sculptures depicting the birth of all ages from a salamander mouth. The death of all men in a barren desert. Knighted robots gnashing groves of fruit in their jaws. Solar kingdoms harvested and unmade. Each pantheon layer rising flooded, patrolled by tigers. Polluted by sunk starship vessels. Eyeless giants gnawing the domes. Starfish burning on clock faces. This fountain palace depicting creation rests on the back of the golden four-armed whale god spurting tropical water from rows of blowhole—ready to swallow the entire sea cliff, me, Seven, and the audience into the story meant to drown all sadness.

On screen, Seven and me are still ignoring this sunken miracle. Because of our faces. Because of our faces I felt, just like the audience, that our conversation was more beautiful than all the secrets in the world—and forever out of reach at the beginning of the best story ever told. No matter how many times you watched this movie. No matter how close you got to the screen or how high you turned the volume, you could never hear what we were saying.

The stuffed animal audience and I could've spent the rest of the universe's lifespan discussing the beginning of the film. Debating why all the credits were the title repeated over and over again. About the cause of the scars on the bottom of my left foot. The intent of all the robot machines creeping in that jungle pattern on Seven's Hawaiian shirt. What feeling was created by the reality-shattering ocean shrine and all its carvings. It was certain. Whatever the Angels were searching for, it could be found somewhere in this movie.

I wanted to sit down, hug my monkey, and watch the movie. But that was the point. To keep me there. The Robot in the film held a bleeding lion head—what would *she* think of me if I sat back, relaxed, licking wet popcorn while the rest of my friends struggled to stay alive? There were more heads in need of decapitating. After all, I was the real lion killer. Maybe someday I'd be the one handing Duke Ellington's head to *myself* on set, the Robot on screen, before I slipped away into the crowded studio. Lost. Looking for other dreams to belong in.

I left the theatre. In the science room, a spiral staircase led up around fossil displays to the topmost crow's nest lookout. I ran around its curves, past the prehistoric reptile ribs and windows and solar panels until I was on the observation deck with a view of the whole museum preserve.

In the far future, archeology witches will uncover an iceberg temple on some far-off planet, discovering the original incantation that describes how Summer's Final Goodbye can only be summoned every 350,000 Earth years. Between summonings the dragon sleeps. Not in the north pole or Antarctic, but at the coldest point cold can be—a total spatial tundra of freeze that permeates all subzero temperatures. These wizard dragon dreams play out across all coldness on all worlds. Even in sleep, Summer's Final Goodbye wages war, its will imparted

241

upon every frost crystal and flake of snow. When summoned, Summer's Final Goodbye shares its dreams with whatever
world it materializes on. Using antlers of carved magic and
blessings from God herself to terraform its new habitat in a
manner suitable to take control of its unconscious adventures
and deliver salvation to the warm-blooded.

To the always moving.

This is what I saw atop the Super Ultimate Treehouse. A newborn ultraboss from the end of a long, confusing videogame.
Pink smoke billowed from the park buildings and two helicopters circled Summer's Final Goodbye, chain guns firing in
solid streams. The dragon roared with hail and antler lasers,
severing projectiles and a few soldiers still parachuting in,
with all of the *Grand Laramidian Gulch* under its divine
telekinetic control.

The woolly mammoth statue rampaged. Impaled paratroopers rotted on its tusks, and the fur elephant made crude
cave paintings by bashing them on an ice wall beside blazing
helicopter debris.

With a cone party hat cocked sideways on its slow head,
the giant land sloth tore the legs off a soldier above that frozen
koi pond, the soldier sucking on the end of their pistol. The
twelve-foot-tall sasquatch replica peeked out from behind a
tree to watch, nibbling the nub of a soldier's arm.

Small, nimble velociraptor dinosaurs hunted with coord-
inated pack behavior, herding a squad of five paratroopers into
a tight circle on a mound of snow. Then a towering two-footed

carnivore with twin head fins bit them all at once, which set off a grenade and plastered fossil fragments and plastic entrails across the white dune. The only soldier to survive the prehistoric rumpus had a weird helmet, one that looked like the head of a killer whale.

Finally—crying their tears onto its black head and lazy tentacles—the fountain swans circled the octopus kite soaring over the neighborhood. Then the invertebrate kite swiveled its giant peeper and took control of its arms. Against the wind, the midnight octopus wiggle-swam across town, over a cliff, and disappeared out of sight.

Seaweed banners flapped from a pink flipper arm. The appendage scooched a whole building clear across the park, smashing it against a cliff as the fin scrabbled for purchase. Next, the head appeared. Jurassic. Triangular. Designed for eating megadolphins and hypersharks. Turns out the Drowned Leviathan was not done gasping after all. Black kite tentacles wiggled from the monster's mouth and belly wounds, surveying, grasping, dragging the sea monster prince forward. The head fluke of the octopus rose through a gash on the beast's back to make a dorsal fin with a pouted eye. Kite tentacles contracted inside the aquatic dinosaur's chest to beat its heart, pumping blood through salty veins. Soldiers were pincered between Summer's Final Goodbye and the Drowned Leviathan as deranged, extinct animals galloped through the trees and bushes.

The last helicopter was caught naked in the knife-fight.

With kite tentacles used as stilts, the sea monster rose and chomped down on the tail rotor. Pink gore squirted from the creature's gills and heavy mouth to douse groups of paratroopers, flooding them in molten bubblegum bile.

A single soldier ran through the forest of noodling parasite tentacles, dodging waterfalls of monster blood, blasting off the lower jaw of the land sloth with a machine gun. Looking over his shoulder, the whale-helmeted paratrooper bolted—if it even was a *he*—sprinting blindly across the street in the same way a dumb kid stares at a butterfly while pedaling a tricycle, unaware that they are careening off the sidewalk into a gutter. The whale soldier stepped in a deep hole where Mackenzie's mailbox clam had once stood, and they tripped blowhole first into a ditch as the last exploding helicopter tumbled down the street and rolled over them in a flaming cartwheel.

Then a window broke below me. Toby cleared out the glass with a dinosaur bone from halfway up the staircase. He leaned out and looked on at the destruction orchestrated by his videogame's final boss.

"I should've taken it easier on you," I told him.

Toby made a farting noise. "It looks bad, but have some faith, my sad and malfunctioning Robot. It took me a while, and it was especially hard considering half the buttons were toast, but it's time to strap on your diaper." Tobes hefted a silver weapon onto his shoulder. Winged angels decorated its barrel. They were touching each other's private parts. The launcher hummed from their mouths, deep and lonely, and Toby told me what it was. "This is a *Sin Ray*."

At that he pulled the trigger and beamed a purple pulse of unholy particles right through the dragon's snowdrift heart.

The halo above Summer's Final Goodbye *screamed*. Burst into flames. Sent the dragon's soft serpent body crashing to the ground where it coiled up like a rattle snake and snapped at gusts of wind, confused and scared. The land sloth fell with a paw hooked in its mouth. An unmoving sasquatch got torch-ed with a flamethrower. With a last bellow from its trunk, the mammoth reared and got its fuzzy elephant belly punct-ured by a split palm tree as the octopus kite deflated inside the Drowned Leviathan—its last breath escaping not as a gasp, but a whimper that wafted streams of seaweed. Head slumped, a spike of iceberg jutted through the Drowned Leviathan's plated skull and out that empty, rotting eye socket.

The orca-headed soldier crawled out of the ditch with their whale helmet shoveling snow slush. They just barely missed one of the falling stone swans.

I decided to call 'em Lucky.

Lucky studied the ice dragon for a second and then crossed themselves like people do at church. Tapped their head, chest, then both boobies. They tossed a grenade into the body coil of Summer's Final Goodbye. Pulled out a handgun. Snowflakes vaporized into steam and an amethyst shrapnel-shard punctured their whale helmet from the blast, but Lucky was undeterred, they fired away and shot off a laser antler that fired beams of light through the dragon's hide. A few remaining soldiers emerged from the exhibit rubble and helped out, signaling to one another to coordinate their fire.

Toby cheered from below, but I couldn't celebrate with him. He didn't know our mission was fake yet. We were still being swallowed whole by the Mouth of God. Any victory here wouldn't matter in a handful of weeks.

I found Seven's newly gifted telescope at the edge of the deck, gazing hopeful into the Mouth for answers.

"Robot."

I heard Sevs panting behind me, but I ignored him. One of the focus dials on the telescope had a wad of gum on it, and where it came from and how it got there was a mystery to me. I gave the nob a turn and touched the chewed lump to make sure it was real.

"Your hide-and-seek software appears to have been upgraded," he said.

There was no way I was going to turn around and look at him. Not without something smart to say, anyway.

"Why do you care, *Eight*? Last I heard you weren't in the mood to find *anything*." I pointed to the sky to enforce the point. There wasn't a thing he could say to make me feel better. I wanted him to try though. He gave the war unfolding on the ground a casual glance. Neither upset nor worried, happy nor sad. Just gave it a big whatever-that's-not-very-important-to-me shrug and then leaned on the handrail to stare into the sky.

"It would almost be a shame to stop it now. The light is so beautiful, don'tcha think?"

"No. I want to find the switch and shut it off. I thought you wanted to do that too. Wanted to watch me implode the sky's whole stupid face into an oblivion of curved sorrow —the greatest upside-down frown ever known." I ripped a magnolia flower off a branch sticking through the crystal deck. Inside the petals were streaks of color. Waxy. Made with crayons. And blood, too, whale blood and Mike blood.

"Well, if you're going to curb stomp the heavens, they need to be closer," Seven told me. Here we were, still partying in this end of the world horror circus because our friends gave up their lives for ours, and all Sevs could do was be the smartest of uncaring armpits left alive. I hugged the railing and watched Lucky climb up exposed dragon ribs—then empty the tank of a flamethrower straight into Summer's Final Goodbye, gun-tip speared in its sacred lips like the ice dragon was sucking on the straw of a juice box. "It's okay to be mad at me."

"No," I told him. "This isn't about you. Everything here —this deck—this treehouse—all of it—was built by me. Blueprinted out in my imaginatorium. I wanted it more than anything. Even more than I wanted the Conductor or Mike's life."

I wiped blood on my dress. Flicked a drop over the railing.

"Seven, this telescope is here for you. I would've given up everything for it to be here, for you to look through it and find what you wanted, what my dad wanted too, but it turns out I'm a big stupid idiot for believing you—just another dumb kid you have to lie to because I can't handle your grown-up truth. So why don't you keep going with it? Tell me it'll all be alright, like you always do. Keep telling me we'll make it out alive until we're all vaporized into nothing and I'll keep believing you even after I've disintegrated into a wisp of *fucking* diaper ash."

Seven's seas froze solid. He shifted uneasy and I heard the salty ice crack with hurt. I looked over to the hulking scope and imagined how its slow spin could track the missing puzzle pieces waiting in space. Lights blinked to life on its control panel.

"Seven, all I want is for you to look through it. No matter what. It's the only thing that will save us. Please, promise me you will. Promise you'll pretend for me—like I've pretended about so much stupid crap for you." 247

I nudged him toward the telescope. Seven grabbed the control module and started typing away, and the scope purred and swiveled its white neck. He pulled the gum on the focus knob and the pink stuff stretched the whole length of his arm, meaning it'd been freshly chewed. The mess stuck to his hand as he bent over to look through the lens. He stargazed deep into the universe's secret hiding places, and it was strange, because it felt like the universe was staring back. But not our universe—another one. Breathing heavy behind me with the scent of meat. Drooling animal life. Prowling in the gap of stillness that comes before a pounce.

I turned and was greeted by the head of a wolf god. White and vehicle-sized, fur blowing in a breeze. Hackles raised with sharp hairs where Ed sat petting the beast. Her finger brushed the front of her lips shaped to silently *shhh* me.

Ed's hair didn't blow in the wind.

Black strands of it weaved around each other in their own perfect tangles, shiny and smooth. At first I couldn't make it make sense, so I pulled at my own hair as I levitated off the deck and was tractor-beamed toward the wolf's jaws. Its snout opened wide, incredibly wide, splitting all the way apart to reveal a technicolor orb—the same rainbow eye painted on that river bridge with the girl astronaut screaming into oblivion—the same multi-color sphere on the caped dead hero by my tarp banner—and the sticker on Ed's water bottle, too. The flashing ball inflated in the wolf throat with a pupil stretching wide, neon colors spinning in thick bands ready to watch me fall into its iris forever. Seven's eye was glued to the telescope lens, and I almost shouted out to him because, once again, I needed saving. *Of course* I wanted to be saved, pulled away before getting sucked into the White Guardian's wolf realm of eternal annihilation, but I saw Seven wiggle and pet his telescope as he focused the lens.

He'd found it, the astronomical anomaly that could save everyone.

So. I held back. I covered my mouth with a hand to make sure I stayed in hush mode as Ed's Angel eyes watched me be eaten. I stared into her Halo, that sphere throbbing as the ghost-core of an unbelievable wolf. Before me was the world inside Ed—the Black Bandit—the *Angel*—and I slipped beyond teeth and gums and everything I'd ever known into the corruption of her soul stream.

CHAPTER FOURTEEN

You're Saved ((~GONG~)) There's
Nothing Left to ((~GONG~)) Be Afraid Of

E d unzipped me. That's the best way to describe it. My arms bent in broken zigzags through a monsoon of colors. They scrolled past me, or through me, or made me them, but I was definitely moving forward. It's strange, becoming a color. You'd think if you were drowning in a vat of molten crayon fluid that it'd hurt—being churned into paint and dye—but it doesn't. It feels good. The colors swirled around me. Vibrated. And I saw a special color twitching in a kind of static between the others, a shade that shouldn't be there, or maybe always had been. That was Ed, I knew, and I felt her warmth as she spread over the other hues. Her light ripped a hole through the rainbow vortex, and the place her color searched for appeared before me. I felt it becoming real, using my blood to give life to itself.

The reality that appeared was the Sculpture Garden. But not the Sculpture Garden I knew. We were back a billion years before my toddler feet ever plopped down on its curved meadows and valleys. A prehistoric, untamed, pure version in an age long past. Botanical toymaker habitats interlocked with pinnacled orchard shrines, coral laboratories, and witch-spell altars swirling with cloud glyphs. Ecosystems made of mythological zoo animals roamed from exhibit to exhibit, licking, grazing, migrating in herds with their brainwork bubbled and floating freely around their bodies like giant microorganisms. Stilt-legged ghost urchins polished corners of fantastic statues and hoisted banners of the most beautiful blue I'd ever seen—a blue that rippled with color from all reptile lagoons, sweaters for baby boys, and the painting of a conductor's baseball cap blown wild and sky-splitting into clear mountain air that only existed inside my memories. This Garden was newborn with fresh art budding in groves, a perfect paradise at the dawn of the Fountain Heart—a realm now laid naked and wide before a cataclysmic intruder.

Ed was trespassing.

She used me as a key, hijacked my dream DNA like a parasite, surfed on my overloaded robot spine right into a sacred chamber she was forbidden from entering. Laser defenses on the Fountain Heart's moon opened fire, filling the Garden ring with electric-mercury light. Ed was no longer in her human form though. Her body had changed to a massive orange-sheened diamond bursting with leaves and winding arms of kudzu. Light beams pinged off her gem tip as she attached vines and bushes to the Fountain Heart and its moon, 251 absorbing robed worshipers lined around the craters there, funneling their blood into golden amoeba embryos that bloomed from corkscrews of her rainforest canopy. Exhibits in the Sculpture Garden's habitat caught fire, forced to offer their souls to Ed's new forest planet. She was growing a precious flower, some new organism or reality. A home for the color that exists only when all other colors sacrifice themselves so it can be born.

And let me tell you.

I dangled at the top of Ed's carnivorous jungle feeding frenzy. Beheld her hedges and vines devouring the Sculpture Garden with such glowing majesty that even the most royal of princesses, and cutest of kittens, would bow down before her spangle. It almost made me want to stay and become one with her garden eternity. Almost.

Ed set up the Super Ultimate Treehouse as a stage for our deaths. Not because she hated us. Well, I mean, maybe. But I think she did it because she was afraid of being our friend. Of getting close to things you know you're gonna lose some day. Every word she said and step she took was calculated to lead us to our dirt naps and me into that wolf mouth. Ed wanted Mack and Allie and Toby and me to all be alone, so that we'd never have a chance at understanding one another—to connect with the ones we loved—because that's what would save us all, winning her over to our side. She made us live through her fears because they were too tough to deal with on her own. Just like God, because if there is one, it only made people so they could deal with all the suffering and sorrow that God's big, heavenly slug-butt was too afraid to face alone.

That's for babies and for whiners. Yep yep.

That's how I knew she didn't stand a chance. Knew Ontology's End would slice through Ed's monkey jam on its path to existence's dramatic conclusion. I clenched Tycho Brahe. Imagined as hard as my hamster brain could pretend. A small splash of familiar sunrise peeped out of Tycho's plush back, leaking from Nappy Sir Sleeps-a-Lot, and that starshine transformed Tycho into a wide-browed baby shark. Spat clean from my imagination. Squiggling in my hands. Eyes soft and worried on the ends of its hammerhead. It was obvious to me what needed to happen.

You're saved, I thought. *There's nothing left to be afraid of.*

Then I bit into the shark's throat. Spilled liquid red salt onto my tongue as a blood-prayer summoning. Tattooed waves curled around my arms and elbows. A rubber giraffe-shaped inner tube inflated around my waist. And with a triumphant flex, I let loose the swollen blue hills of Tide from my skin. Seafoam bubbled around me on wave peaks as a great sphere of ocean horizon spread across the sky, dwarfing the Sculpture Garden and gaining Ed's geodesic attention with fine sheets of rain. From that wet depth, the impossible black frisbee head of Ontology's End emerged with dinosaur-killer jaws quivering for extinction, opening dead-moon wide to welcome me inside, to reunite me with my blood—the red ink which gave the monster the name to end all names—already flowing through its temple-heart.

Swallowed, I sloshed through brine and vessels and was pumped into the cerebral cortex of Ontology's End. My vision multiplied through a dozen eyes. My arms and fingers split and stretched and divided. My lungs boomed, breathing in time with the flapping of raked gills.

253

It was sandcastle-stomping time.

With our bodies combined, silver starfish armor materialized to helmet the continent of *our* head—a jet-black starship housing cursed ocean organisms in its scars and blowholes. Our tentacles spooled over one another, impatient. Wetness spilled through our fingers. Washed over our stubbed flippers and arms and towering dorsal fin. So. Brutal, sharp, and drowny, we plunged with a roar down the unstoppable surf of the Tide. Its black current waterfalled us into a full-blooded-sea-monster-head-ram against Ed's gem body, sending her diamond and bush tentacles crashing into the Sculpture Garden where they landed with a splash of tidal mud.

Perched on that moon, we popped Ed's golden embryos into tang that drooled from the corners of our mouth. Then I figured it out. Why it was my responsibility to be the Curator of the Sculpture Garden. It was because I was the monster that destroyed the Garden's inner sanctum in the first place. I was doing it right then, right there. All my dreams were punishment. Cleanup duty for what was about to happen next.

Ontology's End and me pounced on the Garden ring. Bit down on Ed's crystal as she fought for purchase with shrub and branch. But her vine grip wasn't enough. We hammer-thwacked her into the ground and then galloped—smashing her mineral core through coral fortresses, glades of spiraling swamp trees, and valleys of wizard dens in tall pyramids. Yes. We rampaged over the gardenscape, but more than just that, we trampled on my most cherished memories of spending time there.

We pierced Ed's gem on a bell tower in a palm-swept oasis.

Uprooted from the sands, the white spire stuck out both sides of her geode body like an arrow through the head of a very unfortunate duck. When Duke Ellington hunted me through that office building for two days, I spent my nights dream-herding a naked crab into that bell. But the bell was broken then—in the future. Sunk in a sand dune. Cracked down the middle from this very fight. And after I led that crab into their new bell-shell home, I left for a while—and came back to find a cyclops heron plucking out the crab's digestive tract through that very crack. A crack made because in our thrashing, the bell clanged over and—

(((~GONG~)))

—over again.

Pods of six-finned dolphins got catapulted as we plowed through layers of aqueducts and mangrove rivers, their porp-oise eyes beaming wide to behold our battle. When I dozed off in social studies class (((~GONG~))) I spent my naps chasing those weird water mammals, doing my best to pet 'em. They were blind in my dreams though. Always fleeing from my footsteps and playful coos. But now their dolphin peepers were wide open. Absorbing sharp photon rays as Ed sheared off one of me and Onto's arms with focused emerald energy that was (((~GONG ~ GONG ~ GONG~))) so bright, it not only blinded the gentle flipper swimmers tumbling around us in the present, but punched through time to sear the eye holes of all their not-yet-born babies, which is why in my daydreams they always shied away from my voice. Why they cried in pain when I cornered them to pet their blowholes.

Then came what I called the Goodbye Well.

(((~GONG~)))

A crater-ecology puzzle of pathways and moss that I solved by attracting insects that leaked water from their plump bellies. The behemoth rain bugs were drawn to the sad cries of an infant salamander newt, freshly separated from its mother by yours truly. I placed the squirming baby at the crater's base, something I did back when my only baby brother was in his hospital incubator box for the last night. Tubes all stuck out of his small mouth ((~GONG~)) and veins shining in the moonlight. I was so scared that I ran away and slept underneath a gurney in an abandoned wing of the hospital while my dad looked for me so I could say goodbye and mom was still asleep but I was too afraid ((~GONG~)) I was too busy weeping in that dreamscape impact crater with my face pressed against the slick amphibial infant as insects drifted in clouds ((~GONG~)) pouring clean water from their tummies ((~GONG~)) springing up tufts of soft moss to cradle me like a blanket as grass swallowed the gummy salamander whole ((~GONG~)) sucking the baby from my hands beneath the greenery where its ((~GONG~)) slippery glands and spotted skin decomposed—then sprouted with a bouquet of infected red bulbs that smelled like the sadness of an empty operating room, flowers drooping like the heads of hopeless doctors.

(/(/(/CRACK/)/)/)

Onto's End and me reared back with Ed's crystalline body glinting and flailing against the planetarium sky. Then with the grace of a starship—we collided face-first through layers of lightning jelly-cone forest, crumbling full treetop temples, splattering fungus monkeys, creating the crater that would become the softness of the Goodbye Well.

Ed managed to infiltrate our gills and break away, propelling her punctured jewel around the ring in fans of atomized rainforest. She landed on the Sculpture Garden's central core to rest. Cleaning dream guts off her facets with those mutant bush limbs. A tiny shard fell from her gem face —the shard that would one day become my Super Ultimate Treehouse. Ed's geometric body absorbed energy from the tide pool and glowed in bright silver pulses, her plant appendages blooming again. Spreading spores and pollen from white flowers.

Fused deep in Onto's brain core, I didn't gain any knowledge. I didn't learn a single thing. But I inherited something—a forsaken instinct. That primal hunger Mike spoke of, I felt it there. Knew that it wouldn't be the one to eat me, but that *I'd be the one to eat it*. Ontology's End and I asked the ecosystems housed in our blubber for forgiveness. And then we roared. Roared so loud their souls separated from their shells and slithering bodies to form a bubble-sheen barrier, a forcefield that deflected Ed's laser beam attack and splayed its pink disco terror through the Garden ring. Vaporizing schools of manta giants in calm pools. Plasma-slicing crowds of delicate robed curators and the lance knights protecting them. Volcanic powder pyroclasted the inhabitants into terracotta statues along blasted watchtowers, mystic bathhouses, and castle walls—blister-scarring the exhibits meant to give the Fountain Heart its memories and purpose.

Ed slumped, exhausted. Me and Onto's End took the opportunity to fluke ourselves through flooded debris and shredded ecosphere, leaping off an observatory to grasp Ed in our jaws. And oh, did we ever chomp on her. Breaking ridgelines 257 of teeth. Crunching our molars to dust. We even grabbed our own face, pressing with a dozen of our own arms to bite down even harder. But Ed remained a steaming crystal fortress. Impenetrable. We relaxed with her hanging loose, a tired golden retriever with a squeaky toy in our mouth. And then something strange happened.

Ed *sighed*. Which, I know, sounds weird and doesn't make sense. How does a diamond parasite with bush tentacles make a sigh? It was—I imagine—what being on a first date is like. When you have nothing to talk about but are sitting across from one another at a small table in a crowded coffee shop and you're too embarrassed to bring up a new topic, or tell your crush you think they're cute, so you just stare at your date's coffee with some kind of unspoken shame and see the surface of your black drink ripple from the invisible force of their disappointment.

So. Ed wrapped tendrils of vine around our head. Spread branches in spirals around our hyper-aquatic god muzzle. And with the will of a whole forest of tall trees ready to be mulched into seed debris by heartless machines, she closed our mouth around her with more strength than our sea monster muscles could muster on their own. With a sick crack, her body broke into a thousand splinters of rock candy that soaked our gums. Angel blood, the holiest red you can imagine, erupted in a fountain plume that geyser'd with the same beautiful spray as the first and only time I touched my baby brother in that plastic hospital box. His fleshy hand holding on to my finger. Ventilator machine disconnected and making wheezes. His eyes a clean well of thoughts looking up to me, hoping for the best big sister in the history of all sisters as he took his first organic breath. Such a *big* and *brave* one. But his small mouth quivered. Tried to hold back but wasn't able to. He winced and gushed up his precious newborn kool-aid in a little spurt of foam and spittle. My hand on his chest, I felt his lungs pop. The same way you could *feel* the sound of a horse's leg breaking underwater on a smooth stone. A sound like shouting your first thought, your first magnificent "*Hello!*" from the bottom of a well, but only ever hearing the echo of your sister's footsteps running down an empty hallway in return.

Ontology's End and me separated. I think Onto's End thought me out of its brain core as the Sculpture Garden flooded with Ed's blood. I dream-teleported back into that tunnel of color and clutched Tycho Brahe as he returned to his stuffed-monkey-form after being a hammerhead shark. Sword tips appeared beside me, one by one in a large circle, and they buzzed through metal plating hidden behind the pretty bands of light. A hole opened in Ed's Halo and silver smoke and paint poured out. I leaned over and vomited crayon juice through the opening as I flew over the Super Ultimate Tree-house, rejecting the world Ed desired to create in one long stream of puke that splattered in a rainbow on the ground. A puddle from the swans' crying spread out on the lawn with the white wolf soaking in its wetness, ribs poked red and fresh from its chest.

In the puddle's reflection, I saw Ed's Halo, which had turned into the ship I was riding in. The orb stretched out in a

259

long, sleek torpedo with a white ridgeline of wolf fur for a bloody mohawk. Racks of rocket boosters fired from its tail end. Uneven, pizzicato, trumpets blaring out of tune. The Halo started to spin out of control. I passed over the last of the soldiers standing in a glacial pool, torching the pink skull-horns of Summer's Final Goodbye, burning them like trees in a turquoise pond. They watched me float by. Past the wreckage of the park. Over the rotting Drowned Leviathan. Then circle back to the lawn littered with my friends.

Seven stood on top the treehouse, yelling at Ed with Onto's End drawn and snaking behind him in twisting metal streamers. The sword form of Ontology's End stretched out and curved in all the possible paths the blade could take, through all the different times and spaces it could inhabit, so that they all joined into our reality under Seven's control to become the long and curved path to our salvation. He pointed with his free hand to the telescope and Ed laughed. Onto's blade ribbons clanged back into proper-sword-position, and Seven spun 'em as hard as he could at Ed's face. She caught his swing. Flung Sevs backward into his telescope. All at once, the magnolia blossoms fell from the tree. Cupped leaves drifted between Seven and Ed like the final frame of some classic movie.

Then Ontology's End extended, pushing Ed right through the deck railing as the weapon shot out and stretched five stories all the way to the ground. More sword lengths branched off and stabbed through her wrists and legs, then they all retracted back into a single blade.

Seven spotted me. He waited until the Halo circled around closer, bracing himself as the Super Ultimate Treehouse was split in half by a blast from an unknown weapon. My dream home toppled close enough for him to *imagine* jumping off the viewing platform. *Pretend* he landed on the falling spiral staircase. Seven predicted his path, running around a thick branch as it twisted and fell toward me. With one great make-believe leap and then another to the far end of the crystal house, he saw himself throw his sword like a spear through the air in a perfect arc that ended at the back end of Ed's Halo. It was possible. Barely. But that's all it took for Onto's End to spring into action. It cut through all the worlds of failure where I was whisked away into capital *F* forever. Worlds where the sword fell short or hit the Halo on its butt end or Seven rolled his ankle running to the tip of the teetering branch and plummeted to his death. Ontology's End found a possible truth where physics and fate lined up just right for him to save my life. It made this universe the one where the sword hit its mark.

The blade curved its long neck along that single path, lopping off the Halo ship's rocket nozzles, and I was greeted with wind and open sky as I crashed into the tree trunk, emergency ejected into the swimming pool, where water poured out on the lawn to leave me and eeking dolphins floundering about in the grass.

Ed rose to her feet in front of us. Will was on her in an instant, his Angel weapon sputtering magma so hard it dented the ground. The ring glowed white hot and Ed tried to dodge the attack, but she caught some of the invisible blow and her left arm melted with a blind-maiden, broken-back-bone shriek. She uppercut Will in the stomach with her good arm and he crumpled. Things got quiet and still. I found myself listening to a whispered hiss from a toilet leaning out of

261

the crystal trunk. A gumdrop canary perched on its ceramic seat, then drowned itself without a sound.

A rock hit Ed in the back of her head. She turned and faced Toby.

"If I'd known," he said to her. "That you were one of them. I would've let a boulder fall and crush you. Even if it killed all of us."

The remaining paratroops walked out of the bushes with their guns aimed at her, about five of them, all covered in blood and shredded kelp. Lucky looked particularly badass as they shouldered a rifle and tapped the whale eye on their helmet. Hands cupped under my armpits and Seven lifted me to my feet. Ontology's End hummed gentle by my shoulder. Ed was surrounded.

"If Mike were alive, I'd owe him twenty dollars," Will said with a cough, "because you've turned out to be the biggest asshole left alive."

A soldier fired a shot into Ed's chest, but the bullet just beaded and fell flat on the ground with a thud. More guns opened fire, and Seven and me crouched to make sure we weren't hit. Mackenzie and Allie crawled up from behind to watch the show.

Ed checked on her Halo. It frizzled in colored static from the broken and confetti-plastered plating of its hull. The vessel was cratered and smeared on the lawn in all the pretty patterns of a class-nine spaceship wreck. She dismissed it with a wave of her hand. Gave a tiny knock with a knuckle to her mini-door earing. Then she glanced at me, saddened that I chose not to give birth to her color.

Without replying to Toby, not even with a shrug or guilty

half-abandoned gesture, she covered her heart with a hand. Ed's mouth bent with the spine decay of a 100-million-year-old reptile.

"Robot. You need to know that the birthday wish I made—*all I wished*—was for everything you ever wanted to come true."

A sword blade emerged from her hand. Hundreds more sliced out from her belly and arms and legs and neck. Seven had his eyes closed as he imagined stabbing Ed over and over again in the most violent fashion possible. Out of breath. Screaming. Calm and crying too. Every path Ontology's End could've traveled into and through her body was found and taken. The blades whirred so fast they blended into a bubble of silver, shivering with slender sword filaments until the metal blister deflated with a catastrophic clang that tossed Ed's Angel parts all over the lawn. There wasn't much left of her. Just shredded limbs. Some silver goo and shiny internal organs. But her head and chest were still attached. Barely.

Our group didn't know what to do. We were hurt and abandoned. There was nothing to be said. Nothing that would unpop Mike and the Conductor's skin bags. Nothing that could unbetray the union of our hearts. With the moment shriveled like a worm on a summer sidewalk, I decided to go about keeping my promise to my friends—to Ed—and to the stars above, what was left of 'em anyway.

A pile of costumes from the theater room lay flushed out and sopping wet on the lawn. I nudged the heap of fabric and then formed a plan which would certainly cause Ed's brain to eat itself into any number of dead-Barbie oblivions. With a big tug, I tore free a costume stuck to a pipe and turned it into

263

a ragged cape. A cloak with its hood shaped as the head of a *narwhal*, its fine yellow horn sparkling with glitter.

I slung the cape around my shoulders. Flipped the kiddy narwhal head over my own. It looked like one of those dumb animal-hood towels you find in grimy seaside trinket stores. You know, the marketplaces with half the hermit crabs dying in a chicken coop, lopsided racks of stink bombs and dud fireworks, lousy water guns, and more stupid cartoon bikini-lady shirts and painted sea shells and shark teeth than you could ever buy. I bobbed my new horn up and down. Peered hard with my blubber face to show Ed one clothed eye as I dropped to all fours on top of her body pile, squishing her liquid-mirror alleluia guts through my fingers. I still had salt flowing in my blood. Still was a little *too* much sea monster and not enough human.

Ed's narwhal mama had returned. I growled—shoved my costume horn through Ed's jaw. Then I bit into her exposed heart organ like a polar bear eating the face of a grandfather clock—tearing and swallowing Angel flesh as her torso caught on golden fire.

She tasted just like birthday cake. Red velvet with silver icing.

Ed's astonishment and terror were clearly at a peak because she did something I never thought she'd do. Something I found sort of funny at the time. She screamed.

Treehouse branches and leaves and rooms and decorations all dissolved into white Cloud Maker snow under the spell of Ed's cries. The motes swarmed her broken Halo ship. Electricity hummed and wove alive through the wreckage. Taffy lumbar and candy skulls and crystal shards and fossils chattered and combined. The mess floated over Ed's shimmering, screaming face while the museum exhibits broke down and joined the strange storm, the Drowned Leviathan and octopus kite drifting as deflated hot air balloons, splitting open in midair so their white insides could flow with the massive cloud. The disintegrated carnival of chaos flew higher and groaned with the sound of full on *Piku Bo-Bebop Tucan Maru*. Tiny rocks rained down around us, and I spat out a strip of Ed's Angel meat onto her golden, horror-seized half body.

Will fled with Allie kicking and flailing under his arm, reaching out for Merlin 2.0 as a shadow spread across the ground. Our new dog had inherited the original Merlin's bad legs, which were clearly broken from the candy-wolf attack. Merlin 2.0 was unable to crawl away as the Super Ultimate Treehouse, museum rubble, and Angel debris hardened into a boulder, a red and dusty dinosaur tomb, a true avalanche heart the size of the entire lawn. The crag fragment was striated like the canyon walls with bands of rock grating against one another. Merlin 2.0 scooched to Ed's side. Tucked his tail. Whimpered while sniffing her sparkled armpit.

We all escaped in time to watch the slab of bedrock fall right onto our wizard-dog apprentice. Press him deep into the ground along with the geological formation of Ed's soul, her blister-evaporated body, and the hopes of a normal life. The boulder settled. Grass confetti fluttered. A trickle of water oozed out a crack in the rock—no doubt from one of the fountain swans still trapped inside. The leak stopped though, as the birds didn't need to cry anymore. Toby, both hands on the rock and trying to push it with all his might, finally remembered how.

CHAPTER FIFTEEN

*You Do Not Need to See
a Thing to Know That it Is There*

There was a small rock stuck in my shoe that I rolled back and forth by wiggling my foot. It hopped in my shoe-shoe train for a hitchhike right after the Mouth of God opened. The rock was my little secret, something only I could feel. The reason why I sometimes hobbled along in the back of the group. Why I hid the limp it gave me by adopting distraction techniques—cute hand flourishes or dramatic spin moves performed on my good foot. Other pebbles made their way into my shoe over the months, but I picked them out and only left the one, which made me feel bad at times, depriving my rock buddy of any friends. Seven knew how my real dad died because I told him. But the only other thing that knew was the little stone in my shoe. The rock wedged itself in there as I ran across a dirt parking lot to him, my one and only Popsicle, right as he was killed. Not by an extradimensional being with superpowers. Or a floating death machine. But by a guy with a baseball bat on rollerblades.

The man jumped out of a car as my dad tried to charge his phone by a lamppost, and the guy bashed in his face with a home run swing. The batter grabbed the phone and drove away. Surprising, I know, him being able to use the brakes and gas pedal while wearing rollerblades. I hope he careened into a toy store. Flipped over into the skateboard section and caught on fire with all the Barbie dolls giggling in their flimsy box cages. But I guess the rollerblade guy didn't see me sitting by a bush, reading a picture book about a penguin who leaves their group, which is called a waddle or colony if you didn't know.

In the book, this one penguin starts running toward a mountain very far away so they can climb to the top all by themselves. Without their family. Without any friends. I ran like the pengy and slid on my knees to try and wake my dad up. But his snooze button was permanently jammed, and all I got was blood on my hands and shirt. I was never going to get *that* goodbye. Not a dramatic one with him going cold in my arms. Not a regular one like when you're drinking orange juice at the kitchen table on a Saturday and he kisses you on the top of your head, whispers something silly in your ear while he steals some of your cereal, and then heads out the door.

I rolled the rock around in my shoe when I got *that* feeling again. When a hard goodbye was said, or when I stood in the empty space where one should've been. The silence that clung around Ed's boulder made one of these moments. We hung out around the enormous rock, taking a break, trying to un-paralyze ourselves. Trying to figure out what'd happened, what we needed to feel. Some of the army men dropped flares on the ground and orange smoke drifted up and over a cluster of trees. The military squad huddled together discussing something, and occasionally one would raise their voice or glance over at me. Our waddle was strung out on the lawn, just a bunch of traumatized penguins sunbathing. Seven held Mack and Toby. They buried their heads in his chest as he rubbed their backs. Will cleaned wolf blood off Allie's glasses. We were shaky and confused, staring at thick and twisted tree roots or burning flares. Trying to read hidden words in their bark patterns or find ghosts in the smoke.

A worm wiggled on the grass, disappeared. Birds chirped and fluttered. Life moved on somehow. The air smelled mummified, smelled like a sarcophagus where the inside is wet and jeweled and filled with heavy stories that can never be told anymore.

After passing through this transitional Life-Age of obs-erving grass and leaves and our dead friend's ginormous gravestone, the soldiers broke their huddle and lined up. Lucky took point in the middle. The closed whale lips of their helmet split, showing us rows of teeth as the helmet's jaws opened. Lucky's face came into view and *he* sucked juice from a straw inside the helmet.

"Well, we have rescue inbound," he said, "so normally I'd tell you guys to relax, but we've got some business to attend to first." He pointed to me. "We all saw what happened. That *Sky Stealer* tried to capture this girl. None of us have ever seen that, and Elbow here has seen a tuxedoed werewolf play a cello concerto *while* it vomited up a flaming porcelain rabbit. A flaming porcelain rabbit infected with a deep-space sea snail. So, you get it. Elbow's been down the shitshow hole and even he's impressed." The soldier beside him named Elbow gave a nod and spun his sunglasses around a finger.

A girl soldier stepped forward shaking. Pointing at me. "That girl was *eating* the Sky Stealer. I saw her eating it."

My group stepped back and stared at me. I shrunk. Wiped silver slush from my mouth with a shameful backhand.

"So here's what's going to happen," Lucky continued. "You're all beat to shit, upset, and sad. We get that, we really do, but we can't let our enemy get ahold of whatever this little girl has that they want. If it's that important to them, then it's dangerous, and we can't let that get used against us. Okay? We just lost a lot of buddies and so did you, but I really believe we need to add another body to the pile. All in favor, raise your rifles."

Lucky's whale-mouth helmet closed clean around his head. Three of the four soldiers around him cocked their guns and aimed them at me. Seven tossed Mack and Tobes to the side and Will tripped over Allie and fell. Lucky looked around at his teammates, the ones who agreed I needed to be put to sleep in the fashion of a no-legged cat with a biting problem, and then he put a gun to one of *their* heads. One of his buddies that had their weapon pointed at me.

Lucky fired a bullet into his friend's ear to blow their brains out the other. As the soldier fell, Lucky pulled a shotgun from their back, pumped a shell into its barrel, and then erased an astonished look from another soldier's face.

Elbow was the only one besides Lucky who hadn't raised

269

his rifle. He put his sunglasses on and then slit an army girl's throat, which I'd never seen before—not an army girl, but a full-on throat slitting. It was weirdly gentle. The way her blonde hair swept over the wound to turn the color of curtains pulling closed at the end of a fantastic play—one you fell asleep during and only woke up at the end of.

Lucky removed his whale head. He gave Elbow a thumbs up and then came to my side. Dirt smeared his cheeks and his smile showed me a big chip in his front tooth. Sweat dripped off his short hair from being inside the helmet so long, and it smelled like he could use a good spray down. He reminded me of some kind of cartoon character. One that appears late in a show after a major conflict and does their best to try and make everything okay. You know, the kind of character that smiles instead of crying when they cast the ashes of their best friend over the sea at sunrise.

"Sorry to scare you like that," he said, "but me and Elbow were outnumbered. They all wanted you toast. They really believed that nasty stuff I just said, because they were all morons, and morons aren't going to help us stay alive—right?" His sidekick, Elbow, was apologizing to the rest of the group for making such a scene in front of the kiddos.

I wiggled a loose tooth, a permanent one that probably chomped a little too hard while I was merged with Ontology's End. "I wasn't scared of your friends. I'm more afraid of the Tooth Fairy than I was afraid of those clowns."

"Well. If I see the Tooth Fairy fluttering her ass sparkles around these parts, I'll blast her into pixie dust. I didn't get anything for the chipped part of my front tooth."

I gave him a high five. "Thanks, I think fairies are dumb. I eat fairies for breakfast. I feed fairies to angry stray cats. I wear dead fairies as earrings, and sometimes, sometimes I just spit on trees because I think fairies might live in 'em. But hey—if you let that tooth-obsessed minimunchkin live, I'll lend you half of whatever she gives me for my molar." He poked at his chipped tooth and then we shook hands. "So. What's your name and where'd you get that helmet?"

"I'm Garrett." He rubbed the snout of his helmet and gave it a pat. "And I found this baby a while ago. It was some nerd's motorcycle helmet, although it's sort of like a knight's helm, too. Made after a character in some cartoon or comic book, but it's pretty cool. There's a speaker for my voice and all kinds of information pops up on the inside, like the speed of objects and how far away things are. It even has a backward-facing camera so I can see what's behind me." He put the helmet back on and tapped some buttons along its mouth. "What's your name?"

"The name's Robot, and . . . " I closed my eyes. Gave my forehead a smack. So much for having a real name anymore. I'd officially been brainwashed. "Garrett, I'm glad you're not a jackass."

"Well, so am I. Robot? It's nice to meet you. I'm glad you didn't get kidnapped by the bad guys. Do you know what's been going on here? And if you *do* have some kind of super-power the Sky Stealers want, that's awesome. You should probably keep it secret for a while longer though. Even if it's really cool."

I rolled the rock in my shoe up to my toes and let it snuggle up between my big toe and its neighbor.

"The only superpower I have is being a broken skin bag of a human being. And maybe summoning swans."

271

"*What?*" Garrett grabbed my shoulder. It hurt. He shook his whale face back and forth, then held a finger to his orca lips. "Yes. Definitely. Do not tell anyone about that. Especially the man that is about come meet us. Corporal Lox, our leader. No swan talk. Okay?"

Okay. Weird.

"Sure thing, Shamu. Well, we lost three of our friends. One of them turned out to be an Angel, one of 'em you call a Sky Stealer. A lot has happened in the last few days. It's sort of hard to get out right now." Garrett pulled out a chewing gum wrapper from one of his vest pockets. He put it in my hand and held a finger up to his helmet to shush me.

"When you feel like spitting it all out, put it in that wrapper and give it back to me. And remember. You don't know anything about swans."

A buzzing sound drew near and two aircraft scattered leaves as they circled the boulder. One was a slick helicopter painted pink, yellow, and white like it was a retro-fashion ski boot—or an R/C toy meant to blast slime and tennis balls at cartoon kaiju. The other vehicle was a plane with engines that rotated up on its wings so it could land vertically. Big-time military stuff. A tall man wearing a long jacket dropped from the hoverplane's sliding door. The wind died and I rejoined my waddle while Garrett lead him over to us. The clothes under the man's jacket were shredded, taped over with armor, then patched some more. His beard made him look like he should have an eye patch on, pirate style, but he didn't. Just a cigar sticking out of his mouth. He didn't look pissed, more like a sorely disappointed parent staring at your report card.

Seven gave the man a fake-looking salute, rolling his eyes,

leaving his wrist limp like he was about to start a puppet show. "Hello, your majesty, how's the kingdom holding up nowadays?"

The man kept his ice cubes cool. This guy was way too mature to get ruffled by Seven's sassy-pants—probably even if Seven called his mother a pajama-wearing, platypus-headed stack of pancakes in a dumpster.

"Dr. Oulglaive," he said. "If you killed these pilots, I will take you up in that plane and let the kids watch you fall out of a cloud."

Lucky threw his arms out in a baseball umpire's safe sweep. "Corporal, Elbow and I took them out." Soldier Garrett toed blood on his fallen teammate's face. "Sir, Elbow and I ghosted them because they would've put their face into a bear trap if I'd shit in it first and told them it was ice cream."

The Corporal pulled out a pocket watch and flipped its clasp, then closed it without checking the time. He glanced over at Ed's boulder. Its geological bands shed bits of dust here and there.

"Abari, what happened here?" the Corporal asked. My new bud, Garrett Lucky Abari, gave his commanding officer a blank whale stare.

"If I had to write down what I witnessed, it's safe to say you'd be surprised, sir. Much worse than we predicted the Origin would be."

"More than Elbow's werewolf concert?"

"We found an extended audience," Lucky said. "They wiped out the whole platoon. All our wings. Some sort of parade float reanimated a sea monster the size of our base. An albino dragon froze Mei and ate her. Booe and Lawrence

273

were gored by a woolly mammoth, a giant land sloth ripped Shane in half, and a pterodactyl the size of our 'copter speared Bald Tommy—"

"God bless that bald bastard," Elbow said.

"Damn straight, he was a good kid," Lucky said.

"Abari, you mean a *pterodactyl* killed Bald Tommy?" the Corporal asked.

"Yes sir, mid-parachute with its beak. I repeat, a *flying dinosaur.*"

"Actually," Allie said, "pterodactyls are avian reptiles, not flying dinosaurs."

"Strike that, sir. An avian reptile." Lucky nodded to us. "And that wasn't even inside the Origin. This group was smack-dead in the epicenter when we showed up. The Origin core seemed to have even worse causal-reality violations inside. They fought through the whole thing though, ended it too. Even the kids. I'm pretty sure that hero over there saved us with some sort of high-powered weapon."

He pointed to Toby.

"So wait," I said to the Corporal. He looked at me and it was familiar—him seeing me, not the other way around. He somehow knew Seven. It was obvious those two wanted to punch each other's faces off. But I really wanted to ride in the helicopter because I never had before, so I tried to smooth things over between them. "Did the werewolf-bunny thing really happen, with the cello and everything?"

Elbow didn't say anything. But he cradled an imaginary instrument and dragged an invisible bow across its strings.

"So, I see you found the girl," Corporal Lox said to Seven. "Best friends forever." His tone was the same as a monkey exterminator saying *awwww* before they flamethrower'd a pair of primates huddled together in a bathtub.

Lucky spoke, probably to break up the staring contest between Corporal beard man and Sevs. "They call them Angels, and one of their group turned out to be one, pretending to be human."

Lox pointed at Ed's boulder with his cigar. "Did you pinpoint the source of the Origin?"

Elbow shook his head. "It was definitely here, but the source originated from behind a wall of shrubs," he said with a thumb-jab over his shoulder, "and we didn't make it through in time before the Origin congealed into this boulder. Again, their group was inside."

"Excuse me, inside what?" Lox asked.

"I don't know—inside the core of all metaphysical, goddamn fucking creation, sir."

Lox contemplated the embers on the end of his cigar. "Once we've analyzed the boulder, we're out. If they want to come along for the ride that's fine, but you are under no circumstances to waste another bullet protecting them." The soldier pair gave a full salute, and the Corporal headed back to his hoverjet with Lucky and Arm Joint headed to the bright ski boot helicopter circled with sputtering emergency flares.

Will took out his harmonica and sat between Mack and Toby, playing it slow and soft. Saying he was sorry through the notes. Allie cleaned off her Page Master dagger on one of the dead soldier's pant legs. Seven flicked the frozen shape on Onto-

275

logy's End and stared into its black core. He sheathed the sword and looked around. At his feet. At a bird chirping. At the sun. All to stall having to talk to me.

I'd had it with him. I took off Ursa Minor from around my neck and threw the pendant. Pretended I needed to sneeze so he couldn't tell the beaver dams in my tear ducts were about to cave in and drown all the wood chewers. Seven picked up my necklace. Came to my side and sat down. Twirling the stars around his fingers. Then he took off his own stars and held both our constellations together.

"You deserve all the stars, Robot." He looped both of them over my head, and I let him. "You're the only one keeping them alive. The only real astronomer left on the planet."

"I *hate* you. I don't have enough words to tell you how much I hate you."

"I read a story once about a robot who felt the exact same way."

"What did the robot do?"

"Forced some people to fight a giant bird monster with a water pistol, it was some real nasty business."

"Sounds like me. But I wouldn't give you a super soaker. I'd tie your shoelaces together and cover you in peanut butter and birdseed."

"Ouch," Seven said. Rubbing his arm.

"Yeah. *Ouch*, you goddamn platypus. You lied to me!"

"I didn't know what else to do."

"What was your big plan for when the Mouth of God showed up? Huh? What were you gonna do with us?"

Seven blushed. A phenomenon as rare as the Mouth of God itself.

"Well, I thought maybe I'd take us all to some power station. Somewhere with a control room and a bunch of computers. Then I'd maybe turn on some large generator that made a lot of noise . . . and make you guys get in a blanket fort—"

"A *blanket fort*? You, you're kidding me. You thought we'd just crawl into a blanket fort? Make us hold hands and chant an astronomy prayer? How stupid do you think we are? And don't you know Mackenzie is *claustro-fucking-phobic* —she would've peed all over us!"

Seven laughed while taking a drink from his water bottle. A real laugh. A laugh that sucked a mouthful of water into his lungs and nearly choked him to death as he rolled around on the grass wheezing, crying, hiccupping, sputtering out *stop, stop*, as I continued my unsupervised mega-rant about how absolutely infantile he was, how he should be eaten by giant wolves, reincarnated as dead-dinosaur blood in a lousy automobile, turned into emu fertilizer, how he should be haunted by a ghost army made of every child who ever lived and let starlight shine through their eyes to hope against the awe of all the gaping dark above.

Seven finally got his cupcakes back together and stopped drowning to death. "You're the best, Robot. We were right. We were right all along. I can't believe it. We're alive and we were right."

"Right about what?" I licked my finger and poked it in his ear. Smacked him on the cheek.

"About abandoning the Great Seeker," Seven said. Staring into the Mouth of God's golden mist hiding behind blue sky. "That's how I know Corporal Lox."

"Wait. What?"

"The country was under martial law. Uh, I guess it still is. But the military took control of anything to do with deep space observatories. Had to do recon and prepare for *The Attack*, because those military types have no imagination, thought aliens were gonna post up on the moon and shoot lasers at us so we could have a real digestible, refined, easy-to-understand war that they could all become heroes in. But headquarters got nailed by an Angel—the first one we'd ever seen. We had to sacrifice the entire launch complex to kill it. Engineers knocked an experimental heavy launch system onto its side and fired the whole vehicle, booster-and-all, straight into mission control. A whole space shuttle just blasting sideways down a runway. You really should've seen it. The entire tower facility exploded into a bright white thundercloud spewing lava. It was like watching an animal being born."

Seven remembered and got quiet. Picked at a splinter of trauma inside his palm. I had to tap him on the shoulder to get him talking again.

"Space Camp?" I asked.

"Yeah, that was Space Camp."

"Anyway," he said, looking over to Mackenzie and Toby, "I was the only one left who was familiar with the ground systems for the Great Seeker, well, mainly what to point it at. Corporal Lox held a gun to my head and told me to keep the observatory in orbit. The crew was already running low on food up there. They were terrified. I told them the shuttle meant to bring them supplies was gone. Used to obliterate an exo-universe organism that just randomly appeared and that nothing made sense anymore. They weren't getting help. But Lox was insistent they continue observations. For a while, I was too. And they did make some incredible discoveries. Everything I've told you is owed to what those astronomers did up there. All while starving to death and bleeding out of every hole in their bodies. But the Great Seeker had its limits. Progress plateaued. Biology and psychology rendered all but two of the crew useless."

Seven had my backpack. He dug out my dinged-up, scratched-to-heck dinosaur walkie-talkie.

"*But then we heard you,*" he said with a click. Bit down on the antennae.

My blood vibrated against my skin. Prickled mountain ranges sprouted on my arms where a million invisible rocket ships launched, each carrying a lone astronaut on a voyage they could never return from.

"Command had access to radio detectors across the country, monitoring all Family Radio Service frequencies for anyone who might still be out there with information. Basic-ally, an old government spy network. You pinged one of the sensors, Robot. You kept pinging it every night."

There was nothing I could say. My mouth was a telescope throat humming with blackness and spots of starlight that struggled to twinkle.

"I recorded all of your evening transmissions and played them for the astronauts on the Great Seeker. Your rants about squirrels being assholes. How the gaps between forest leaves make you sad. When you found Allie by those heaps of refrigerators falling from a Miracle and the both of you ate oranges all day. That time you saw a hundred cats climb up a tree and caught all the runts that got knocked off so they didn't hit the ground and die. All your commentary about people crawling into crocodile mouths, your late-night golf-cart rampage through that toy store, how you found that dying boy and pet his forehead with Sir Tycho Brahe's hand—we heard it all. The Great Seeker loved you, Robot. Everything about you. They wanted to save you more than anything. You were all that mattered to them. So. We deboosted the Great Seeker on a slow trajectory. Triangulated your position. I torched the control systems and bolted from the facility as perhaps the last true traitor to the nation. The night I found you and Allie was the same night the Great Seeker reentered our atmosphere—right over our heads. That was their message to you, Robot. On fire with the hope that you'd be the one to save us in the end. I found all that mattered to them. All that mattered to me. All that matters at all anymore."

We were quiet for a while after that. My hand snaked through grass and tried to hold his out of instinct, but I retracted it. It was too soon. My absolute anger at Seven steamed out of my skin, leaving just the scalded emotional circus rides of our relationship as a reminder of his lie. I sorta hated myself for that. How easy it was to start to forgive him. For his make-believe plan to save us. How he'd given up on the mission before he even found me. But those astronauts, they'd known me. Heard all my ramblings about the collapse of the universe. And then they transferred their power to me by crashing through the atmosphere, burning all their wishes at once so I could maybe have mine come true. I couldn't understand. The situation was too grown-up for me.

Too complex and filled with feelings and doubt and hope that when combined made a very confused-looking hippopotamus in my imagination. It made me embarrassed. The pretend hippopotamus. How it couldn't walk well with five legs or shiver off the pesky birds pecking at mud berries on its back, or even hold its breath underwater for more than two seconds.

It was a very me kind of hippo.

"I hope it was worth it," I told Seven, "that telescope I imagined." He spun me around. Hard. On my butt to face him. I didn't realize my hands were holding my face.

"I don't have enough words to tell you how incredible your telescope was. You've really listened to me, listened to your dad, all our lectures about photons and space-time and uni-verse-membrane fabrics."

"I mean, maybe."

"The Great Seeker would've never been able to see what we needed. All those astronomers, every astronomer ever— Galileo, Rubin, Kepler, Herschel, Hubble, Hawking, and Tycho friggin' Brahe—I'm telling you, if they knew about the telescope you imagined, what it could do, what it *did* do, they'd all have set themselves on fire for eternity to keep us looking through its lens."

"What did you see?"

"It's a secret." I punched him in the ear before I could even think. "Okay, okay! Sorry," he said, rubbing his hearing lobe. He held me at arm's length, I guess because my punch really hurt him.

"I swear to Mackenzie. I will bite you."

Seven nodded. Massaged my shoulders a bit. "It's hard to explain, but sometimes astronomy is more about what *isn't there* than what is there."

"Explain. But better. Please." I squinted. Imagined Seven at the bottom of a classroom atrium, all the seats empty except for mine. He cleared his throat. Wrote, *the most important lesson I can ever teach you* on the chalkboard.

"You do not need to see a thing to know that it is there."

"You do not need to see a thing to know that it is there?"

"Yes." Seven made his hand claw-swipe across my tummy. "When I was your age, I lived near the beach. Lots of marsh. Subtropical rainforests. Plants with fronds big enough to hide under during rainstorms and not get wet. This path called the Greenway ran through twenty miles of that forest and wetland, and for a while it wasn't even paved. It was just this sandy, muddy trail. Totally untamed. Walked on more by deer and boar and awkward shorebirds than by people, really."

He blew into his fist and cupped palm, making the lonesome *coo coo* call of some jungle pigeon.

"One day a newspaper put on their front page that a leopard was sighted along the Greenway, which is crazy. Leopards don't even live on this continent. I thought it was stupid. How would you put it—*total burnt pancakes*. Well, one day I took off on my bike down the Greenway, running over puddles on purpose, chasing frogs, just being a complete wild animal on this path. Roaring. Proclaiming my invincible boyness to the woods and swamp."

"Then you saw the leopard."

Seven pressed his mouth into a straight line and patted my head.

"I saw Miss Pinkberry's black polka-dotted pig at the top of a tree. Swaying in the wind against vines and summer sky. Its organs oozed on banana leaves and the sand path. That pig's ribcage was *plowed* open. Its skin plastered over a felled pine tree."

I covered my eyes with my hands. "You do not need to see a thing to know that it is there." I restored my sight but found Seven covering his own peepers.

"Robot. I didn't see anyone else but us up there. No other life. No *traces* of life. No fallen intergalactic empires. No wayward drifting nomadic colonies from long-extinct solar systems. No satellites orbiting moons or planets. No cities. No houses. No subterranean lairs or basements and no animals, no alien dinosaurs rampaging around ocean-paradise worlds or amoebas clinging to deep-water thermal vents. Nothing. I checked everything. I checked them all—from the dawn of time onwards. That's what your telescope did. I saw every-thing, and I didn't see a single peep of L-I-F-E."

"I don't get it. You didn't see anything, so what is it you know is hiding there? What's waiting to eat?"

Seven flatlined his mouth again, disappointed. Gave my head a single, firm pat. Stared at me and didn't stop staring.

I said it. "Just us."

"Just *us*," he repeated.

I pointed to the sky. At the warm yellow dot that poked through our atmosphere, even during the day.

"The golden bubblegum core up there—is that Miss Pinkberry's prized polka-dotted pig?"

"You know that most special thing you've been looking for?"

"No," I said. "Answer my question."

"Come on, listen. That one door inside you—the one lead-ing to that very special place?" He pretended to turn a door- 283 knob back and forth. I grabbed his hand and twisted it, then nodded. "Well, I found the door the Angels want to open. Kind of like yours. I know where it is, but I don't know what they're hoping to find behind it." I pulled my hand away, and some of the bubble gum that was on the telescope stuck to my hand. Seven hadn't wiped it off his hand yet, or had tried to but couldn't.

"Is the door far away?" I asked.

"Yes, farther than anyone's ever been before. You and me, we're gonna go there and give it a knock. That is, if you'll come with me. If you still want to."

I swished my cheeks to make him think I was a little un-certain. "Maybe if we can resolve the main issue between you and me, then yeah. I'll go with you."

"Main issue?"

Now it was my turn to give him the—*you couldn't possibly understand*—stare down. "Our main issue is that you don't believe in the Tide. You can't see it coming because no one ever has, not even the Sky Stealers. Like how you made fun of those multiverse, nerd-bearded astrophilosophers back in the day at NASA, it seems hard for you to believe in the nonsense dream logic hyper-gnawin' at physics and spacetime. But I have to. I have to wear an innertube around my waist and kick over everyone's safe and cozy blanket forts. Because the Tide has been low. Every Mouth of God and Angel and human has been piddling on a dry beach making pretend castles. Digging up extinct seashells." I held an imaginary conch shell to my ear for the Conductor.

"But if you put one of those shells to your ear, you can hear it roaring. A foam rising in the distance. Teeth pushing through waves. Monsters from ancient seas that'll rip you apart in their whirlpool jaws—and I'm one of 'em. That sea-shell roar is mine. I'll be the monster so that none of you have to be. I'm the only thing that can float out there in all that deep. So hold on to me. No matter what. Even if I drown beneath you, use my body to keep your head above water."

I wiped Seven's face with his own hand to clean off the residual astonishment.

"I'm sorry," I said. "Just figured we should tell the truth from now on."

Seven pinched some dirt and dusted me. "You're right. You don't deserve anything less."

"Well, I sort of deserved it," I told him. "Being lied to."

"Why?"

"Because I lied to you, too."

"About what?"

I held Tycho Brahe's head up so he could watch the sky. "About believing I'm strong enough to save everyone, pretending it's not scary to try and do all the stuff I thought you were doing for me."

"Well, you're doing a better job of being the universe's savior than me, for sure," Seven said. I tapped Ontology's End.

"Your sword is cool. You should use it more."

Seven winced. "I'll try. It's not easy though. I'm afraid it will get too wild and poke through you." He jabbed me in the tummy with his index finger.

"Are we okay?" I asked.

"That's for you to decide. I'm the fuck-up here."

"Yeah you are. You said I was too old to have a stuffed animal. You're a monster." 285

"That was mean." Seven shook his head and wiped underneath his eye. "I was scared. I didn't know what I was doing. I know that's stupid, but I'm stupid, too. A bad grownup. Always have been."

"Well," I said, "it's up to Tycho to forgive you for that, not me. I'm fine." Seven smiled true. Which hurt. Because all of that was a lie. But I just wanted to feel okay, even for a minute.

"Just don't mess up your leopard-spotting duty," I told him. "If you see that jungle cat anywhere, let me know."

Seven cupped his hands and held them to his eyes as a pair of binoculars. Scanning the sky. Then Ed's boulder. The helicopter. The aftermath of the *Grand Laramidian Gulch* strewn about the lawn. And then he pointed them at me. Looking hard through imaginary lenses, and he didn't look away again.

Lucky pulled a crate off the helicopter and passed out food bags to Will. He gave the kids some juice packs, which were pretty hard to open. Lucky tried his hardest to punch a hole through the plastic pouch, even took his helmet off to really concentrate, and ended up squeezing the thing so hard it sprayed all over his face. Mack wiped the mess off Lucky with her sleeve and then sucked the juice out of it. Allie pulled Mack's arm down and began to lecture her, I guess about germs, because she picked up a handful of dirt and wiggled her fingers like an amoeba. It was good, seeing us getting a little back to normal.

We'd met and lost people dozens of times. Like the people in the Fiesta Car on the train with their brave moose-sweatered leader, Captain Frumps. Groups of survivors were baskets of kittens we'd find and hold onto, sharing hugs and meows and taking care of 'em, trying not to get too attached because the basket always ended up getting run over by a minivan. But Mike and the Conductor were different. Ed, too. They'd found special places in our hearts. Shared wisdom and secrets that bushwhacked new paths to the core of our souls. We weren't going to shake them off like fleas. We were going to suck on our sleeves and collars like Mackenzie, because we didn't want to let go of the only pieces of them that were left. Their tiny amoebas clinging to our shirts and skin.

I noticed that all my kid friends were left alone to talk among themselves for the first time in days. No adult ears to hear and judge and try to make 'em feel like everything was going to be okay. I could see them figuring out, again, that they didn't know the world for what it really was. I headed over to help carry the burden of that knowledge. We stood around and looked at each other. Tired, sweaty, bloody, and sad. No one knew what to say, so I took a different course of action. I stood by Tobes and nudged him with my butt over to Mack until they were standing side by side, and then I pushed Allie over, made sure they were snugged tight against one another, and then I wrapped my arms around them—as much as I could anyway—and tried to pick everyone up, but all I did was squeeze 'em so tight that Mack-a-Doodle farted. Toby and Al Pal squirmed, probably because their faces were so close they were almost kissing.

"Knock it off, Robo-turd," Tobes muttered.

287

"You're making me have to pee," Allie said.

Mack's head was squished between their bellies.

"Tinkle away, Al Pal," I said, "because I'm not letting go until I squeeze the sad out of all of you and make you happy. Ya better cheer up real quick before Mack gets nervous and passes gas again."

"Robots," Mackenzie said, "I can't hears you because it sounds like Allie and Toberkin's tummies are making poop. It's loud."

Normally such a comment would have us laughing good, except for Mack, who didn't really understand this wasn't a normal thing for her to have said. But we didn't laugh. Allie and Toby gave weak smiles, acknowledging the humor without feeling it. That was okay. It was all we could expect for now. I let go and eyed Allie's jeans to make sure I hadn't burst her bladder. Mack looked at us, wondering why we'd gotten a little happy and she hadn't. I slipped Tycho Brahe from over my head and fastened him around her neck.

"He told me he misses the way you suck on his ears." Tycho held his head up high, proud to sacrifice his hearing holes for a small amount of comfort. Mack clamped her mouth around one of them and slobbered away.

"There's no juice in there." Toby scratched Mack-a-Doodle's head. "Let's get you another drink pouch." He put his arm around her and headed to the supply crate. Classic Toby. Acting tough even though he was shaken up like a rattlesnake in the hands of a sugar baby. I knew better though. But I'd give him some time before I talked to him.

Allie stared up at the boulder, studying it hard, or maybe imagining that our tree home was still intact somewhere inside the rocky tomb.

"I'm sorry I made you sign the agreement forcing you to invite everyone to the house," I told her. "If I hadn't, then it would've only been you and me and the Super Ultimate Treehouse. No one would've gotten hurt." Allie looked at me and rubbed a red splotch on her shirt.

"I killed something. A lot of somethings," she said.

"I noticed. Ya know, you're at the top of the food chain now. The sun in the sky and the white in the clouds." She took her glasses off and nibbled on the frame. That thought hadn't occurred to her yet. "Don't feel bad about it. Pretend it's like nature gave you the ultimate high five." I held my hand up, and she contemplated completing its circuit, then made a fist and jabbed my palm.

"No. Nature gave the ultimate high five to Mike and the Conductor. Smashed them flat. Is it our fault? If we hadn't wished for the Super Ultimate Treehouse would Mike and the Conductor still be okay? Would Merlin still be sniffing the back of my knees." She sucked on the top of her sweater.

"I don't know, Lord Bookworm. I don't know how we're supposed to hope for things when that hope grows teeth and tries to snack on your monkey ears. Who gives a hot dog if we made it out with all our lives and all our fingers, when not all of us did? You're smarter than me. Way smarter. I'm sorry, you're going to have to think about all of that. Figure it out, feel all the feels and then clue me in. Because I'm an idiot. Because I wanted a dog for us, a playground, a home—and that's just it, there aren't any homes anymore."

Allie tilted her head and held it there, listening for some secret in the leaves scraping on the boulder. Bullets tinkling into a crate. She nodded and then took me by the arm. Held

289

her glasses so the sun curved in their lenses and warmed my
hand with a small yellow dot.

"The Train Captain and Mike cared," she said. "They
gave up all their hotdogs—Merlin, too. Not because they
didn't want them, but because they believed in you. You're
different, Avery. So different that all those soldiers formed
up into a firing squad to execute you, an eleven-year-old girl
with a stuffed monkey around her neck and a narwhal cape."
I'd forgotten the cape was still fluttering against my back. I
wondered why it didn't dissolve with the rest of the treehouse junk. "It's safe to say you have something special,
probably even in your spit. This thing, I think we're all ready
to sacrifice everything to protect it. Mike and the Conductor
and Merls were just the first to charge ahead, torches lit in
the darkness to lead the way."

I grabbed the sunspot in my palm and hugged the breath
right outta my best friend. It was hard for me to breathe, too,
with the added weight of all the belief from her, from all our
friends, alive ones and buried ones. I wanted to say something
smart and meaningful, but I ended up nibbling on her sweater
collar, like she would've done if our places were switched.

"You're the best, Wolf Queen." I bit her shoulder to
initiate the binding of our new pack.

Toby sprawled out on the grass with his hands behind his
head and shoes off. Just lounging in a classic relaxation pose.
He wasn't fooling me though. I sent Allie on a secret mission
and then sprawled out beside Toby, mocking him down to the
one untied shoelace on his left sneaker. He ignored me, like he
always would when I tried to talk to him about something
serious. *Razor-filled dinosaur popsicles*, maybe it wasn't even

time to talk about something heavy. I rushed into it with Al Pal, but I still felt the shark mouths of Seven's telescope lie nipping at the inside of my chest. Toby's crush on Ed had been so real that it'd crushed her in real life. She didn't even wave goodbye to him. Ed was colder than Summer's Final Goodbye—she would've frozen it so bad the dragon would've gone and put on a fuzzy hat, marshmallow jacket, and mittens.

"You totally leveled my ultimate boss—Summer's Final Goodbye," I told him. A compliment was the rarest of red gems, one held by a golden monkey hidden in my temple of things I could give Toberkins. I knew he was going to eat it up. "I would've never thought of how to beat it."

Toby rolled his head to look at me.

"You don't have to pretend you like me now because I lost the only girl around that did. I can handle it."

If there ever were a spear, invisible and sharp, that spun itself around the outside of our solar system, then proceeded to dive right through Pluto, plunge into the gasses of Neptune and Uranus before it shattered Saturn's rings and bulls-eye bored Jupiter's great red hole, only to pierce Mars' lonely heart and scrape by the craters of our moon to finally lodge firmly in my soul, it was then that it happened. Of everyone in our group, I gave Toby the hardest time. I wailed on Seven most days, but it wasn't so bad for him because he was much smarter than me. For Toby it was different. These months must've been torture for him—thinking I genuinely didn't like the way his bananas were put together. Hated his puke and one untied shoelace on his left sneaker.

If my baby brother had lived to crawl out of his plastic

291

hospital cube, *this* is how I would've treated him. I would've been a monster. An unrelentful snot-sucking witch queen. The absolute worst. The most annoying, uncaring, and inconsiderate sister to ever slink from the sea and terrorize the innocent creatures of land.

It seemed clear that apologizing for my constant buttholing wasn't going to put a dent in the metal cage guarding his feelings for me. I'd have to sacrifice something precious to make up for the hurt I gave Toby on a daily basis. A loyal baby goat tied to a spike in the middle of the Tyrannosaur meadow.

Tobes went back to looking at his boulder and I sat up.

"A while ago this stupid pebble jumped in my shoe and has never come out." I took off my sneaker and shook my rock buddy. "Even when I toss my shoe around the sucker just won't leave, but you can hear him in there laughing at me."

Rattle rattle rattle.

"It's bothered me every day of my life, constantly making me mad and irritable, and overall—a big cranky barnacle sniffer. It's my ultimate enemy, the one I'll never be able to beat." I stopped shaking my shoe and the little pebble hopped out onto the grass. My eyes opened wide with grade A astonishment, but Toby didn't look amused. I picked the rock up and handed it to him. "You deserve to have it, to shove it in my face as a constant reminder of what I am to you. It will make me shut up and be nice. Promise."

He took the dirty little fella and held it close to his eye, pinched it between his fingeys. Toby focused on the pebble so it was all he could see. He stood up and dropped the rock into his left shoe, put it on, and fixed the loose string.

"I'm pretty bad at saving people from rocks," he said. The boulder loomed behind him and a wisp of dust snaked off its peak. "I'll try again, but don't hate me if I can't do anything about it."

Lucky whistled—Seven howled like a coyote. His signal for time to go. Al Pal took Toby by the arm and led him to the helicopter while I lay there. Lucky and Seven lifted an ammo crate, with Mack sitting on top, and loaded her into our ride while she gnawed Tycho's ears raw.

I stood up but didn't move. I knew as soon as I did, I'd feel that the rock was gone—knew it wouldn't greet me with one of the six little points on its angled body. With the pebble no longer underfoot, the sole survivor of the day my dad died was gone. It was kept warm by someone else while they missed someone else. If the memory of my dad was one of those survivor kittens we'd found in a basket, then a minivan would be driving over it, backing up, and doing it again. Over and over with every step Toby took. I gave away my last memory of him, my real dad, and knew it wouldn't take long before I couldn't remember how it happened, not exactly, anyway, since the constant poking and pressure of the rock reminded me every minute.

I took that first step, though, because I had to be strong. Strong enough to make Seven believe, to destroy my dad's ghost so Toby wouldn't hate me, and so I could honor the dead and all their hot dogs. My baby brother, too, because my last memory of him didn't exist. I'd been too afraid to stick around and make one.

With Seven's permission, I got to put on a harness clipped to a cable so I could sit right at the edge of the helicopter's open door. Of course, I wasn't dangling my feet, but I could've if I'd wanted to. The boulder stayed put as we flew away, and I watched it fade like a roadside attraction you have to leave behind on a long and unplanned road trip.

I thought about a lot of things. About how the Conductor told me to imagine that corpse hands reaching for the sun were flowers. About the book I was reading when my dad was killed, the one with the penguin who left her home and ran to the mountain so far away. Toward the majestic light glowing atop its peak. How that jawline of frost and rock must've looked like a crown to her. Along the way, the penguin passed by other penguins forever trapped in solid hunks of ice, some even frozen in mid-sprint. Her ancestors turned into gravestones that she hid behind during great gusts of wind. Other penguins were half-eaten by sea lions with their clean spines collecting small dunes of snow. One even swallowed the barrel of a flare gun left behind by an ancient ice explorer to burn themselves alive, tasting the warmth and light they'd never be able to reach. Those penguins were just like her—loners who'd chased after the undying shine that crested the mighty mountain. It was very sad, seeing them all so dead and hopeless, but the penguin didn't let it ruin her journey. The penguin kept on running even though the others couldn't. She'd run until the hope of climbing that impossible slope froze her solid. Even if she only made it a little farther than the other pengys. She'd go on so that when the sun rose in the morning over that damned tundra, she'd glow as a crystal lighthouse for the next penguin who tried.

I pulled out my dino walkie-talkie and clicked the switch:

"Hello, my obliterated orbital oracles, my dead-astronaut ghost knights searching for things I can't know in all the places I can't go [blip] Emotion level for the day is Impaled-Sea-Monster Funeral Ceremony [blip] And you're all gone. But it doesn't feel right to stop talking to you. To stop telling stories to the sky. Because one of these days the Mouth of God will erase all these words anyway. Letters in their flat patterns will perish first [blip] That's why they've always been curled up in all their mysterious rune shapes, shivering and wiggly. They've been scared [blip] They've known the Mouth of God was coming to burn 'em up one noun and verb and adjective at a time. The ideas they connected will die next, and at that point this story won't stand a chance, turning over its last page into lava and star-spit pyroclasm. The Mouth of God, without a dead-dolphin-doubt, will set our books on incredible golden fire. It'll blaze and unbind all these novel spines.

"So [blip] Tell me. When that happens where will this story exist? In you? In me? Scrawled somehow on the fluctuations of microphysics lapping at the shore of forever? Tickling probability's great duck-billed butt cheeks? Telling our tale through the ultimate energy-conclusion from the tiny particles shoved around by Mackenzie's fart, or maybe a stick Toby threw in a river or a book Allie left at home? A star Seven forgot to name and then suddenly remembered while putting a band-aid on my knee? It could be like that. Our plots and feelings just change shape. All that matters is the change they make in the world, not how the change was made. But maybe that's not right. Maybe our story only exists here. Right now.

In the present. A single moment that can be divided forever, just like a heart, until the pages are so far apart there's nothing left to feel.

"I'm feeling everything for you now. For as long as I can. So, sleep well and gentle and good up there. Sleep for all the salamanders and sea birds. Sleep for me [blip] because I'm afraid to now."

ACKNOWLEDGEMENTS

Undying thanks to Drew Tapp, John Knight, Ben DeCorso, and Romina for helping get these words nestled in their pages. I'd like to thank the eyeholes of Jordan Long, Hannah Hyatt, Kaighn Morlok, Allie Briggs, Hunter Moss, Adam James, and Mom and Pop. A great and special hug to Ori Toor for sharing his imagination with this story. But most of all—I extend my eternal gratitude to the children of Laurel Hill Kaleidoscope and hope nothing but the best adventures find all who were there with me. May you all dream forever wild and free.

To the jellyfish I left behind:
I hope you got what you wished for.

ABOUT THE AUTHOR

Justin Hellstrom likes thinking of the sea and wayward starships. One time he saw a transdimensional event. His desk is littered with plastic dinosaurs wearing cone party hats. He's the creator of *The Great Chameleon War*, the *Singularity Playtime Saga*, and other fictions which will appear at the inter-reality rift of DeadPondSwan.com. If he could tell you a story, he would tell you this one.

CPSIA information can be obtained
at www.ICGtesting.com
Printed in the USA
BVHW082023080721
611457BV00008B/349

9 780578 858036